Room *for* More

BETH EHEMANN

CRANBERRY INN SERIES, VOLUME II

ALSO BY BETH EHEMANN

Room for You

Room for Just a Little Bit More

Room *for* More

BETH EHEMANN

CRANBERRY INN SERIES, VOLUME II

Montlake
Romance

Published by Montlake Romance, Seattle

www.apub.com

Amazon, the Amazon logo, and Montlake Romance are trademarks of Amazon.com, Inc., or its affiliates.

ISBN-13: 9781477828991
ISBN-10: 1477828990

Cover design by Shasti O'Leary-Soudant / SOS CREATIVE LLC

Library of Congress Control Number: 2014957575

Printed in the United States of America

This book is dedicated to my "Roomies." You guys cheer me up on bad days and make the good days awesome. Thank you for making me one grateful landlord.

PROLOGUE

Kacie,

I can't do this anymore. I'm leaving. Actually, I'm already gone. I listened to you when you said things would be great. They're not great. They suck. I have no freedom, I have to work all the time, and I never get to see my friends. This is not what I wanted and I've had enough. Sorry.

P.S. As a favor, I already paid the sitter and left you $100. Good luck.

Zach

Good luck?

I stood in my kitchen, staring down at the black letters, trying to force my brain to believe that I must be reading them wrong. My hands started shaking uncontrollably and my chest tightened as I sprinted to our bedroom and ripped the closet door open—nothing but empty hangers on his side. As I pulled his empty drawers out of the dresser completely, throwing them to the ground one by one, it hit me.

He was gone.

Really gone.

How could he do this? How could he do this *now*, after three years? Our twin girls were turning one next week. Didn't he want to be here for that?

The bile started to rise up in my throat as I put my hand over my mouth and ran to the bathroom, getting there just in time. After I was done emptying my lunch into the toilet, I sat back against the bathroom wall and pulled my knees up to my chest, putting my head in my hands.

"Are you okay?" Christina, our babysitter, asked quietly as she appeared in the doorway.

Without looking up at her, I asked flatly, "Did he say anything to you?"

She sighed. "No. He just paid me and said he left a letter for you on the counter, to make sure you saw it."

A letter? He scribbled that bullshit on the back of a Lee Auto Parts receipt. That could hardly be classified as a letter.

I couldn't believe it.

Sure, we got pregnant much earlier than we should have, and while it wasn't planned, we were making it work. It certainly hadn't been easy so far, but I'd thought that this was forever. That *we* were forever. I never imagined he would leave us, and certainly not like this.

Maybe I could stop him, make him change his mind. I jumped up off the bathroom floor and rushed past Christina, heading straight for the kitchen counter where I'd left my purse to find my cell phone. My fingers were shaking so badly I could barely dial his number.

One ring, two rings, three rings, voice mail.

I dialed again.

One ring, voice mail.

He knew I was calling. He knew I was calling and he was sending me to voice mail. Where was he? What was going on?

My knees felt weak and my head light, like I might pass out, but I managed to make my way over to the kitchen table and sit down.

Christina followed me into the kitchen, though she looked like she would rather be anywhere else. She was white as a sheet and nervously playing with the buttons on her sweater.

"Go home, Christina. Thanks for watching the girls." I was biting my lip so hard I tasted blood, but I didn't want to break down in front of her.

She let out a huge sigh as relief crossed her face. "Um, okay," she stammered. "The girls have been napping for about an hour, so . . . if you need anything, call me tonight." She started to make her way out of the kitchen, but she stopped halfway and turned back toward me. "Are you going to need me tomorrow?"

I let out a long breath that I had no idea I was even holding in.

"I don't know . . . anything. I'll call you."

"Okay." She hurried over and threw her arms around me, but I couldn't feel a thing. I was numb.

"I'm so sorry, Kacie."

She let go and turned to walk out the front door, the floorboards creaking behind her as she went.

My mind started replaying all the memories of the last three years with Zach like a movie in my head, scene by scene. We'd met at a bonfire after a football game, and I knew that night that he was the boy I wanted to spend the rest of my life with, or so I thought. We'd had a whirlwind high school romance, full of steamy make-out sessions in his truck, sneaking out for late-night walks, and lots of skinny-dipping in the lake. We'd dated for a little over a year before we found out we were pregnant.

Then, when I was eight weeks along, we got the shock of our lives: twins.

I'd almost fallen off the table when the ultrasound technician beamed at me and said, "I hope you're ready for two!"

"Two what?" Zach said.

I didn't say anything. I knew. My wide eyes stared at the two little flashing lights on the screen and I needed no further explanation. The next few minutes were a blur as the tech explained to Zach what was happening. I was too busy falling madly in love with the little beings currently occupying about as much space as two gummy bears in my belly. I wasn't prepared for one baby at eighteen years old, let alone two, but I vowed that moment that for the rest of my life they would be the most important things in it.

I figured Zach would eventually share my excitement and feel the same way.

Wrong.

My first hint should have been halfway through my pregnancy when we received the news that we were going to be blessed with two girls.

Immediately, I started picturing two little girls in matching pink outfits with bows in their hair, asking me to paint their nails when they were old enough. And how lucky were they going to be to have each other? Built-in best friends. I was elated.

Zach?

Not so much.

"Seriously? Shit. If I have to go through this, I was at least hoping for boys. Fuck," he mumbled on the way home while I sat in the passenger seat rubbing my protruding belly with a smile on my face. I just knew that as soon as he held them, he would feel the way I was feeling.

They were born eighteen weeks later, weighing in at just five pounds each and absolutely perfect. Zach was as supportive as I expected him to be during delivery, at least in the moments he wasn't busy texting on his cell phone. My picture-perfect fairy tale was quickly shattered. Our first fight came when the girls were only eight hours old.

"You want to *what*?" I scowled at him. I could feel my face turning red with anger.

"Calm down, Kacie! It's no big deal. The guys just want me to come out for a few drinks to celebrate becoming a dad."

"But they were *just born*!" I hissed back at him, trying not to focus on my mom in the background, shaking her disapproving head at him.

"I was hoping you were going to stay here in the hospital . . . with us. I thought that was the plan."

"Babe, I'll only be gone an hour or so. Then I'll come back and stay here with you tonight," he responded, flashing that megawatt smile that I swear got me pregnant in the first place.

"We've waited nine months to meet them. How can you leave *now*?" I looked down at the two little pink bundles sleeping peacefully, one in each arm. Tears started to well up in my eyes, but I was determined to keep them there.

"Jesus. They're not going anywhere, Kacie. They'll still be here when I get back. I just want to see the guys, have a cigar, and celebrate, okay? Come on, just for a little bit," he cooed, turning on the charm. "Then, when I get back, it's just you and me and them. We can sit and talk about how awesome our future is gonna be together."

He knew just how to get to me. "Fine, just for a couple of hours. When you come back, you're here with me one hundred percent, okay? No more phone, no more distractions, just us. Right?"

"Sure thing, babe!" he said as he kissed my forehead. He was out the door before I could say anything else.

I spent the rest of the evening trying not to make eye contact with my told-you-so mom, who hadn't been a big fan of Zach from the moment she met him. I had been going to great lengths to sugarcoat things to make it seem like he was as excited as I was about starting our own family. I obviously couldn't lie anymore, nor did I need to. She could see it.

Zach never came back that night.

Instead, he showed up the next morning, still wearing the same clothes and smelling like he'd slept in the bottom of a beer bottle. I made him run in and shower in my bathroom while my mom was downstairs in the cafeteria getting herself some coffee.

I should have known right then that it was the beginning of a very dark, lonely road.

But I didn't.

Call it denial. Call it stupidity. I put my blinders on and pushed through, determined to do everything in my power to keep my family together. I was hopeful that he would eventually fall as deeply in love with Lucy and Piper as I had, and want to be with us forever. When the girls were only a couple of months old, we looked at engagement rings. My stupid, naïve self thought he had secretly bought one and was paying it off, when in reality he was planning his escape. I felt like such an idiot.

The baby monitor lit up on the kitchen counter, bringing my trip down memory lane to a screeching halt. I walked over and turned the volume up. The girls had woken up from their naps and were babbling and giggling to each other. The sound of their sweet voices usually made my heart swell with joy, but right now each little cackle coming from their bedroom was another blow to my already weak heart. What was I going to tell them when they were older?

Tears slid down my cheeks, and the stream quickly turned into an ocean. Sinking to the floor in my kitchen as the world below me fell away, I sobbed and sobbed until I couldn't cry anymore. I leaned against the cabinet for what felt like hours, wondering what my life was going to be like from this point on. I made a silent promise to myself and to my daughters. I would never go through this again. They deserved better; so did I.

I had my girls, and they were all I needed. Failing them was not an option. Suddenly I was on my own and had to figure out how to not only provide for, but grow and nurture two little girls. It was all up to me. So I did what any normal nineteen-year-old, suddenly single mom would do.

I swallowed my pride and called my mom.

1

KACIE

"Zach? At the hospital? Are you serious?" Lauren shrieked so loud into the phone I had to pull it away from my ear for a second.

"Obviously." I sighed. "I wouldn't joke about something like *that*."

"He totally fell off the grid. I haven't heard a word about him since he left. And I certainly had no idea he was a paramedic!"

"Me either. Needless to say, I was stunned."

"What did he say? What did *you* say?"

"Nothing. I ran. Shocker, huh?" I chuckled nervously. "I pretended to get sick and sprinted to the bathroom. This other nurse, Darla, had to take over the patient while I sat on the floor of the bathroom stall having a full-blown panic attack for fifteen minutes. When I came out, he was gone."

"Did you tell Brody?"

"Not yet. This just happened yesterday. I haven't even processed it yet. Nor do I have any idea *how* to tell him."

"You told Alexa, right?"

"Nope. You're the only one who knows so far. Lucky you, huh?" I waited for her to laugh. She didn't, so I continued, "Anyway, I can't tell anyone. My mom's first instinct will be to pack us all up in the car and move across country, and I'm worried that Alexa will go to the hospital and kill him."

"You know she's going to lose her mind when she finds out, right?"

"Alexa? Yeah, I know." I sighed. "Which is exactly why I can't tell her right now."

"Kacie!"

"I'll tell her eventually, just not yet. You know how she gets, Lauren. She's so protective of us and hot-headed when it comes to Zach. Promise you won't tell her?"

Lauren sighed. "It's not my news to tell, so of course I won't. I just don't like this."

"There might not be anything to get worked up about anyway."

"What do you mean?" she asked.

"Maybe that'll be the only time I'll have to see him. Who knows? With any luck, I can put my hours in and escape without ever having to see him again."

I sat back on my bed and stared up at the ceiling, trying to force myself to believe the lie I'd just told Lauren. The odds of me not seeing him again over the next couple of months were slim to none.

"Oh God, Kacie. I don't even know what to say," she said.

I had been friends with Lauren long enough to know exactly what she looked like at that moment, even from 4,700 miles away. Her blue eyes were as wide as saucers while her long, perfectly manicured hands were over her mouth. I could hear the wooden floors creaking beneath her feet as she paced her apartment.

"What's going on?" Tommy called from the background.

"Zach is back!" she called to him.

"No shit!" he exclaimed. "Did Brody kick his ass?"

"He doesn't know yet."

"Oh shit. When he finds out, he's going to kill him. Ask Kacie not to tell him until this season is over so he doesn't go to jail, okay? I have a lot of money riding on him."

"Shhh!" Lauren hissed at him. "What are you gonna do, Kacie?"

I took a deep breath and exhaled loudly. "I don't know. What can I do? If I request a hospital transfer now, either I'll end up in a field I don't want to be in or they could make me wait till next semester to switch and finish my hours, which would delay my graduation. I'm stuck."

"Do you want me to come home?"

"Yes," I said sarcastically. "Please hop on a plane and travel halfway around the world because I ran into my ex-boyfriend. I love you, but no."

"You know if you said yes, seriously, I would be on a plane in an hour," she said softly.

"I know you would, and I really do love you for it."

"So . . . how did he look?"

"Lauren!"

"What?" she squealed defensively. "I didn't mean, like, were you checking him out. I just meant it's been a long time. How did he look?"

"I don't know. The same. Older. He had a baseball hat on, so I couldn't see much."

"Kacie . . ."

"What?"

"I know you. There was a 'but' coming."

She does know me well.

"God, Lauren . . . those eyes. Those big brown puppy-dog eyes that both the girls got from him . . ." I sighed. "They haven't changed one bit."

"Do you miss him?" she asked slowly. "Any sparks?"

"Hell no!" I screeched, lowering my voice when I remembered Brody was just a couple of rooms away. "Brody on his worst day is a thousand times better than Zach on his best day. It's not about missing him; I was just caught off guard, that's all."

The bedroom door flew open, startling me, as Lucy came flying in. "Mom, can you make us eggs?" she whined. "Brody said he'd do it but we had to pay him a hundred dollars. We don't have any money."

I shook my head and laughed. "Sure, honey. Just one sec. All right, Lauren, I gotta get going. I've got some hungry hungry hippos and a blackmailing boyfriend on my hands. Plus, I have to work again today."

"You do? Oh, God."

"Think positive, Lauren. Think positive."

Am I reassuring her or me or both of us?

"Are you going to tell the girls?" she whispered into the phone.

"You know she can't hear you, right?" I laughed, winking at Lucy, who was sitting at the end of my bed, staring at me. "And the answer to that is a big fat no. I'm hoping he just goes away. Think it's a possibility?"

"Um, no."

Lauren and I said our good-byes and I followed Lucy out into the kitchen. The closer we got, the stronger the bacon smell got, and all was right in the world again.

Brody was standing at the stove with his back to me. He had on a blue T-shirt that was just tight enough to accentuate his toned back and shoulders. Those same blue pajama pants he'd worn the first time I'd stayed at his house hung loosely from his hips. The memories of our first morning together made my cheeks flush. I walked up behind him, slid my arms under his, and wrapped them around his waist. I laid my head against his back and closed my eyes as the familiar smell of him calmed my nerves.

"Good morning." A light chuckle mixed with his surprised tone.

"Don't move. This is nice." His back vibrated against my cheek as he laughed harder, squeezing my hands in his.

"Do you have to go to the hospital today?" he asked.

The knot in my stomach returned. I was dreading heading into my bedroom and putting my scrubs on. I was dreading driving up to work and seeing an ambulance parked outside. I was dreading seeing Maureen again, who probably thought I was a total flake after yesterday.

"Unfortunately, yes."

"Why? Quit. Stay home with us. You don't have to work. Who needs a degree these days anyway?"

"Not a chance, but you're sweet." I squeezed him tight one last time and turned around to the fridge.

"Why not? Do you ever want to be a stay-at-home mom?"

"I don't know. After *him*, I swore to myself that I would never depend on a man again. It was embarrassing to move back home and rely on my mom to feed and take care of us."

"What about when we have kids?"

I spun to face him, nearly dropping the eggs that were in my hand. "What?"

"Down the road, when there are dozens of little Brodys running around the house, do you want to be home with us?"

"Dozens of little Brodys?" I chuckled.

"Why not?" He grinned.

"Uh, I can think of a few reasons. My poor uterus, for one." I poked him in the chest.

"Okay, fine. Not a dozen, but at least like . . . six." He wiggled his eyebrows. "After that, we can just practice—a lot."

"I'm definitely down for the practicing." I batted my eyes at him. "And what do you mean, at home with *us*? You'll be traveling most of the time."

"Yeah, but not forever. Eventually I'll retire and do the full-time-dad thing."

Crossing my arms over my chest, I cocked my head to the side and looked at him skeptically. "Since when does staying home with kids all day interest you?"

He looked over at the girls, who were watching a movie in the living room, and shrugged. "Since them."

I grinned at him as my stomach flipped. "You're too good to be real."

"Nope, I'm real and I'm all yours." He reached over and grabbed my T-shirt, pulling me in close to him.

"Until next week," I pouted dramatically. "Then you have to start practicing every day and we won't see each other much. Add in games and you'll forget who I am."

I was not looking forward to his season starting. My subconscious knew it was coming, but I was purposely not thinking about it. I'd gotten so used to seeing him often over the last couple of months, this would definitely be an adjustment.

"It'll be tough, but we'll still see each other," he said, lifting my chin up to face him. "We'll just have to make an effort to really, uh, make good use of the time we *do* have together."

I set the eggs on the island and shoved my hands up the back of his T-shirt, pulling him hard against me. "I like the way that sounds, Murphy."

"I love it when you call me Murphy." He groaned as he trailed kisses down the side of my neck, stopping at my collarbone.

"Really? I'll have to remember that," I cooed.

My glance panned over to the clock. "Holy crap! I gotta hurry." I rushed over and tossed a pan on the stove.

"Go. I got this." Brody came over and grabbed the handle of the pan.

I tried to snatch it back from him, but he held it high above his head so I couldn't reach it.

"Stop." He laughed. "I admit that I'm better with a hockey stick than I am with a spatula, but I can handle scrambled eggs. Go get ready. You can pay me back later." He wiggled his eyebrows up and down again.

"Deal." I smiled and started out of the kitchen, but he caught my wrist and pulled me toward him as he bent down to kiss my lips.

I quickly turned my head to the side and covered my mouth, mumbling through my hands, "I haven't brushed yet."

"I'll take my chances," he said, gently pulling my hands away from my mouth. "Pay the toll, stinky."

2

BRODY

"Lucy, are you dipping your popsicle in *syrup*?"

She grinned at me and nodded, clearly proud of herself.

"Great." I laughed. "At this rate, you'll be diabetic by noon. Your mom's already going to kill me if she finds out I let you have popsicles with your eggs and pancakes."

"We won't tell!" Piper grinned, red juice dripping off her chin.

"You guys rock!" I leaned over and high-fived her. "Okay, my little Twinkies, next on the agenda: what do you want to do today?"

"Play Barbies."

"Watch *Sleeping Beauty.*"

"Build things with Play-Doh."

"Play Mario Kart."

"Can we paint your nails again?"

I got dizzy looking back and forth between the two of them as they spit out more things than were possible to accomplish in one day. "Whoa, whoa." I held my hands up. "I might need to write this down. Are we taking naps at all? Please?"

"No!" they squealed in unison.

"I have an idea. Mom was running late today and didn't pack a lunch. What if we go to the hospital and surprise her?"

Smiles lit up both of their faces as they nodded furiously.

I looked down at their plates of brown, gooey syrup mixed with red popsicle juice and bits of scrambled egg and sighed. "I'm gonna clean up breakfast while you guys play for a few minutes, okay?"

With that, they hopped down from the island and ran toward their bedroom.

I had just about finished scrubbing the egg pan when Sophia and Fred came into the kitchen.

"Good morning!" Sophia said cheerfully.

"Hey! You guys just missed eggs and bacon."

"No problem. We'll make something in a little bit. Kacie leave already?"

"Yep, a little while ago. She was in a hurry and didn't make her lunch, so I thought the girls and I would drive up there and surprise her, if that's okay with you?"

"Of course it is." Sophia walked up and lightly cupped my face. "You're a good man, Brody."

"It's my mom's fault." I winked at her.

An hour or so later I was showered, dressed, and ready to walk out the door of my guest room when my cell phone chirped. It was Viper.

V: Hey, Shit-for-brains. Where are you?

What's up, numbnuts? I'm at Kacie's.

V: I figured. Went by your house and you weren't there. You ever coming home or what? Gonna work at the inn full time as the new cook? Should I buy you a pink apron?

Shut it, asshole. I'll be home soon, and I'll be ready to go on opening day.

V: You better be. Your contract is up this year. If you play like
you left your brain, and your dick, up there your ass is gonna get
traded and shipped out of state.

Awww, Viper. Do you care about me?

V: Fuck off. Get in shape. Win us games.

Love you too, pumpkin.

There was truth to what Viper was saying. It *was* an important
year for me. I had pushed it from my brain for as long as I could, but
I couldn't ignore it any longer. My current contract was up, and if I
wanted to stay in Minnesota, I needed to be on the ball this year.

No mistakes.

No fuckups.

I also needed to work on finding a new agent. That thought sat in
my stomach like a lead weight. Sighing, I shoved my phone in my back
pocket and headed out the door.

Lucy and Piper were fidgeting excitedly on the bench by the front
door when I got to the bottom of the stairs.

"You girls listen to Brody and don't act up. Got it?"

They listened closely and nodded as Sophia lectured them on behaving. I couldn't help myself. I walked up behind Sophia, making silly
faces and hand gestures as she continued. Lucy and Piper covered their
mouths and tried hard not to giggle, but they weren't successful. Sophia
spun around and caught me with my tongue hanging out of my mouth.

She shook her head and smiled at me. "Maybe I should be giving
you the lecture."

"Oh, trust me, I've heard it hundreds of times. It's never helped
before." I grinned at her as I walked over and opened the front door for
the girls. I grabbed the booster seats that were waiting for me there, the
girls hugged Sophia good-bye, and we were off.

We pulled up to the hospital, and I turned and peeked at the girls in the backseat. They stared at the big white building in complete awe. People hustled in and out of the main entrance. A man wheeled a woman out the front door as she held their new baby in her arms. An ambulance quickly pulled up to sliding doors in the side driveway, which I assumed led to the ER.

"Have you guys ever been to this hospital before?"

Lucy shook her head.

"I've only been to that one when that man hit me in the lake," Piper said.

Her innocent comment made my chest tight. When I thought back to that day, to her lying on the ground and all that blood around her, to Kacie's face as she knelt over her, to her tiny body lying motionless in that big hospital bed . . . I still wanted to punch things. Preferably that asshole's face. Hard.

"This one is much bigger. Pretty cool that your mom works here, huh? You guys gonna be nurses like her when you grow up?"

Lucy nodded while Piper twisted her little face, thinking.

"I want to be a hockey player like you," she said proudly, with a big, toothy grin on her face.

"You do? That's awesome. I can put in a good word for you. I know some people." I laughed back. "Come on, guys, let's go find your mom. She's gonna be so surprised to see us."

They hopped out of my truck and each grabbed one of my hands as we went inside.

We followed the red signs that led us to the ER.

"Hi there, can I help you?" asked an overly cheery woman with a big smile.

"Uh, hi." I walked over and leaned on the counter she was sitting behind. "We're looking for Kacie Jensen."

Her eyes grew wide as she bit the corner of her lip, trying to keep her smile in check. "Hang on, I'll page her for you." She turned and said something into the phone before turning back to us. "You guys can sit over there if you want. She'll be right out."

I stared at her curiously for a second before Lucy tugged my hand, pulling me over to the waiting area.

Before we even sat down, Kacie rushed around the corner with a concerned look on her face.

Holy shit, does she look hot in her light blue scrubs. Maybe I can get her to give me an exam later.

"What's going on? Is everything okay?" Her eyes scanned Lucy and Piper top to bottom before she turned to me.

"Yeah, we're fine." I reached over and squeezed her shaky hand. "We just thought we'd surprise you for lunch."

Her brows were furrowed in confusion as her green eyes searched my face, trying to process what I'd just said.

"Surprise?" I held my hands up and shrugged my shoulders, not sure she was happy to see us.

"Are you mad?" Lucy asked nervously.

Kacie's head snapped over to Lucy and her face instantly relaxed. "No, no, baby. Not mad at all, just shocked. I thought something was wrong. You just scared me, that's all." She pulled Lucy and Piper in for a big hug. "I'm so glad you guys are here. Thank you." She looked up at me and smiled, but it didn't quite meet her eyes.

"You okay?" I asked.

"Yep, fine. I'm ready for a break anyway. Let's get out of here for a while, okay?" She looked around nervously and led us toward a long hallway. "I'll be back in a bit, okay, Darla?"

The woman behind the desk smirked and nodded, still staring at me.

"Where are we going?" Piper asked after a minute.

"The cafeteria. Is that okay? Mommy needs coffee, bad." Kacie smiled as she slipped her tiny hand in mine.

Once we were in the cafeteria, Kacie seemed back to her normal, happy self. Lucy and Piper had chicken noodle soup while Kacie and I sat and talked.

"You sure you're not hungry at all?"

"Nope. I'm good." She lifted her coffee cup to her face and closed her eyes as she inhaled. "This is perfect."

"Sorry about the food. We were going to stop and get you something, but two little people I know kept asking me to stop the truck so they could pee." I cocked an eyebrow at Lucy and Piper.

"Uh-oh, they do that. I should've warned you." Kacie gave each of them the "mom look."

"It's okay." I winked at the girls. "I just feel bad that you aren't eating."

"Oh, don't worry about me. Darla always has extra food. I'll steal something from her in a bit."

"Is that who was sitting at the desk just now?"

She nodded and took a sip of her coffee.

"What do you think of her? She kept looking at me funny."

"She just thinks you're hot." She giggled. "I don't really know her yet, but from what I've seen so far, I like her. A lot, actually. She's sweet and really funny. Sometimes inappropriate, but mostly funny."

"Inappropriate, huh?" I shook my head. "Sounds like the perfect woman for Viper."

"Do you think Viper will ever get married?"

"No way."

"Who's Viper?" Lucy asked.

"Uh . . . Viper is one of my friends." I chose my words carefully. No way could I ever accurately describe Viper to a six-year-old without scaring the hell out of her.

"Does he play hockey too?" Piper chimed in.

"Yep. He's on my team."

"Why did his mommy name him Viper?" Lucy scrunched up her nose in disapproval when she said his name.

"That's not his real name, baby, it's just a nickname." I laughed quickly. "His real name is Lawrence Finkle."

Lucy and Piper shoveled their soup into their mouths, seemingly unaffected by what I'd just said. Kacie, on the other hand, stared at me with her mouth open.

"Viper's real name is *Lawrence Finkle*?"

"You didn't know that?" I cocked my head slightly to the side.

"No!" She gawked at me in disbelief. "That's like . . . the nerdiest name *ever*!"

"Finkle Tinkle," Lucy said to Piper before exploding in laughter.

Piper crossed her eyes and responded, "Finkle Tinkle Winkle."

Lucy threw her head back and laughed so hard the vein in her neck popped out. A second later, Piper joined her, giggling hysterically.

I looked at Kacie and tilted my head toward the girls. "Easy crowd, huh?"

She didn't even hear me. She was too busy staring down at the two laughing hyenas with that mommy glow all over her face. If anyone ever asked me to, it would be really hard to describe exactly what love *looks like*, but I got to witness it firsthand every time Kacie looked at her girls. The way she loved them made me love her more, if that was even possible.

A moment later, she came out of her Twinkie coma and looked at me, her eyes red-rimmed. "Seriously, thank you for this. You guys just made my afternoon a thousand times better."

I grabbed her hand and pulled the top of it against my lips, not kissing it, but holding it there. We were at her work *and* with the girls, so I was trying to be respectful, but I needed to have physical contact with her.

We sat hand in hand, listening to the girls chatter about how excited they were to start school and what they were going to be for Halloween.

"Wait, you already know what you want to be for Halloween?" I asked incredulously.

Kacie squeezed my hand gently and winked at me. "It'll change at least a hundred times between now and then."

"What are *we* gonna be for Halloween?"

She frowned at me curiously but didn't respond.

"Oh, c'mon! We have to dress up! I do it every year anyway; now I have a real reason," I exclaimed, waving toward Lucy and Piper. "Granted, I might have to tame my costume ideas a bit, but I'm cool with that."

The girls rattled off all of the princess names before moving on to farm animals.

"So what do you think *we* should dress up as?" I repeated.

Her eyes slid from the girls back to me. "I don't know. What do you think—" She stopped talking midsentence and the color drained from her face as she stared at something over my shoulder.

"Kacie?" Following her gaze, I spun around in my chair, but there was nothing there. By the time I turned back around, her face had gone to the opposite extreme. Her cheeks were red and flushed as her eyes darted all over the room nervously.

"What's going on? Are you okay?"

She looked at me, but her eyes didn't meet mine. Her mind was somewhere else. "Yeah," she stammered as she rubbed her face. "I'm okay. I think I'd better head back. Maureen just walked by and I don't want her hating me any more than she already does."

I didn't say anything, hoping she'd elaborate. Instead, she gave me a fake smile and turned her attention to the girls, obviously not wanting me to ask any more questions.

"Let's clean up so Mommy can get back, okay?" Kacie stacked their soup cups and silverware on the tray and stood to throw it in the garbage. She was about five feet from the table when the tray slipped out of her hand and everything crashed to the floor.

"Stay here one minute," I said to the girls as I got up from the table and rushed to help her. I reached for the soup cup in her hand and noticed she was trembling. "Kacie, your hands are shaking. What the hell is going on?"

Sighing heavily, she sat back on her heels with her shoulders slumped, looking at the ground. "It's Maureen. I think she hates me."

"Why would she hate you?"

"I don't know. She's just . . . so intimidating." Her face lifted as her eyes finally connected with mine. "It's hard to describe. This one person has your whole future sitting in their hands and they can either make you the happiest ever or completely squash you. And they have no clue how powerful they really are. Know what I mean?"

I reached over and tucked a wavy piece of hair behind her ear. "I know exactly how that feels."

A small smile crept across her face. A real smile.

I needed that smile.

3

KACIE

My stomach was still in knots as I kissed the girls and Brody good-bye.

"Hey, you sure you're okay?" He squeezed my hand, concern evident on his face.

"Yeah." I sighed. "Just wishing I were leaving *with* you guys. I'm jealous."

"Go. Quit. Dozens of little Brodys, remember?" He wiggled his eyebrows up and down.

"Tempting, but I can't. Independence, remember?" I lifted onto my tippy-toes for one last kiss. "I gotta go."

The girls waved on their way out the door. I leaned against the wall and watched them for a minute as they passed through the extra-wide automatic hospital doors. The sun was shining bright outside and their dark silhouettes made their way hand in hand, out to the parking lot. They walked in slow motion, as if I were watching a movie. In that moment, I wanted to run out the door after them and jump in Brody's truck, never having to go back to that damn hospital again.

While we were sitting at the table, innocently talking about Halloween costumes, Zach strolled down the hallway behind Brody. I don't think he saw us, but it sent my nerves into a complete tailspin.

I felt like a sitting duck in that damn ER. At any moment, he could come in with a patient and I would be face-to-face with him again. And eventually, I would be forced to talk to him. Lauren had grilled me on why I hadn't told Brody that I had seen him, and though I knew I should have, now wasn't the right time. Brody and I only had a couple of days left of being together before his training started, and I wanted to enjoy them. Zach working at the same hospital as I was would make him feel protective and edgy, and I didn't want us going into our first season apart full of tension.

My running shoes squeaked against the cold tile floor while I walked quickly through the hallway connecting the main building to the emergency room wing. I was so lost in my thoughts about timing and the irony of my life that I didn't notice the big wooden door to my right swing open until Zach grabbed my arm and pulled me inside.

"Get the hell off me!" I snapped, jerking my arm free.

He pushed me into the janitorial closet and closed the door behind him, blocking it so I couldn't leave.

"Was that them?" His face was panicked, his dark brown eyes drilled into mine.

"Was that *who*?" I responded, irritation dripping from my words.

"Them. At the table . . . our girls."

My eyes widened as I fought the urge to lunge forward and strangle him with my bare hands. "They're *my* girls, *not* yours," I spat at him through clenched teeth.

"That was them, wasn't it?" His voice was gentle.

"No, genius, I was having lunch with some other random six-year-old twins. Get out of my way."

He crossed his arms across his chest and stood firm. "Why won't you talk to me?"

"Why?" I yelled incredulously. "I can think of five years' worth of reasons. Now move it!"

"Kacie, please. I have so much to explain." He took a step toward me, causing me to instinctively back up against the shelves of cleaning supplies behind me. "Can we meet up after work today? Just to talk? I'll buy you a cup of coffee."

"Coffee? You abandoned us for five years and you want to buy me fucking coffee?" My heart was pounding so hard I thought I might die of a heart attack right there. I grabbed on to the hem at the bottom of my scrubs so that I didn't reach out and punch him in his damn mouth.

"I just want to talk to you. Please?" he begged with sad, pathetic eyes.

"Sure, we can talk—in five years!" I rushed past him and pushed the door open. "Eye for an eye, asshole!" I called back before the door closed.

Tears were rolling down my cheeks by the time I reached the ER, though I didn't know why. I wasn't sad. I was mad.

So. Fucking. Mad.

My hands shook so fiercely I didn't know how I was going to be able to insert an IV, check someone's pulse, or even write my name for the rest of the day. I wanted to run. Run straight to the bathroom, splash my face with cold water, and regain my composure the best I could, but I was already late from my break. I slid quietly back into the Square and asked Darla to update me on patients.

"Nada," she said, spitting pieces of chewed-up turkey sandwich all over my sleeve. "It's been really quiet. Lady with a UTI in one, guy with a broken wrist in three. Let's hope it stays like this for the rest of the day."

I smiled at her, praying to all that is holy that what she said would be right.

No more patients today, at least not ones that have to come in by ambulance.

Darla's eyes sparkled at something over the desk. I looked up to see Zach leaning against the counter, glaring down at me.

"This isn't over," he said sternly, pinning me to my chair with his intense eyes.

I swallowed hard and looked down at the desk, not wanting to make a scene in front of Darla. When I heard his footsteps fade, I looked up at Darla, who was staring at me with her eyes as wide as they could possibly go.

"Don't ask." I sighed, dropping my head into my folded hands on the desk. "And you have bread hanging off your bottom lip."

"You know by saying 'don't ask,' that means I'm definitely going to ask."

"It's nothing. Let's drop it." I sat back in the chair and crossed my arms.

"Or we can pick it up." She giggled.

"You're strange, Darla, but I like you." I peered at her out of the corner of my eye.

"I like you too," she said quickly as she took another bite. "Now spill it."

"It's nothing. He's just . . . someone I used to know."

Darla didn't say anything. She just sat, staring at me and chewing loudly. It was then that I realized maybe she could give *me* information.

"How long has he been an EMT? Do you know?"

"Hmm . . ." Her eyes drifted up to the ceiling as she pulled her brows in, thinking hard. "It's hard to tell because he may have worked for other companies before, but he's been coming here for about a year, I would say. Yes, definitely a year because he was at our holiday party last year. He came with one of the nurses he was dating."

My stomach rolled. Not a jealous roll, but an annoyed, I-can't-believe-he's-moved-on-with-his-life-like-nothing-happened kind of roll. This hospital was roughly thirty minutes from my house. He'd been thirty minutes away from us for at least a year. Had he ever thought about us? I supposed he could have assumed we stayed in Minneapolis, but he knew my mom was my only support system. He had to have known I'd go home. Then panic started to set in.

What if he's going to stop by? What if he's going to force me to talk to him, or worse, try to see the girls?

For a moment, I started to seriously consider quitting this job, saying "screw it" to my degree, packing the girls up, and moving far away.

"Hey! Did you hear me?"

I jumped as Darla's bellow brought me back to reality.

"I'm so sorry, Darla. What were you saying?"

"You weirded out for a minute there. Does it bother you that he was dating someone?"

I scoffed. "No. Not *at all*."

It bothers me that he still lives in Minnesota. I would prefer somewhere like . . . North Korea.

"Well, if it makes you feel any better, they broke up shortly after the holiday party. Apparently the girl he was with was caught making out with someone else in the bathroom at the party. Then she quit. That was it." Darla reached in her lunch bag and pulled out a bag of cookies.

I swear all Darla does is eat.

"Anyway, that's all I really know—other than he's hot!"

I coughed, backwashing a mouthful of water back into my bottle.

"Sorry. You don't think he's hot?" She waited for my answer, but I was too busy choking. I just shook my head no. "That boy makes me want to turn into a jaguar."

"A what?"

"A jaguar. You know, a woman who goes after younger men?" She wiggled her eyebrows.

"You mean a cougar?" I laughed.

"Yeah, yeah, that's it. I knew it was one of those feline animals." She shoved a cookie in her mouth, a devilish grin slowly creeping across her face.

"What?" I asked nervously, unsure I wanted to hear the answer.

"I was just thinking about that sexy young man and what he could do to this old pussy—cat."

She giggled uncontrollably.

Barf.

"Okay, I've heard enough." I stood up and walked around to the other side of the counter.

"Where are you going?" Darla was still chuckling.

"To chat with the woman in one about her urinary tract infection. That's gotta be more fun than listening to you purring like a cat." I stuck my tongue out at her and walked away while she continued laughing at herself.

4

BRODY

"Well, well, look who decided to show up!" Viper called out as I walked into our locker room at The House. Our first practice started in ten minutes and I'd barely made it on time.

Good start, idiot.

I'd stayed at Kacie's until the last minute. Actually, way past when I was supposed to leave, but it wasn't my fault. Sophia and Fred took the girls out for doughnuts unexpectedly. Kacie and I don't have a lot of alone time, so when she chewed on her bottom lip and gave me a little look with those sexy green eyes, suddenly nothing was more important than burying myself inside her one more time.

"Shut it, Sally." I glared at him. "I told you I'd be here and I am."

Big Mike and a few of the other guys were putting their pads on and lacing their skates up. I went around the room shaking hands and getting filled in on everyone's summers.

Big Mike's wife, Michelle, had finished the first part of her pregnancy and wasn't puking anymore. They would be finding out what they were having in a couple of months and he was beyond excited about it. Who knew a father could be that proud before the baby was even born?

Louie, our backup goalie, and his girlfriend had broken up—again. He vowed to be a bachelor for the rest of his life and asked Viper to show him the ropes and all the best clubs around Minneapolis. Viper was all too happy for the new project. God help the both of them.

Viktor's nine-year-old son had checked another kid into the boards at his peewee hockey game and was suspended for two games. The kid needed five stitches to close his chin, so in Viktor's eyes, it was completely worth it. That crazy bastard spent so much time in our penalty box, he should've had his mail delivered there.

"What have you been up to, Murphy?" Louie asked as he slammed his locker shut.

"Uh, nothing, really. Spent a lot of my summer up north at my girlfriend's place."

"That's right. I heard you were all pussy crazed over some chick."

Louie was young and had a big mouth, so I cut him a little slack, but any more vulgar comments about Kacie and I was going to have to show him exactly why I was the captain of the team. I didn't like people talking about her like she was one of Viper's insignificant whores.

"Pussy crazed is an understatement." Viper laughed. "I barely saw this guy all fucking summer. Thought I was going to have to file a missing persons report."

The locker room erupted in laughter as Viper walked over and slapped me on the shoulder before shaking my hand. "You know I'm just giving you shit, bro. Good to see you." He leaned in suspiciously for a hug and quietly said, "Coach was looking for you a while ago. Just a heads-up. He was mumbling and kicking garbage cans, bitching about not taking this season seriously."

I sighed and ran my hands through my hair in frustration as Viper went back to the bench and finished lacing up his skates.

Might as well get this over with.

"Come in!" Coach Collins yelled after I knocked on his office door.

"Hey, Coach."

He looked up from his paperwork and stared at me for a second before leaning back in his chair, folding his hands behind his head. "Murphy. Wasn't so sure I'd see you today."

"Come on, Coach. You knew I'd be here. I've been here every day for five years."

He rocked back and forth slowly in his chair, his face set in a stern glare. "You're right, you have. I just normally see you around here more in the summer. You were a little . . . absent this year. It worries me."

"I know—"

"I don't think you *do* know," he interrupted. "These guys, they depend on you, look up to you, even the older ones. You're the anchor of this team, Murphy."

"You think I don't know that?" I tilted my head to the side, a little shocked by what I was hearing. "This team always has been, and will continue to be, my top priority. Yes, I have other things going on outside the rink right now—"

"I've heard." He rolled his eyes.

"What the hell, Coach? Why the attitude? I said I'd be ready by opening day and I will be, just like I have been every other year. So I have a girlfriend. Big deal. Most guys on this team are either married or have girlfriends. Why am I getting the third degree?"

Coach Collins stood and walked around his desk slowly, stopping right in front of me. "Brody, you have been with this team since the minute you graduated college, and I've been with you longer than any other player on this team. You grew up in Minnesota. You have ice crystals and pine needles in your blood. You are Mr. Minnesota Wild. I've watched as you grew into a man and, eventually, a leader right before my eyes. I love you like one of my own sons." He took his glasses off and rubbed his eyes with his fingertips in exhaustion as he continued. "Your contract is up this year, and I only have so much control over what happens in the front office. If you don't perform, they're going to trade you, and just the thought of that pisses me off. Not only do I not want to lose you as a player on this team personally, but I think you're talented and you deserve to finish up your career here, in *your* state, however many years away that might be."

While I appreciated the coach's—and Viper's—concern, it was a nonissue for me. Kacie didn't complicate my life, she simplified it. She made me want to do better.

I looked him straight in the eye, attempting to drive home my sincerity. "I'm good, Coach. I promise." I extended my right hand to him.

He looked down at my hand, then back up at me, nodding slightly as he shook it.

"I hope so, Murphy. I don't want to lose you."

"You won't. And thank you for considering me one of your sons." I tried not to laugh. "Now, can I borrow twenty bucks? Me and Viper wanna go see a movie later."

Coach rolled his eyes and pushed me toward the door of his office. "I'm not sure which one of you two idiots is going to give me a heart attack first." He walked around behind his desk and sat down as he pointed to the door. "Out. Go block things. I'll be down in a bit."

The first practice of the season always kicked my ass, and this year's was no exception. I work out hard in the off-season and keep in shape, but actual practice is a different kind of workout. Knowing that it was an important contract year for me, I felt even more pressure to block every single shot and focus harder than I ever had before.

After getting home and taking Diesel for a walk, I sat down on the couch and saw that I had a missed call.

I dialed my mom back and smiled when her cheery voice picked up. "Hello, my favorite son."

"Your *only* son," I teased.

"If I had ten sons, you'd still be my favorite."

I laughed. "How are ya, Mom?"

"Good. Busy, busy as usual. How about you?"

"Exhausted. First practice was today and my legs are on fire." I pushed my palms into my sore quads, trying to give them some relief while suddenly wishing Kacie were going to school to be a massage therapist instead of a nurse. "I'm dreading standing in the shower after this."

"Poor baby. Sounds like you need a little R and R."

"Mom, I've only had one practice." I laughed. "I'm not quite in need of a break yet."

"You work hard, Brody. You could always use a break. When do Lucy and Piper start school?"

"Uh . . . a couple weeks. Why?"

"Your dad and I were thinking we'd really like to get to know Kacie and the girls better. The hospital wasn't exactly the ideal location for our first introduction, and other than a few phone calls here and there, we haven't really talked to her since. Would you four want to come spend next weekend here?"

Kacie and I hadn't even approached the topic of her bringing the kids to *my* house yet, let alone my parents'.

"Oh, God, you're not going to interrogate her, are you, Ma?"

"Absolutely not!" she snapped. "But I'd like to get to know the woman who has stolen my son's heart . . . and all of his time."

Ah, so that was it.

"Ahhh, so that's what this is about. Mom, if you want me to come home for a weekend, just ask."

"Of course I miss seeing you, but I do want to get to know Kacie and the girls. I promise, no ulterior motives here."

"Okay. Let me talk to her and have her look at her work schedule, and I'll get back to you tomorrow, okay?"

"Sounds good! One more question—will you be in town two weeks from Friday? I have to come into the city for my scans, and since it'll be a long day, I was hoping I could stay there. Maybe a mother-son sleepover?"

My stomach dropped. I knew these scans were normal and just a precaution, but I got anxious every time she had to have them. Though I would never admit it to her, I had never completely let go of the fear that her cancer would come back. I'd feel better in a couple of weeks when she got the all clear from her doctor.

"Of course, Mom," I said flatly.

She sensed my tension. "Honey, relax. These are just routine scans."

"I know, I know. This will be fun. I'll grab a bunch of movies and cook you dinner." I tried to sound upbeat.

"That sounds perfect, actually."

"Great. I'll pick up *Saw*, *Texas Chainsaw Massacre*, *Night of the Living Dead* . . . wait, do you like Freddy or Jason?"

"Anything with Meg Ryan in it."

"Mom," I whined, "she's in chick movies. I don't want to watch chick movies, especially not with my mother."

"You want Toll House bars?" she threatened with a laugh.

Mmmm. Toll House bars.

She knew my weakness.

"Evil, Mom. That's evil." I sighed. "*You've Got Mail* or *Sleepless in* . . . wherever?"

5

KACIE

Completely exhausted from work, I came home and made dinner for everyone, even though it was the last thing I wanted to do. My mom never batted an eye when I asked her if she would watch the girls for me while I worked, so cooking dinner was the least I could do. Things would be easier in a couple of weeks when school started for them.

I tucked the girls in and collapsed on my bed, hugging my cell phone while I waited for Brody's call. I'd gotten so used to having him at the inn, it was hard not being able to run up to his guest room and snuggle up with him for a bit.

My text alert went off and I jumped, not realizing I'd dozed off.

B: You still awake?

I didn't waste time texting back; I needed to hear his voice.

"Hey." A big sigh sounded in my ear as he answered the phone.

"Uh-oh, that doesn't sound good." My heart sank.

Does he know something about Zach? No, there is no way. Right?

"Sorry, just a long day." He yawned. "I'm glad you're still awake."

His yawn was contagious. "Barely."

"How was work?"

Awful. Terrible. Horrendous.

"Good. There was a five-car pileup. That was exciting."

His husky laugh tickled my ear. "Sometimes I think I should be worried about the weird things that excite you."

I giggled. "What about you? How was practice?"

"It was okay. I probably won't be able to walk tomorrow. My quads hurt *so* bad."

"Mmmm, sounds like you need a good rubdown."

"You have no idea. I would sell my soul to the devil himself to have you here with me right now."

"Me too, Brody. This is harder than I thought it would be. How are we going to make it seven, eight months?"

"We'll just have to make more of an effort to carve out time for each other. Maybe tomorrow, as soon as practice ends, I'll grab D and head straight up there?"

I paused for a second, excited at the thought but not sure we had space. "I'll have to check with Mom; I don't know if there are any rooms available." The girls knew that Brody and I were together now, but I still didn't think it was appropriate for them to know we were sleeping in the same bed, so Brody stayed in a guest room when he was here.

A suspicious laugh filled the line. "You check with her and get back to me."

"I feel bad, though, making you drive all that way for just one night."

"Kacie, I'd drive twenty hours for just one kiss from you." Hearing him say that made my belly warm. How was I so lucky to snag the greatest guy in the world? "I'd expect a little tongue with that kiss, but you get my point."

I laughed loudly. "There's the Brody I know and love."

"I want to see you, though. It's only been a couple days and I already miss my girls—all three of you."

"We miss you too. I'll check with my mom in the morning and get back to you, okay?"

"You do that." I could tell he was smiling.

"Okay, I'm off to bed."

"All right, babe. Dream about me. I love you."

"I love *you*, Brody."

"Good morning!" I bounced into the kitchen.

"Hi?" Mom said, turning to face me from the stove. "What's with you today? You're unusually perky."

"Nothing. Just excited to see Brody tonight." The girls had already finished eating and were coloring at the island as I walked over and kissed them on the tops of their heads.

Mom rolled her eyes and chuckled. "It's only been a couple of days since you two have seen each other."

"I know." I went over to the stove and scooped up some scrambled eggs onto my plate before I sat with Lucy and Piper at the island. "I'm pathetic."

"A little, but it's sweet." She winked at me.

"Wait! Before I get too excited, is there a guest room available tonight?"

Mom turned back from the stove with a blank look on her face and stared at me. After a second she pulled her brows in and tilted her head to the side suspiciously. "Did he not tell you?"

I was confused. "Tell me what?"

A slow grin grew on her face and she slowly shook her head. "Oh, that boy. You better hold on to him, Kacie."

"What are you talking about?"

"When he told me about you being uncomfortable, um . . ." She glanced at the girls and back at me. I could tell she was trying to speak in code because of them. ". . . being roommates at night, I told him that he was welcome to a guest room anytime he wanted one. I said I'd save one for him." She walked over to the island and put her hand on her hip while I continued shoveling eggs into my mouth. "He insisted I not be out any money because of all this, so he prepaid for one guest room for an entire year. Three hundred and sixty-five nights."

My mouth fell open as my fork dropped to the plate, making a horrible clanging noise. "He paid for a *whole year?*"

She nodded. "A whole year. He's crazy about you, girl, and clearly confident in your relationship—at least for a year."

"Be right back!" I jumped off the stool and ran to my bedroom, grabbing my phone off the nightstand.

You paid for a whole year?!?!?

My foot tapped impatiently for two minutes as I waited for his response. Finally, my phone beeped.

B: You talked to your mom, huh?

Why didn't you tell me?

B: What? And miss this moment? Are you kidding? Surprising you is one of my favorite things in the world, Kacie. Well, that and watching the look on your face when you come.

My stomach flipped as I read his last text. That man was perfection.

B: You still there?

Oh, shit.

Sorry, I'm here. Just thinking about . . . you. Everything you've done for me, the surprises, the gestures. I have no words. How can I ever repay you for all you do for me?

B: Well, you could repay me tonight by showing me that look I was talking about.

Uh, abso-freaking-lutely. You might see it more than once. ;)

B: Holy shit! The winky face! I've been working for that elusive little bastard for months now!

What?

What?

B: Never mind, I'll explain later. Gotta take poor Diesel out. He's standing at the front door with his leash in his mouth, glaring at me.

Okay, love you! Can't wait to see you tonight!

B: Love you too, Kacie.

I went back out to the kitchen with a smile cemented on my face. Mom was bent over, loading the dishwasher as I sat back at the island in a daze, happily eating cold eggs.

"Give me these. At least let me warm them up," my mom hissed playfully when she stood up. She put them in the microwave and turned back to me, trying not to laugh. "What has happened to my little Kacie? She's all grown up and madly in love."

I felt my face flush, but I didn't care. "I totally am, Mom."

"I can tell. You're glowing. Happiness looks good on you." She walked over and kissed my cheek as she set my plate down in front of me. "I've never seen you like this, not even with Zach."

My stomach rolled as I tried to force the eggs to stay put. His name used to freeze me in my tracks and annoy me; now it terrified me. The first year after he left, I prayed every day that he would realize his mistake and come back for us. The last four years, I'd prayed every day that he would stay far away, and that the girls would belong to just me forever. The room started to spin as my breathing increased.

"Uh-oh, what's with the face?"

"What?" I tried to sound as normal as possible.

"Don't 'what' me, Kacie Jensen. I know you. You clam up when I mention him, but you don't look ill."

My brain started arguing with itself. I didn't want anyone to know I'd seen him. If I said it out loud, it made it seem more real. I wanted to take that secret, lock it in a box, and bury it in the middle of nowhere. Maybe then it would stay hidden forever and my life would never change. On the other hand, I desperately wanted someone to talk about it with. I hadn't seen Alexa yet, and I knew she was going to lose her mind and try to kill him. Telling Brody was out of the question right now. Lauren knew I'd seen him, but she lived on the other side of the world for the next year. I couldn't just grab the phone and call her every time I needed to talk about it.

"Where are the girls?" I craned my neck, looking for them in the family room and down the hallway.

"When you were in your room, they got dressed and went outside to rake leaves with Fred. Spill it."

"I saw him," I said in a barely audible voice.

"Him? What him? Zach?" Her eyes opened so wide I thought they might fall out of her head. "When? Where?"

I sighed. "At work. He works there. Well, kind of. He's an EMT, so I've seen him a couple of times."

She didn't speak. Her mouth hung open, her green eyes still wide as can be, her face completely frozen in shock.

"I saw him my first day. I was in a room waiting for a patient, and two EMTs brought her in. He had his back to me—I didn't recognize him from behind. When he turned around, I almost died."

"That son of a bitch," she growled. "Have you talked to him since you saw him? I can't believe you didn't tell me about this sooner, by the way."

"I ignored him the first time I saw him. Actually, I freaked out and hid in the bathroom. Then last week, the day Brody brought the girls to the hospital to have lunch with me, Zach saw them. Us. Sitting together, having lunch." She sat at the island across from me with her chin resting on her hand, mesmerized by every word I was saying. "Anyway, on my way back to the ER, he grabbed me, pulled me into a janitorial closet, and asked me about them. He wanted to talk to me, even offered to buy me a coffee."

"Wow," she said, shaking her head back and forth. "You should've taken him up on it."

"I should have?" I couldn't believe what I was hearing.

"Yes. You should have ordered the biggest, hottest coffee on the menu, then thrown it in his face."

"Mom." I let a slight giggle escape as I rolled my eyes. "Fun as that would have been, it's slightly violent."

"But fitting." She curved her lips into an evil smirk. "What does Brody think about it?"

I covered my eyes with my hands, ignoring her question.

"You didn't tell him yet?"

I just shook my head, still hiding from her.

"Kacie! What are you thinking?" She crossed her arms across her chest.

"I know, I know." I sighed. "I'm going to tell him. Soon."

"You better," she demanded.

"Anyway, I don't know what to do. I can't exactly ask for a transfer or it'll delay my graduation. I just have to do my best to avoid him until I'm done." I swallowed a huge lump in my throat as tears stung my eyes. "I'm so scared, Mom. I don't want him back in our lives. Can he take the girls?"

Mom got up and hurried around to my side of the island, pulling me in close. "Honey, he will never, ever take those girls. Do you hear me? He hasn't been around for five years. No court in their right mind would grant him any sort of custody. The most he could hope for would be minimal visitation, but if I have to sell this damn inn to hire the best lawyer in Minnesota, so be it."

Court. Custody. Visitation.

Those were things I hadn't even thought about. The knot in my stomach was so big and heavy, I felt like it might crush me. I thought telling my mom about Zach would make me feel better, but she had brought up things I wasn't prepared to deal with. The last thing in the world that I wanted right now was a court battle.

My head dropped down to my folded arms on the island and I sobbed.

6

BRODY

After another mediocre practice, I was frustrated and stressed and decided I needed to take care of something that had been disrupting my focus.

I showered at the rink and drove straight to Andy's office. My palms started to sweat as the elevator stopped at the forty-second floor and the doors opened. The Shaw Management sign stared me right in the face. I hadn't spoken to Andy since he'd shown up at my condo right after Piper's accident. Everything between us was fine that day, but it wasn't like us to go this long without even a harassing text. I also couldn't remember a time in my whole life when I was nervous to talk to him.

Andy's secretary, Ellie, was sitting behind the large granite desk.

"Brody!" she sang cheerfully as I walked out of the elevator.

"Hey, Ellie. How are ya?"

"Really good, thanks." She smiled and batted her fake eyelashes at me. I had never seen teeth as big as Ellie's. They were like white Chiclets in her mouth. She glanced at her computer screen and frowned slightly. "Is Mr. Shaw expecting you? I don't have anything on the schedule."

"Nah, he has no idea I'm here. Is he busy?"

She looked down at her watch. "He's in a meeting with Brice Foster, but they should be just about done. Do you want to wait a minute?"

"Sure." I walked over and slumped down in one of the oversize black leather chairs.

Before I even had time to pick up a magazine, his office door swung open and the hottest up-and-coming college baseball player walked out.

I stood up and rubbed my damp palms on my jeans when I caught Brice's eye. He was a little over six feet tall, but skinny as hell. Someone needed to plump this kid up if he was going to make a run at a professional sports career. He had long hair, brushed off to the side like that annoying Bieber kid, and a baseball hat propped on the very top of his head.

Who the hell taught this kid how to dress?

"Brody Murphy?" He said my name excitedly as he extended his hand.

I smiled politely and shook it. "Nice to meet you. I've heard great things about you."

He grinned as his eyes went wide. "Wow! That's awesome. Can I take a picture with you?"

"Sure. Ellie, would you mind?" I called out, but Brice shook me off.

Brice waved at Ellie to sit back down. "I got it. We'll just do a selfie." He held the camera out in front of us. "Ready?"

"As I'll ever be." I sighed, putting my arm around his shoulder and flashing a quick smile.

"Thanks so much!" He grabbed my hand and shook it quickly before rushing off.

I looked at Ellie, who watched Brice walk into the elevator. When he was out of earshot, she looked back at me and rolled her eyes. "Cute kid."

"If you say so." I laughed.

I heard Andy on the phone, so I turned the knob quietly and slipped inside. His back was to me as he stood looking out the window with his phone at his ear. Being the boss had its perks, especially when it came to offices. You could've played a full-court basketball game in there. A seating arrangement off to my right looked more like a high-end living room than office furniture. I parked my ass on the brown leather couch and propped my feet up on the coffee table while he paced back and forth, still oblivious that I was there.

"No. You have more than enough. Send the bill to my assistant and I'll pay it, but I'm not giving you any more cash, Blaire."

Wait. What?

I cleared my throat to get his attention. When his eyes snapped up and caught mine, I grinned at him and flipped him off. He rolled his eyes and pointed toward his phone. "Look, I gotta go. A client just walked in, a real pain in the ass."

I picked up the *Sports Illustrated* with Brice Foster on the cover and threw it across the room at him.

"Yeah. Yeah. Whatever. Set it up with my assistant. Bye." He turned the phone off, tossed it on his desk, and ran his hands through his hair. "Jesus, how did I deal with her all these years?"

I laughed loudly. "I've asked myself that about a hundred times."

He walked over and offered his hand to me as I stood up. He got closer and I swatted his hand away. "Fuck your handshake," I said, pulling him in for a hug. We both sat down and, for the first time, I could see how exhausted he was. He looked pale and had dark lines under his eyes.

"You look like shit. What's going on?" I linked my fingers and tucked them behind my head.

He rubbed his eyes with his palms and shook his head. "Being a single dad is tough."

"Single dad?" He officially had my attention.

"Yep. We're done." He leaned back in his chair and crossed his arms over his chest. "Actually, I'm done. I left. If she loves that ridiculously ugly castle house so much, she can have it."

"What about Becca and Logan?"

"I took them with me."

My mouth fell open. "You did?"

"Yeah. I sure as shit wasn't leaving them there with her. Of course, she argued, but only because she would've looked like an even bigger bitch letting me take them without a fight."

"Wow." I leaned forward, resting my elbows on my knees. "How did you get her to let you take the kids?"

Andy looked at me and rolled his eyes. "You know how Blaire is, Brody. Money talks. Instead of ten thousand a month in child support, I offered her thirty in alimony. She couldn't sign those papers fast enough. Gloria helped me pack up the kids' shit, and we left. I'm renting a house in town until I figure out what I want to buy. A real house—one that they can actually play in." He sighed. "Gloria has been a huge help. I pulled the kids out of day care and I'm paying her double to be with them during the day. They seem so much happier. Me too."

"Holy shit, dude. I had no idea all this was going on. Why didn't you call me?" I felt awful that my best friend of twenty years was going through so much and I'd been so clueless.

He shrugged. "Last time we talked, you had a lot going on with Piper's accident and all. You didn't need my shit weighing on you. Besides, I'm good. Better than I have been in years. You know what the worst part is?"

I shook my head.

"We've been out of the house a full month and Becca and Logan haven't asked for her once. How pathetic is that?"

"Has she asked for them?" I asked cautiously.

"Today, finally. She asked if they can spend the weekend at her house, with Gloria, of course, because God forbid she be alone with them without a nanny for longer than ten minutes." He exhaled loudly. "It's fine, though. I have work to catch up on and house hunting to do."

"I'm so sorry about all this." I was trying to ignore the knot in my stomach. "You know I've never been a big fan of Blaire, but I never wanted you to be a single dad either."

"Oh, I know that. I got the best parts of her in Becca and Logan, so for that reason, I'm glad I was with her for the last few years. Now that I see how she is, I know what *not* to look for next time." He laughed.

"Well, you sound pretty content. I'm happy about that."

"I'm glad you stopped by, actually." He stood up and walked over to his desk, picking up a piece of paper. "I have the contract termination ready for you to sign. As you know, it doesn't go into effect for sixty days, and should there be any team negotiations or if you need a new contract in that time period, of course I'll still help you out with that."

He handed me the paper and a pen and sat back down across from me.

I stared down at the legal bullshit, not understanding a damn word of it.

"Go ahead, sign it. Business is business, Brody. No hard feelings."

"Fuck this," I said, ripping the paper in half. "Regardless of your marital situation, no one has my back like you, Andy. They never have and they never will."

"Brody, listen . . . you made your decision and I completely respect that."

"I was pissed off."

"You had reason to be," he argued back.

"You're damn right I did. Even so, this is not what I want." I set the ripped-up document on the table and stood up. "Take that. Shred it, burn it, do whatever the hell you want with it, but do it after dinner. Let's go to the Bumper. I need a burger and a beer with my best friend."

A smile spread across Andy's face as he stood and grabbed his suit jacket out of the closet. "You're on."

He opened his office door and let me go first. I clapped his shoulder as I walked past him. "To celebrate, I'm going to let you buy me dinner."

A few hours later, I took Diesel for a quick walk and crawled into bed, exhausted from staying out too late with Andy.

My phone chirped.

K: Are you still coming?

FUCK! I got so caught up that I forgot I was going to go to Kacie's tonight.

Baby, I'm so sorry. I had an unexpected dinner with Andy and just got home. I totally forgot.

K: Oh, that's okay. I get it. :(

No. No. No. Not a SAD face!

I feel bad, Kacie. I'm so sorry. Let me make it up to you tomorrow?

K: No problem. I understand. I'm tired. I'm gonna head to bed. I'll talk to you in the morning, okay?

You're mad.

K: No, not at all. I'm a little sad, but things happen. Just don't forget about me tomorrow, all right?

Forget about her? Holy shit.

Kacie, I could never forget about you.

Except for tonight. Ugh. Way to go, Murphy. You idiot.

K: It's fine. I'm gonna head to bed. I'll call you in the morning, okay?

Okay. I love you.

K: Love you too! :)

I felt like a total dick and that fake smiley face kicked me right in the gut. Call me in the morning? I was going to redeem myself and do her one better.

7

KACIE

Sleep had just about taken over when I felt myself jerk awake. I grabbed my phone off the nightstand to check the time and realized I had three missed calls and five texts. All from Brody.

B: Surprise. Come to your front door.

B: You gonna come let me in or what?

B: Kacie??? Did you fall asleep?

B: Wake up! Me and Diesel are sitting on your porch and one of us has to pee . . . bad.

B: Never mind, we both pissed in the woods. Wake up! I want to see my girlfriend tonight!

Every nerve in my body tingled with pure excitement as I jumped out of bed and flew through the house. The last text had come in almost an hour ago, and by now it was completely dark outside. Slowly, I pulled the wooden door open, squinting as my eyes adjusted to the porch light.

I prayed that he hadn't decided to head back home. When I spotted him, I covered my mouth with my hand and tried to stifle my laugh.

Brody was sound asleep on the porch swing, Diesel curled into his side. He was sitting up with his hands clasped together, resting on his stomach. His head was resting on the back of the wooden swing, his mouth slightly open as he snored quietly. A bouquet of pink and purple gladiolus sat on the swing next to him. As I walked over, Diesel lifted his eyebrows and peeked up at me.

"Hey, buddy." I reached down and scratched the soft black fur on top of his head. His tail wagged in excitement.

The thumping of his tail against the wooden swing caused Brody to shift, but not open his eyes. I walked around to the back of the swing and stared down at him. He hadn't shaved in a couple of days and his stubble accentuated his strong jawline, framing his face perfectly. I cupped his face in my hands and brushed his cheeks with my thumbs. His stunning green eyes fluttered open, blinking in confusion.

"Why are you upside down?" he asked.

"Why are you sleeping on my porch?" I planted a gentle kiss on his lips before I walked around to the front of the swing and sat on his lap.

He wrapped his arms around my waist and pulled me in close. "Because you wouldn't open the door."

I turned in his lap and swung my leg over his so that I was straddling him. "I'm sorry. I fell asleep. What are you doing here?"

"You said, 'Don't forget about me.'" He shrugged. "That was like a direct challenge to prove to you that wasn't possible, so Diesel and I jumped in my truck and here we are."

"Don't you have hockey in the morning?" I mumbled as I gently kissed the side of his neck, slowly inhaling the sporty smell of his cologne and tasting his skin against my tongue. A low groan climbed from deep within him, vibrating against my lips as it escaped his mouth.

"I do. I have to leave before the sun comes up, but what you just did right there makes it all worth it."

"Just that neck kiss?" I giggled as I pulled back, looking at him. "Wow, you're easy."

"You have no idea." He crashed against my mouth, holding the back of my head with his hands. It was a feral kiss. I don't know if he still felt he needed to prove that he wouldn't forget about me or if he was just caught in the moment, but he claimed my mouth like an animal, and I wasn't about to fight it. I kept up with him the best I could, but he was relentless, aggressively exploring my entire mouth with his warm tongue.

"Wait. We can't do this here, not on the porch." I pulled back. My chest was heaving, my lips tingling. His erection pressed against the inside of my thigh and I knew we both wanted the same thing, but my mom's porch swing wasn't the place.

"Come on." He gently eased me off of him. My face flushed when he stood and reached into his pants, adjusting himself.

He took my hand and led me off the porch, letting go at the bottom of the stairs as he walked to his truck. Diesel followed us down the steps and sat next to me as we watched Brody dig around in his backseat for something. A few seconds later, with a blanket tucked under his arm, he grabbed my hand as he hurried past me.

"Where are we going?"

He turned his head to the side slightly, not saying a word as a sly grin tugged at the corner of his lips.

I didn't ask again. I had a pretty good idea where he was leading me.

It was dark outside, which made the walk through the backyard difficult, especially with bare feet. I was cautious, worried that I would step in a hole or on a stick and completely kill the mood between us.

"What's wrong?" he whispered loudly.

"Nothing. I'm trying not to step on anything," I whispered back, not looking up at him. "I never put shoes on."

With that he turned and scooped me up, tossing me over his shoulder.

"Put me down! What are you doing?" I giggled.

"You're going too slow, and the faster we get down there, the faster I can have you," he growled as he slapped my butt.

We got to the beach and I waited for Brody to set me down, but he continued marching right over the sand and onto the creaky wooden pier.

"We're going on the pier?"

He set me down gently and cocked his eyebrow at me. "Correction. *Our* pier."

I tilted my head to the side and frowned at him, confused. "Our pier?"

"Yeah, it's where we had our first dinner. Remember? As friends?" He rolled his eyes and grinned. "It was on this pier that I learned there was something incredibly special about you. It was also on this pier that I realized I am meant to have more in my life than just hockey."

"Am I the *more*?" I looked up at this sexy man, in complete awe of just how lucky I was to have him.

"You're absolutely the more." He rubbed the pad of his thumb softly along my bottom lip. "You're more than more."

I caught his hand in mine and gently kissed his palm as he stared right through me.

"And right now, I'd like to have *more* on *our* pier."

I plucked the blanket from under his arm and barely had time to open it before Brody had me on my back, his full weight on top of me, kissing me with an unapologetic neediness. We took our time, slowly kissing and savoring each other for as long as we could stand it.

He pulled back and licked his lips while he slowly studied my face. "God, I didn't realize how much I truly missed you until I was with you again."

"I missed you too," I replied breathlessly as I shoved my hands up the back of his shirt, feeling his muscles roll and flex beneath my fingertips. "Don't stop kissing me." He clasped his lips over mine again and the spark that burned constantly between us exploded into fire.

Pulling me up into a sitting position, he grabbed the waist of my tank top and lifted it over my head.

His eyes went wide as he stared down at my breasts. "Holy shit. You don't have a bra on."

Overcome with sudden shyness, I bit my lip and shrugged, trying to cover myself with my hands. "I was in bed. I don't normally wear a—"

All coherent thought drained from my brain like a burst dam as Brody pushed my hands away and clamped his warm lips around my nipple. My head fell back and a moan slipped from my mouth.

His tongue moved painfully slow, making circles around my nipple until I was pushing my breast farther into his mouth, desperate for more.

"Someone's needy tonight, huh?"

"Mmhmm," I sighed.

He gently pulled the elastic band of my pajama pants out, just far enough to tuck his hand inside. "Let's see just how needy you are, huh?"

I don't know if it was the crisp night air or the fact that we hadn't seen each other in a couple of days, but I felt like I was going to burst, and he hadn't even touched me yet. Desperate for the release only he could give me, I spread my legs to give him easier access.

He dipped his fingers inside my panties and made slow circles around my most sensitive spot. The faster he swirled his fingers, the faster I panted, hovering deliciously close to my orgasm.

"Wait." I pinched my legs together, pinning his hand in between them.

"What's wrong?" He scrunched his eyebrows in confusion.

"I'm close. Really, really close, but . . . I want you inside me."

It was almost completely dark out, but I could see his lips roll into a devilish grin when what I said registered in his brain. I lay back on the blanket, and in a matter of seconds, his pants were off and he had a condom on, hovering at my opening. He tucked his arm under my head like a pillow and slowly pushed his cock inside me. It normally took me a second to adjust to the feeling, but tonight I was so wet and so ready that I started grinding back against him immediately. He sensed how close I was already and pushed in and out of me with a fast, hard rhythm. With each thrust of his hips, my backside rocked against the wood boards of the pier, creating a squeaking serenade over the quiet lake. His deep, low moans tickled my ear as he grew close too.

"God, Kacie. You feel so good." He sounded erotically pained.

My fingers scratched against his back as he moved in me faster and faster. His hands curled around my shoulders, pulling me against him as he groaned loudly. The way he sounded when he came was just what I needed to push me over the edge. I called out over and over so loud, Brody tried to cover my face with his shoulder. His body went limp, lying on top of me while we caught our breath. After a minute, he rolled off of me and propped himself up on his elbow.

"I think I was too loud," I panted, staring up at the stars.

Leaning over and kissing my shoulder, he laughed quietly. "Uh, you were definitely vocal."

Throwing my arm over my face, I cringed internally. "I couldn't help it."

"It's *our* pier, I told you. It's magical."

8

BRODY

In the morning, I jumped out of bed before the sun was up and headed down to the kitchen. Kacie was sitting at the island, half-asleep and curled around her coffee cup.

"Good morning." I kissed the top of her head.

She grunted back without looking up at me.

I laughed. "Little tired today, are we?"

"Beyond." She blew on her steaming coffee and scoffed at me. "And I'm still mad about losing my favorite tank top."

Last night, after lying on the pier, talking for hours, and having sex one more time, we got up to get dressed and one of us realized the other one had accidentally tossed her tank top into the lake after he peeled it off of her. Knowing it was her favorite one, I felt bad, but the sight of her trying to cover herself as she ran up to the house was well worth the cost of a truckload of new tank tops. Of course, I couldn't let her sneak through the house like that. Halfway up the yard, I took my T-shirt off and put it over her head. It was about eight sizes too big and went to her knees, but she'd never looked sexier.

I poured my own cup of coffee and sat down next to her. "If it makes you feel any better, I have about thirty mosquito bites on my ass."

She was taking a drink and nearly spit it out as she covered her mouth with her hand.

"Oh my God." She tossed her head back and laughed hard once she swallowed her coffee. "Do you really?"

"Hell yeah. I was scratching all night," I pouted.

"Awww." She reached over and nuzzled her nose into my neck. "Want me to kiss it and make it better?"

"You'd kiss it for me?"

She pulled back and shrugged. "Sure. Why not?"

"In that case, did I say the mosquito bites were on my ass?" I raised an eyebrow at her. "What I meant was that I have mosquito bites all over my—"

"Brody!" Lucy jumped into my arms just as I was about to tell Kacie where I'd like her to plant her lips.

Kacie elbowed me in the gut as she got up to refill her coffee cup. "Where's my other Twinkie?"

"She doesn't want to brush her hair, so she's hiding in the bathroom." She giggled.

I watched as Kacie bent over and pulled a frying pan out of the cabinet, wondering if she had any idea how truly captivating she was. She had a long gray robe thrown over her Minnesota Wild tank top and gray pajama pants. A few stray pieces of her long copper hair had escaped the messy bun at the back of her head, making her neck look irresistible. She grinned at Lucy's crazy babbling as she slid over to the fridge and grabbed a few eggs. Call me a pussy or a pansy or whatever you want, but this woman's sexy simplicity drove me crazy, and I didn't care who knew it.

"Did you hear me, Brody?"

"I'm sorry, baby. What?" I looked down at Lucy.

"I said I didn't know you were coming today."

"You know what, I didn't know it either." I grabbed a banana from the fruit bowl and started peeling it for her. "I decided late last night to drive up and see you guys."

"Are you staying here with us today?"

"I wish I could, but I have to go home."

Lucy's shoulders slumped and her tiny bottom lip jutted out as her glance fell to the floor, nearly killing me. "I'm so sorry, kiddo, but I have practice today."

Piper skipped into the kitchen and jumped right into the conversation. "Can we come and watch you play hockey sometime?"

I spun on my stool to face her. "Yes! You *want* to come and watch sometime? I would love that!"

"Yeah!" They both jumped up and down, pumping their little arms in the air.

"Maybe one weekend when your mom doesn't work, you all can come and see a game. Maybe spend the weekend at my house?" I rushed through that last part while avoiding eye contact with Kacie.

"Really?" Piper asked excitedly, her eyes almost bugging out of her head.

"Can we, Mom?" Lucy followed up.

"Uh . . ." Kacie looked from Piper to Lucy to me. "Maybe. We'll see, okay?" The girls pouted as Kacie quickly changed the subject. "How do you guys want your eggs today? Scrambled or over easy?"

"Scrambled," they called out before running to play in the family room.

I sat quietly, trying to read Kacie's body language. She was facing away from me, her head down as she whisked the eggs quickly—a little quicker than I was comfortable with, frankly. Women always do things faster when they're mad.

Walk. Cook. Type. Talk.

Watching her arm whip around mixing those eggs had my heart racing.

Was what I said that bad?

"Kacie?"

She jumped at the sound of her name and spun to face me, tears in her eyes.

"Holy shit, are you mad? I'm sorry." I hopped off my stool and rushed around the island.

She shook her head. "No, no. I'm not mad, but me bringing them to your place just makes all of this . . . very real."

"You have two very smart little girls, Jensen. They see us hugging. They've seen me kiss you. They're not stupid; they know what's going on."

She sighed. "I know, and I'm okay with that. I'm just worried about them getting too attached." Her head was facing down, but she peeked up at me with her huge green eyes. "Me too."

"Kacie, get attached. *Please*, get attached. I sure as hell know I am. You're what I want. You *and* the girls. This is it for me." I brushed a fresh tear from her cheek. "I know we're taking our time, especially where the girls are concerned, but you're my more, remember?"

"You're my more too." A tiny smile formed on her pink, kissable lips. "And I don't even have to ask them. They're crazy about you. They talk about you constantly."

I looked over at the two cute little blond heads dancing to Taylor Swift in the family room and smiled.

"Good, because I'm not being cautious. I've thrown myself into this wholeheartedly and I'm pretty damn attached to all three of you."

She grinned and her little freckle-covered nose crinkled just the way I liked.

"Plus, I had to say something to make them happy again, especially Lucy. Did you see the look on her face when I told her I was leaving?"

She bit her lip to keep from laughing at me and shook her head.

"Holy shit!" I threw my hands up in the air. "If she ever looks at me like that again, I'm going to give her whatever the hell she asks for. Pony. Pink convertible. A pony *driving* a pink convertible. I don't know how you fight those looks. They're Kryptonite."

A small giggle escaped her as she rolled her eyes. "You get used to the looks. Sometimes you have to say no."

Gently poking her in the chest, I grinned at her as big as I could. "*You* have to say no. I'm perfectly happy being the pushover. What my Twinkies want, my Twinkies get."

"Oh God," she whooped.

"But I do have a compromise for now, if you're interested. My mom invited us to spend a weekend at their farm before the girls get too involved with school and stuff."

"Really?"

"Yep. This coming weekend, actually. They have plenty of extra space in the house, and we can take Lucy and Piper fishing and horseback riding. There's even a pier on their private lake if you want to take it for a whirl." I wiggled my eyebrows up and down at her.

Her hand smacked me on the chest playfully. "I'll look at my schedule and let you know later."

"Wow." I was surprised. "That was easy. You agreeing to that pier part too?"

The most adorable smirk grew on her face as she walked up to me and pinched my ass. "We'll see about that one. Bring a big tube of hydrocortisone just in case."

My ass was itchy and I was so exhausted on the ride home from Kacie's that I thought I might fall asleep at the wheel. I cranked up Nine Inch Nails and rolled the windows down to keep myself awake as I drove. Poor Diesel was trying to sleep on the seat next to me, but I was playing drums on the steering wheel and singing too loud.

I stopped at home, dropped Diesel off, and grabbed my bag before heading to The House for practice.

"Morning, Princess." Viper grinned at me as I walked into the locker room.

"What's up, buddy?" I walked over and shook his hand.

"Nothing," he chirped. "Wonderful day, isn't it?"

I narrowed my eyes suspiciously. "What's with you? Why are you in such a good mood?"

"Who isn't in a good mood when you wake up with a hot mouth wrapped around your dick?"

"Guess you and Kat are back together?"

"Kat?" He sounded confused. "Oh! She's visiting her sister in California."

"Then who was—" I caught his evil grin out of the corner of my eye and shook my head. "Never mind. I don't want to know."

He laughed loudly as we finished lacing up our skates.

"Viper, my boy, I don't even know what to say to you."

"You jealous?"

"Jealous? Of you?"

"Of all the ass I get."

"No," I said without hesitation. "I'm not."

"Come on, Brody. Not even a little? You've been with Kacie for a few months now, and while I agree that she's smoking fucking hot, you're fucking the same pussy *every* night. Doesn't that get old?"

I thought back to the look on her face the night before when I was buried deep inside of her on the pier. "Not even a little."

"You're so pussy whipped."

"I am." I grinned at him unapologetically. "And I'm loving every minute of it. You'll understand one day."

"Fuck that! I'm staying single forever."

I threw my practice jersey over my head and stared at him incredulously. "You're not single now, idiot."

"Technically, no. But I fuck whoever the hell I want and she never leaves me."

"And what if she did? Would it even bother you?"

Viper frowned and looked at the ground, lost in thought. Had I tamed the beast with that question? Was he actually going to be thoughtful about something for once in his life? He tossed his helmet on top of his big melon and smiled at me. "Nah. I'd have more room in my closet, and I wouldn't have to rush home and wash my sheets before she gets back and discovers I fucked a tiny brunette senseless in our bed last night. And then again this morning." He winked and turned to head out of the locker room.

Okay, maybe he wasn't so thoughtful.

9

KACIE

"Today, please," Maureen huffed.

My hands were shaking as I tried to push a needle into a drunken idiot's arm as smoothly as possible, but it was worse than trying to wrestle pants onto a toddler. I could feel Maureen's hot breath on my neck as she hovered over me, waiting for me to screw up.

"Ow! That hurts, bitch!" Drunk Guy yelled, showering beer-tainted spit droplets all over my face.

Suddenly, I didn't care very much whether it hurt him or not. It's not like he would remember it tomorrow anyway.

I went toward him with the needle again and he yanked his arm back as far as the handcuffs would allow. "Stay the fuck away from me."

"Calm down," the police officer standing next to him said as he pushed his shoulders back down.

"Maureen, I need you for a minute," Darla called from the hallway.

Maureen glared at me. "Hurry up. We have a full house tonight."

Once she hurried out of the room, I narrowed my eyes at Drunk Guy. "Listen, dude. I want to give you this IV about as bad as you want to get it, but it's my job to make your sorry, drunk ass feel better. Sit back, relax, shut your mouth, and I'll get this done as quick and as painless as possible. Got it?"

The officer pulled his fist up to his mouth and coughed, trying to cover up his laugh.

"You're hot," Drunk Guy slurred at me with a lopsided grin.

I rolled my eyes and bent over him to try the IV again. Second time was a charm, thank God. I got him all set up and walked out to the front desk where Darla was sitting.

"How did that go?" Darla nodded her head toward the room I'd just come from.

"Awful. I got hit on."

"Is he cute?"

The corners of my mouth curled down and I frowned at her. "He's plastered."

"That doesn't scare me." She winked. "The drunker, the feistier."

"Well, if you like obnoxious, overweight drunk guys with mullets, he's your man."

The rest of the night moved at lightning speed, and for that I was thankful. As soon as midnight rolled around, I was out of there for the whole weekend. Brody was coming to get us bright and early, and we were heading up to his parents' farm. I'd made the Parenting 101 mistake of telling Lucy and Piper days ago, and they'd been asking every five minutes since then if it was time to leave. I couldn't wait to wake them in the morning and finally say yes!

I was gathering up my things from my cubby when Darla plopped down on the chair next to me dramatically.

"Tired?" I asked.

"Exhausted," she said through a yawn.

"What time are you out of here?"

"Six o'clock."

"Just in time for breakfast. You're almost there." I smiled sympathetically at her. "What are you doing this weekend?"

"Nothing. This will be my first weekend off in months. I'm going to order Chinese and lie in my underwear all weekend, watching trashy reality show reruns." She clapped.

"Did someone say underwear?" Zach slid up to the counter and flashed a cocky grin at us. Chitchat time came to an abrupt end as I grabbed my lunch bag and slipped my hoodie over my head.

"What are you still doing here, handsome?" Darla cooed at him in such a way that it made my stomach roll.

"Not still. I just got here."

"Where's your uniform?"

"I'm not working, just here catching up on some paperwork."

"Good night, Darla. I'll see you next week," I said quickly and turned toward the door.

"Have fun this weekend, Kacie. Give those girls a kiss for me."

Knowing that Zach was standing right there listening to Darla mention the girls made me cringe. It was the colossal white herd of elephants in the room between us, and I was trying desperately not to be trampled by them. I just wanted to put in my hours and be on my merry way so life could be the way it was before.

"Wait up!" Zach called out as the ER doors slid open and a rush of cool night air hit me in the face.

"What do you want?" I asked, walking faster without making eye contact.

He jogged to catch up to me. "What are you guys doing this weekend? Can I see them?"

"No."

"No?"

"That's right. No."

"Just like that?"

"Pretty much." I reached into my purse and grabbed my keys and my pepper spray. The parking lot was well lit and in a safe area, so it wasn't random weirdos I was concerned about; it was the asshole next to me.

"Can I *ever* see them?"

"No."

"Kacie, stop." He tugged gently on my elbow and I stopped and spun to face him.

"I warned you once before not to touch me. This is the last time I'm going to say it. Do. Not. Touch. Me. Got it?" I said as sternly as I could.

"Got it, got it. Please, talk to me."

"No. I have to go."

He didn't attempt to touch me again. He just stopped and watched me climb into my Jeep. I locked the door, started the engine, and pulled out as quickly as I could, praying that my heart rate would return to normal by the time I got home.

"Mom! Mom! It's today, right?"

My eyes bolted open and attempted to focus on Lucy's tiny face, but she was too close to me. I closed my eyes again as I felt them crossing involuntarily. "Yes, baby. It's today."

"Yay!" she cheered loudly as she ran out of my room.

I rolled over and let my eyes drift shut, secretly wishing I'd had three more hours of sleep. When I got home from work the night before, I was so exhausted I went right to sleep instead of packing ahead of time—something completely out of character for me. Clearly Brody's laid-back, go-with-the-flow demeanor was seeping into me. I kinda liked it.

"What time are we going?" Piper crashed through my bedroom door.

"Brody is picking us up at nine o'clock." I yawned.

"He's here!" she shrieked and slammed my door shut again.

"What?" I called out and sat straight up in bed, realizing I was talking to an empty room. I grabbed my phone off the nightstand and blinked several times, trying to focus on the time. 9:12 a.m.

Shit!

I flew out of bed and into the kitchen, where Brody was leaning against the island, blowing on the coffee cup in his hand.

"Morning." Brody cocked a small smile at me.

I stood with my mouth open, my eyes darting back and forth between him and the table where my mom and Fred sat with their own steaming cups of coffee. "I overslept."

"I can see that." He raised an eyebrow as his eyes traveled down to my feet and back up to my face. He walked over and planted a kiss on my forehead. "You're still the cutest thing I've ever seen."

Quickly, I threw some clothes in a duffel bag for the girls and myself, kissed my mom good-bye, and we were out the door.

"Where are you going?" Brody asked as I headed for my Jeep.

"I need to grab Lucy's and Piper's booster seats. Hang on."

"No you don't. I got it covered." He grinned.

"You what?"

"I bought some."

"Booster seats?"

"Yep. *Consumer Reports* said they were the safest and they are super-comfortable. Viper tried them out."

"Wait." I stopped in my tracks and narrowed my eyes at him. "First, you checked *Consumer Reports*? And second, Viper tried them out?"

"Hell yes, I checked *Consumer Reports*. I have no idea what I'm doing when it comes to car seats. And the pictures of Viper are probably on the Internet somewhere. He tried to fit his big ass in one to make sure it was comfortable and some lady videoed the whole thing with her phone." The girls covered their mouths and giggled from the side of Brody's truck. "I actually had to buy three. Two for the girls plus the one Viper broke." He rolled his eyes and walked over, opening the door for me.

I climbed up into the truck and turned around. Sure enough, sitting in the backseat were two brand-new booster seats and Diesel.

Brody walked around and opened the door on his side, and the girls hopped up, settling nicely into their new seats. Every single day that crazy man offered up some innocent text or gesture that made me fall in love with him all over again. Today's dose came in the form of two booster seats.

The drive from my house to his parents' was only about an hour. Brody and I held hands quietly and listened to the girls chatter the whole way. They were so excited to see his parents' farm and swim in the lake. We'd lived on a lake their whole lives, yet they were still thrilled to swim in someone else's lake. We turned down a dirt road and drove along several miles of farm fencing before making a sharp right down another dirt road.

"That's the cutest thing ever," I said as we passed a sign that read Lazy Acres Farm hanging off of a post at the corner.

Brody's lips turned into a crooked smile. "It's always been my dad's dream to have a big farm to retire on. He's wanted to name it that as long as I can remember."

When Brody told me his parents lived in a farmhouse, I pictured a charming hundred-year-old structure that was worn down and decrepit like you would see in the movies. This house was just the opposite. It was a fairly new Victorian-style farmhouse, painted a cheery light green, adorned with small details to make it look antique. White gingerbread trim accented the corners of the huge front porch, and wicker furniture with red-and-white gingham-checked cushions invited you to sit and relax for a while.

I stood on the porch and stared out at the sprawling, immaculately kept property. Every flower was in full bloom, every blade of grass just the perfect length. "This house is amazing!" I muttered incredulously.

"I know. I love it here."

Lucy and Piper, happy to finally be out of the car, skipped around the front yard with Diesel excitedly chasing after them.

"I thought I heard giggling out here," JoAnn said pleasantly as she flowed through the front door, letting it slam gently behind her. She wiped her hands on her apron and walked toward us. "I'm so glad you guys could make it." She reached out and pulled me into a big, warm hug. I gladly squeezed back, feeling instantly connected to her all over again, just as I had at the hospital.

"Hey, Mom," Brody said when she turned her attention toward him. She reached up and wrapped her arms around him as he lifted her off the ground in a big bear hug.

He set her down and she turned and looked out at Lucy and Piper, who were still running around the yard playing. They'd outlasted Diesel, who was lying at the end of the porch, panting in the shade.

"Girls, come here!" I called out, but they didn't hear me over their giggles.

"Oh, don't. Let them play." JoAnn smiled nostalgically their way. "They never stop, do they?"

"Never." I sighed with a smile on my face.

"I tried to get Shae to come home this weekend too, but she couldn't pull herself away from her new boyfriend."

Brody's eyes hardened at his mom's revelation. "She has a new boyfriend?"

"Yep. Ricky May. Apparently he's *the one*."

His face softened as he tried not to laugh. "May? His last name is May?"

She nodded.

"Oh my God, he can't be the one. She can't marry this guy."

JoAnn crossed her arms over her chest and took a step back, cocking her hip to the side. "And why is that?"

"His last name is May, Mom. That would make her Shae May." He held his stomach and fell down onto the wicker couch, laughing hysterically. "I would be bound by sibling law to make fun of her for the rest of our lives."

"I have a feeling you're going to do that anyway." She sighed as Brody reached in his pocket and took out his phone. "What are you doing now?" she asked him.

"Just texting Andy to remind me to run a background check on this clown."

She laughed and bent down, swatting his shoulder. "Oh, Brody. Stop scaring away her boyfriends."

He held his hands up defensively in front of him. "I'm not scaring anyone away, just protecting my baby sister."

JoAnn rolled her eyes and turned toward me. "I was just making lunch. Wanna come help me?"

"I would love to." I looked back at Lucy and Piper as they squatted down, staring at something on the ground.

"Go ahead, I got them," Brody said, following my gaze. "Mom, where's Dad?"

"In his shop, building a picnic table or something." JoAnn waved for me to follow her into the house. "C'mon, Kacie."

"Your house is beautiful!" I cooed once we were in the kitchen.

"Thanks. It's our dream house. Brody built it for us." JoAnn smiled that proud mama smile that I'd worn myself so many times.

I tilted my head to the side and smiled back at her. "He told me. He talks about you a lot, actually."

"I'm very lucky." She motioned for me to sit at the kitchen table. "He's a great son. Not everyone can say that."

"Well, I think he's pretty wonderful too, but I know you had a big hand in that. What was he like as a kid?"

"Oh, goodness." A small chuckle flew from her mouth as she set a tall pitcher of sweet tea on the counter and grabbed two glasses from the cabinet. "Brody as a child. Let's see . . . for starters, he made Dennis the Menace look like an angel." The ice cubes in the glasses popped and cracked as JoAnn poured the tea over them. "He was bold and adventurous and charming, even at eight years old." She slid a glass in my direction as she sat down across from me. "He was all dark brown curls and big cheesy grins. I didn't know a child could smile as much as he did. Hockey has been his life since he was old enough to stand on skates. He wasn't always a goalie, you know."

"He wasn't?"

"Nope. Not until high school, actually. That's when he decided he didn't like relying on someone else to make sure the other team didn't score. He needed the control. Anyway, he made the varsity team as a freshman and asked the coach to put him in as goalie. Coach said no, they had some hotshot senior who had claimed that position, but Brody was persistent. He asked over and over. He was the first one to show up to practice and the last one to leave. One day, about a third of the way through the season, that hotshot got hurt and his coach had no choice but to put Brody in." She smiled and looked out the back window at something that caught her attention. I followed her gaze just in time to see Diesel and the girls run across the yard with Brody chasing after them. Smiling, she shook her head and continued. "That was Brody's defining moment. The other team didn't score once that game. In fact, opposing teams rarely scored on him for the rest of his high school career. College scouts started showing up at his games midway through his sophomore year. He was amazing. Once he was in that goalie box, nothing else existed."

I'd seen that intensity. Before we started dating, I was bored one night and Googled him. I'd quickly become mesmerized by the YouTube videos of him on the ice. He was so focused, so intense. It was as though the second his skates hit the ice, he had the ability to shut the rest of the world out and focus on what needed to be done.

"It didn't come without sacrifice, though. He gave up a lot of his childhood for his love of hockey."

I frowned at her inquisitively. "Like what?"

"Like high school dances. He never went to one." Her eyes grew sad, thinking back to the experiences her son had missed out on.

"*None?*"

"Nope. Not one homecoming, not one prom. He was even voted Snow King his senior year."

"Snow King?"

"Yeah, for the winter dance. The girls ask the boys to the Snow Dance and they vote for a senior to be the Snow King. Brody won and he couldn't even go to the dance because he had a tournament in Milwaukee."

"What are you two yapping about?" Brody bellowed as he came through the back door.

"About you and your boring childhood." JoAnn winked at him.

"Boring?" He collapsed on the chair next to me. "How was my childhood boring?"

I turned to face him. "You never went to any dances? *Ever?*"

"Nope. Wouldn't know how to order a corsage if my life depended on it." He laughed, stealing a gulp of my iced tea.

"That's so sad."

"Not really. Did I miss out on some things? Sure. Has it paid off for me? Hell yes." He shrugged. "Even if I wasn't playing hockey now, I was doing what I loved at that time. I'm not really a plan-for-the-future type of guy. I like to live in the moment."

"You don't say?" I teased, rolling my eyes.

He reached over and caught my bottom lip in his mouth, leaving me reeling from a quick but passionate kiss. I pushed his chest back gently, embarrassed that his mom was still sitting at the table with us. "Brody!"

JoAnn stood up from the table and went to the oven, removing a pan of freshly made chicken pot pies. "It's okay." She laughed. "It's nice to see Brody showing love to something other than his hockey stick for once."

Brody cocked an eyebrow and looked back to me as his mom walked away. Leaning in, he whispered, "I'm not the only one who likes to play with my hockey stick."

I punched him hard in the arm and snapped my head toward his mom, praying she hadn't heard. He laughed and stood up, walking over to the pantry, where he grabbed a loaf of bread.

"What's that for?" I asked.

"Come on." He held his hand out to me. "Let's go grab the Twinkies and feed some ducks."

"Not too long," JoAnn called out as we headed out the back door. "Lunch will be ready soon."

10

BRODY

"Oh my God." I laughed as I opened the wooden door to my dad's workshop and caught a glimpse of Lucy and Piper. They had on clear safety goggles and their little arms were chugging back and forth as fast as they could go, sanding the bench of the picnic table my dad had finished building.

"What?" He held his hands up defensively. "They wanted to help."

"There are child labor laws against this sort of thing, Dad," I teased. Kacie walked over and greeted my dad.

"Hi, Mr. Murphy. Good to see you again."

"No, no. None of that. Call me Bob, please." He bent down and gave her a quick hug. "Good to see you too. And on much better terms this time."

"Absolutely." Kacie sighed. She walked up behind the girls and peeked over them to get a better look. "Are you two behaving?"

"Mom! Back up!" Lucy pushed Kacie's stomach back gently. "Mr. Bob says you can't be in here without protection. You need goggles." With that, she marched over to a big bucket near the door and grabbed two pairs of clear goggles out of it. She handed one to Kacie and then one to me. I laughed and watched Kacie slip the arms of the goggles over her ears and look up at me, blinking fast. Kacie made anything and everything sexy.

Mental note—swipe a pair before we leave. Maybe we can play a game of lonely housewife meets horny carpenter later.

"You too, Brody." Lucy crossed her arms over her chest and tapped her foot impatiently.

"Yes, ma'am." I followed the little drill sergeant's instructions and put my glasses on immediately.

"This is really cool." Kacie looked at the bench closely. "I love the grain in the wood."

"We had to take down a bunch of old trees around the property last year and I didn't want the wood going to waste. I've made a few for local people already. Figure I'll just keep makin' 'em." He shrugged.

Kacie studied his face with a sweet smile. More than likely, she was confused by my father. He was the most Southern northerner you'd ever meet. Living the simple life was all that really ever mattered to him. He never got caught up in the famous part of my life. Mom jumped at the chance to walk a red carpet with me or go to a benefit where she might rub elbows with other celebrities. Dad would rather go through a back entrance and avoid the limelight altogether. When I was a kid, he wasn't the kind of dad who was jumping up and down in the stands screaming at me or the refs or the coaches. The games he was able to come to, he just sat and cheered me on quietly. I definitely got my loud, playful spirit from my mom.

"Hey, you guys wanna take a quick walk? I brought bread; we could feed the ducks."

"We wanna stay here," Piper whined.

Kacie shook her head. "No, no. Come on. We can come back later."

"It's fine by me if they want to stay," Dad mumbled with a pencil clenched in between his teeth, trying to measure a two-by-four.

"You sure, Dad?"

"Sure, they're no bother. Besides, I like having someone else in here with me."

"You okay with that?" I glanced at Kacie, who didn't look convinced.

She crossed her arms and cocked her hip to the side, her eyes darting back and forth between Lucy and Piper. "Are you two going to behave?"

They both nodded excitedly and went right back to working.

"Thanks, Mr. Mur—" She pushed her lips into a tiny smile. "Bob." Dad looked flushed. He nodded once and went right back to his project.

I reached down and took Kacie's hand in mine, gently pulling her toward the door. "C'mon. We only have a little while before lunch."

Grinning up at me, she squeezed my hand and happily followed my lead. I took my glasses off and dropped them in the bucket near the door. When she reached up for hers, I gently grabbed her hand, stopping her. "You should leave those on," I growled, winking at her.

She punched me in the arm playfully after she tossed them in the bucket.

We left my dad's workshop and turned left, following a dirt path down toward the small lake. Our lake wasn't nearly as big as the lake at Kacie's house, but my parents owned this one. The whole thing. Their property wrapped all the way around to the other side and they were the only ones allowed to use it. Every couple of years, my dad stocked it with fish. Even though you couldn't put a boat on it, he liked to sit on a rocker and fish off the pier or the shore.

"Your parents own all this?" Kacie held her hand up to her forehead to block the sun, trying to see across the lake.

"Yep. It's all part of their farm."

"It's beautiful," she murmured. "This whole place . . . it's unreal."

"Want one?"

She whipped her head up and tried to look at me, but she was blinded by the sun. "Do I want what?"

"This." I shrugged. "A farm. A place for the girls to play and grow. I own a lot more property than my parents are actually using. Like hundreds of acres. I could build one for us."

"Oh, Brody. No way. Don't you dare. I was just saying it's—" She stopped suddenly. I turned to face her and followed her gaze to the old, run-down barn way to the left of the lake. "Oh my God. Is that barn yours? Theirs? Whatever."

"Yeah," I answered, completely confused.

"Can we go see it?" She bit her lip and begged me with her eyes.

"Sure. Whatever you want."

The words were barely out of my mouth before she was pulling me through the tall grass and weeds toward the neglected building.

What the hell?

"Kacie, slow down." I laughed.

She turned her head to the side and grinned at me, but didn't respond or walk any slower.

We got to the barn and she stopped so suddenly I almost ran into her back.

"Wow," she whispered, gazing in awe up at the broken-down wooden structure. "Look at how beautiful it is."

I massaged her shoulders gently, squatting so I was just behind her ear. "It's just a barn, Kacie."

"*You* see just a barn. Let me see if I can show you what I see." She grabbed my hand again and pulled me forward.

The dry wood popped and snapped as she cautiously slid the barn doors open. The smell of wood, dust, and old hay rushed into my nose and down my throat, making me cough.

"Look at that. How beautiful is that?" She pointed toward dozens of laser beams of sunshine that escaped through the cracks in the wood, highlighting millions of little dust particles floating through the air. "How amazing is *that*?"

She was staring up at the light and I was staring at her. "What is this? What's with you and old barns?"

"I have no idea." She sighed happily. "But I love them. And when I say love them, I mean I *really* love them. The old wood, the dusty smell, the creaky lofts. And don't get me started on the intricate spiderwebs you find in these places."

"Uh, I distinctly remember a certain cute little copper-headed girl-friend of mine hopping onto the counter in her kitchen just last week because she saw a spider crawl across the floor."

"But I—"

"And," I continued, teasing her, "I seem to remember that same woman screaming for me to pee faster so I could come kill said spider."

She folded her arms across her chest and rolled her eyes. "That was a house spider. It was scary. Barn spiders are harmless."

"And bigger." I nodded my head toward the far dark corner of the barn. "But you're in luck. There's a ladder over there."

"There is?" Her eyes grew wide, excited. "Wanna go up?"

I laughed and nodded at her. "Sure."

She practically skipped across the wood floor of the barn and grabbed on to the rails of the ladder, scampering up it so fast I barely had time to enjoy the view. By the time I got to the top, she was slowly spinning in a circle, trying to look at everything all at once.

"Look at it up here."

I glanced around and saw lots of dust, piles of old hay tucked in the corners, and spiderwebs. Shrugging, I looked at her and shook my head. "Sorry, I don't see the appeal."

"Take a deep breath." She closed her eyes and inhaled. "You smell all this history? Who lived on this property years ago? What were they like? What used to be in here? Doesn't all that excite you? All that . . . unknown?"

"Unfortunately, no. The smell of ice excites me. Interesting to add this to the list of things that make you tick, though, huh? So far it's blood, guts, barns, and lofts." I grinned at her. "Anything else?"

"You." She slowly stalked over to me and curled her arms around my waist.

"What is *this*?" I gladly returned her hug. "This barn really turns you on, huh?"

"Maybe," she cooed. "It's romantic."

"Well, I don't have our trusty pier blanket here, but I'm guessing we can find a nice, soft patch of grass outside. Wanna go down?" I took a step toward the ladder, but she caught my hand and pulled me back toward her.

"Funny you should ask." She raised an eyebrow at me as a devilish grin appeared on her lips. "I would like to go down, actually."

"Wait, what?"

By the time my brain registered what she was saying, my dick was already rock hard.

Kacie slowly sank to her knees, staring at me the whole way with those big, sparkling green eyes. Reaching for the button on my khakis, she peered up at me and rolled her bottom lip between her teeth. She tugged the hem of my boxer briefs down just enough to free my cock and wrapped her tiny hand around it. It was all I could do to keep from blowing my load all over myself like an overly excited fourteen-year-old boy who just got touched by a girl for the first time. The minute she wrapped her tongue around my swollen head, I didn't give a shit about barns or hockey. As she lapped at the tip, my hips instinctively started thrusting. I wanted her to hurry up and slow down at the same time. I shoved my hands in her hair and squeezed. That little tug was like gasoline to her fire as she moaned around me. Kacie flattened her tongue, slid down to the root, and opened her throat, taking as much as she could. She held it there for a minute, swallowed the tip, and I bucked. Reaching around behind me, she gripped my ass to pull me closer as she suctioned her mouth tightly around my cock with a pull so fierce I could blow at any minute.

"Mommy! Brody!"

My eyes snapped open and Kacie jumped up in a flash, wiping her mouth and trying to compose herself. My brain struggled to function again as I buttoned up my shorts.

"Mommy?" Lucy called out again.

"Up here, baby," Kacie called over the railing. "Don't come up. It's not safe. We'll be right down."

Lucy and Piper's feet clomped around the wooden floor of the barn as they skipped to the other side to look in one of the old horse stalls.

"Are you okay?" Kacie licked her swollen, pink lips.

"No," I grunted. "I'm so past the point of no return, it's not even funny."

"I'm so sorry," she apologized. "I promise to take care of it later."

I pushed my legs apart in an effort to keep my thighs from rubbing against my balls. "I hope so. I'm going to be walking like I just got off a horse for the rest of the damn day."

She tried not to giggle as she apologized again. "I really am sorry. Do you have blue balls?"

"No. I have *navy*-blue balls." I groaned uncomfortably. "Feels like I got kicked in my junk. Have you ever heard of anyone dying from this before? If not, I might be the first."

"Mommy, Miss JoAnn said it's time for lunch," Piper hollered.

"Okay, baby. We're coming." She chuckled and threw her hand over her mouth, realizing what she'd just said.

"We were about to," I growled at her as we walked toward the ladder.

11

KACIE

I sailed through the doors at work, still on a complete high from my wonderful weekend with Brody and the girls, determined not to let anything spoil my day.

Famous last words.

"Good morning, Darla!" I sang out as I tucked my lunch bag in my cubby and took off my hoodie.

She took a bite of her apple and cocked an eyebrow at me. "Uh-oh. Someone got some this weekend."

I tried to hide my smile, but every time I thought back to the surprised look on Brody's face when I started to go down on him in the barn, I couldn't help but grin. However, the look on his face a few hours later when I relieved the poor guy's pain and finished what I'd started was even better. Who knew his dad's workshop could be so much fun?

"I don't blame you. With a boyfriend as hot as yours, I'd be on him like a goddamn spider monkey." She giggled, tossing her apple in the garbage.

I laughed and shook my head at her. I really did like Darla. She had absolutely no filter and spouted out whatever came to mind, but she made working here not just tolerable, but fun. The fact that Maureen really liked her, and Darla often talked me up to her, was an added bonus.

"Whose boyfriend is hot?"

My heart leaped into my throat as I turned around to hang my hoodie up. It didn't matter how much time had passed, that voice still sent me into a tailspin, just for different reasons now.

"Kacie's. He's a hockey player, a professional one," Darla chimed back. "I'm waiting. I'll totally take sloppy seconds on that one. He's too hot to pass up."

"Oh really?" Zach said curiously.

"Yeah." She sighed. "Gorgeous brown curls, the dreamiest green eyes you've ever seen, and an ass made for slappin'."

Oh God, Darla, please stop talking. Right now.

"Doubt I'll get the chance, though. From what I hear, he's pretty damn smitten with her."

"What's his name?" Zach asked nonchalantly.

"Bro—"

"None of your business." I spun around, interrupting Darla.

Zach grinned at me, a heart-stopping grin. A grin that I used to love. A grin that used to melt my heart. "None of your business? That's a weird name." He was leaning on the tall counter at the desk, his hands folded in front of him.

"I gotta get to work," I said coldly, walking over to check out the charts.

"Actually, I tried to call you. Maureen had to tweak the schedule a bit. You don't start for an hour." Darla gave me a lopsided frown. "Sorry."

I groaned. That meant I'd have to stay an hour later, and while I had come in to work happy, suddenly I was looking forward to getting out of here and heading home.

"Hey, that worked out nice. I'm about to go on my break." Zach stood up straight. "Can we talk?"

Darla looked back and forth between the two of us. "Do you two, like, *know* each other?"

Four years' worth of anger poured out of me as I glared into his dark brown eyes. How dare he put me in this position at work?

Asshole.

"I'm busy."

"Sweet Darla right here just said that you can't start work for another hour. Come on, please?" His eyes were soft, begging me to hear him out, but I wasn't having it.

"No thanks," I said flatly.

"What's going on?" Darla's eyes were huge, wondering what it was she was missing.

"Kacie doesn't want to talk to me, even though I've been pleading with her to hear me out for a couple of weeks now," Zach answered Darla without breaking my stare.

"Why don't you shut your mouth?" I snapped at him. "You're very good at keeping quiet. Try it now."

Darla's mouth fell open as she slumped into her chair slowly. "Whoa. I don't know the history here, but it's deep, huh?"

"You could say that. I'm the father of her twins," Zach said, emotionless.

My blood boiled. I charged around the counter and stormed past him. "Let's go, dick."

Maybe if I walk fast enough, I can lose him in one of these winding hallways.

"Slow down!" he called, jogging a few steps until he fell in step next to me.

No such luck.

"I can't believe you," I snapped, spinning on my heel to face him.

"This is emotional blackmail. How dare you confront me at work? Who the hell do you think you are?"

"I know that was a shitty thing to do and I'm sorry I did it that way," he apologized halfheartedly, "but I was desperate to talk to you."

"Oh really? Wow." I turned and continued down the hall, still spouting off as I went. "A few weeks of me ignoring you has you desperate, huh? Imagine what five fucking years feels like!"

He shoved his hands in his pants pockets and put his head down, deciding not to argue back anymore.

A very smart decision on his part.

We got to the cafeteria and I marched over and sat down roughly at one of the tables, crossing my arms over my chest. "Let's get this over with, please, so I can go back to my normal, happy life."

He sighed. "I'm going to grab coffee. Want some?"

"Whatever." I rolled my eyes and looked over to my left. A couple was sitting together at a table quietly, holding hands. Tears poured down her cheeks as she rested her head on his shoulder. His lip trembled as he tried to remain strong for her, for whatever they were going through.

Was their child sick? A parent? Had one of them lost a sibling?

That was the hard thing about my job. You usually met people on one of the worst days of their lives. They wouldn't remember you, but you would never forget them.

"Sugar?"

I was pulled from my own thoughts and glared up at Zach. "Don't call me that," I snarled.

He laughed and shook his head. "I was asking if you wanted sugar in your coffee. You used to like it that way; not sure if that's changed."

"I hate sugar in my coffee," I lied, refusing to give him the satisfaction of his memory being right. "I'll take it black."

He set two cardboard cups down and pulled the chair out across from me. Neither of us spoke. I was not about to make this easy on him by starting with meaningless small talk. Sitting there with him was the last place on the entire planet I wanted to be right then. Research tent in Antarctica? I'd take it. Swimming with crocodiles in the Amazon? Give it to me. Crawling across a desert in Egypt? Cakewalk compared to this moment.

"So . . ." He sighed. "What's your boyfriend's name?"

I narrowed my eyes at him and leaned forward. "The only reason I'm even sitting here with you in the first place is because you wouldn't shut your damn mouth with Darla, and I don't want everyone knowing my business. You want to feed me some bullshit about where you've been the last five years? Fine. Suit yourself, but my boyfriend is *not* something I'm discussing with you."

He flinched slightly at my words and looked down at the table. An ache spread through me.

No. Fuck that ache. He deserves this.

"I deserved that," he said.

"Finally, something we agree on." I rolled my eyes and sat back in my chair, my arms still crossed.

"This isn't easy for me either, you know," he said softly. "For years, I've thought about what I would say to you if given the chance. Now here you are, sitting right in front of me, but my brain is paralyzed. I know that nothing I say will justify the decision I made five years ago and I'm not trying to justify it. I just want you to know where I'm coming from."

I didn't give a rat's ass where he was coming from, nor did I want to hear it, but I knew that he wasn't going to back down until I let him explain himself. In that moment, I decided to keep my trap closed and let him get whatever it was out. Then I would let him have it.

"I know you knew I was drinking back then, but you had no idea how much. I was out of control. I would go to work and put in just my eight-hour shift, even though overtime was always available. I couldn't wait to get out of there and go drink."

Remembering back to how much we went without because of how tight our money situation was, I gritted my teeth but let him continue.

"I didn't even need anyone to drink *with* me. I would get a case of beer and just sit in my car by myself and drink. Then I would come home, you would go to work, and after I put the girls to bed, I'd drink until I passed out. It got to the point where I would have to have a beer in the morning on the way to work just so I could get through the day without the shakes."

I sat there, staring at him in shock. I knew he drank—there had been beer cans here and there around the house—but I'd had no idea it had been that bad.

"I was sick. Then one day, I got pulled over and was arrested for a DWI. I should've been put in jail immediately, but if you remember, my mom worked in an attorney's office back then. He worked his magic and got me released and my charges dropped on a technicality. A month later, I hit a car, and the couple inside was seriously injured. Another DWI, another arrest, more charges. That time they stuck."

I was fully engrossed in what he was telling me. I'd had no idea about his arrests.

Who had bailed him out? How had he been able to keep that from me?

"That's when I decided that I was no good for you and the girls. Whatever happened to you three, you would be better off without me. I also knew that if I told you I was leaving because I was such a fuckup, being the devoted girlfriend that you were, you would have fought for us. Most likely, you would have won. Walking away from you and the girls was the hardest and stupidest thing I've ever done."

My heart hurt. Knowing that he was in all that pain and had all those problems and I was so oblivious was rough.

"Anyway, you thought I was at work one morning, but my mom took me to meet with the lawyer she worked for, who proceeded to tell me I was in deep shit. Later that afternoon, Christina came over to babysit and I made a split-second decision. I threw my shit in my car, scribbled a note to you, kissed the girls good-bye in their sleep, and that was it. I sobbed as I kissed them. That night, I drove past the house at least a dozen times, so fucking close to coming home and begging you to forgive me. I pulled in the driveway once. I remember it clearly." He stared at the table, lost in his memory. "You had Lucy on your hip, still wearing your scrubs. You pulled the curtain back to see who it was, but you were blinded by the headlights. I started to pull out of the drive-way and you walked away, assuming it was just a car turning around."

Oh God. I remember that. It was so dark. I prayed it was him, but the car pulled out and I lost all hope.

He sniffed and wiped at the corner of his eye, still not making eye contact with me. "Anyway, after that I spiraled. I moved from couch to couch, drinking a case of beer a day, sometimes more. After a while, beer wasn't enough, so I started drinking more hard liquor. I just wanted to numb everything. When I was sober, all I thought about was you and the girls and all I was missing out on. I chose liquor over my girlfriend and daughters. It was the lowest point in my life, or so I thought."

My eyes teared up and I was thankful he wasn't looking at me. Like him, I'd also imagined what it would be like the first time I saw him after all these years. I'd pictured myself screaming at him, slap-ping him, spewing the most hateful things I could come up with at him. Instead, I was pinching the inside of my arm as hard as I could to try and distract myself and keep from crying. Those four years' worth of anger I'd clung tight to had evaporated instantly into confusion as I found myself hanging on his every word.

"Somehow by the grace of God, and my mom, I was able to stay out of prison. My mom pleaded with me to get help. She offered to pay for rehab, threatened to come to you and tell you everything, and begged my dad for help; but as you know, he was a drunk himself. I was turning into him a little more every day and I was too out of control to notice. One day, I was sleeping on the couch of some girl I met in a bar and my sister found me. She told me that Mom had just had a freak brain aneurysm and died the night before."

I couldn't hold the tears back anymore. Zach had a rough life growing up. His dad was a loser drunk who used to beat his mom up. Finally, when Zach was a little boy, she got sick of it and kicked him out. She worked really hard to raise him and his sister, Tara, on her own and provide a good life for them. His dad was constantly making plans with him and then leaving him on the porch waiting with his overnight bag. His mom never complained about his dad, though. She just worked extra hard to make up for what he was missing from him. In hindsight, she probably loved Zach *too* much and in turn, enabled him to become his father. Zach was as big a mama's boy as I'd ever seen. I couldn't imagine how her death must have affected his already unstable life.

"I tried really hard to stay sober the next couple of days. I helped Tara plan the funeral and put on a smiling face for my gram, but it all became too much and I went on a major drinking binge the night before her services. The next thing I remember is being woken up by loud banging on the door. I opened it and Tara started beating the shit out of me. She pounded on my chest and punched me in the stomach. Then she reeled back and spit in my face." His voice cracked and I had to swallow a sob. "Her boyfriend, Tony, grabbed her shoulders and pulled her back while I wiped her spit off my face with my T-shirt. She was screaming at me, but all her words were blurring together. She turned and cried uncontrollably into Tony's chest. I asked him what the fuck was going on, and he glared at me and told me that they'd been trying to get a hold of me for hours, but I was too passed out. I slept right through my mom's whole funeral."

The sob I'd swallowed worked its way back up and escaped as I clasped my hand over my mouth. Zach reached over, grabbed a couple of napkins from the next table, and handed me one before wiping his own eyes. "Needless to say, *that* was the lowest point in my entire life. My drunk ass was so selfish and so in love with the bottle, not only had I lost my kids, but now I missed my mom's funeral. I checked into an inpatient rehab the next day and lived there for six long, ugly months. While I was there my dad died too, but I chose not to go to his funeral. In my mind, that would have been a betrayal to my mom."

I took a deep breath, trying to absorb everything he'd just thrown at me. "I'm so sorry about your mom, Zach. I know how much you loved her," I finally said in a shaky voice.

"Thanks." An awkward fake smile crossed his lips. "After rehab, I changed my life completely. I started working out constantly, I went to school to become an EMT, and I started a dependency program here at the hospital. I craved stability in my life. My goal was to get myself situated and healed and then come see you. I figured you'd probably be married and maybe have other kids or something, and I didn't want to drum up any hurt, but I was hoping at some point I could earn your trust back and have some sort of role in the girls' lives." His chin quivered. "Please, Kacie. I don't want to be like my dad."

I sat, stunned. That was not at all what I was expecting to hear—any of it. I figured he'd tell me he was young and dumb and selfish, and in a way, he was, but it was so much deeper than that. Then I did something impulsive, without a second thought, something that shocked me to my core. Before my brain realized what my body was doing, I reached across and put my hand on top of his.

"I've craved stability too. We'll figure something out . . . slowly."

12

BRODY

"Holy crap! Are they going off to college?" I stared down at the mile-long list of school supplies for Lucy and Piper, wondering why the hell they needed fifty #2 pencils—each.

"Welcome to school supply shopping." Kacie giggled as she walked over and grabbed a cart.

I looked down at the cart and back at her. "I don't think that's going to be big enough."

She grinned and shook her head. "Oh boy. You're in for a rude awakening. Girls, come on!" Lucy and Piper returned the tiny stuffed animals they were playing with to their bin and bounced over to us.

"They're six. Why on earth do they need one hundred pencils?" I mumbled to myself as I followed along behind Kacie. "I'm twenty-seven. I don't think I've used one hundred pencils in my entire life."

By the time we were on the second half of the list, I was having more fun than the girls, throwing everything not nailed down into the cart.

"Brody, we need regular crayons, not glitter ones." Lucy frowned as she peeked over the edge of the cart.

"Oh, did I grab glitter?" I grabbed six of the biggest packages of regular crayons they had and tossed them in the cart. Lucy reached in to grab the glitter ones and put them back, but I stopped her. "No. We'll get those too." I winked.

Kacie came back from the bathroom with Piper and her eyes got wide once she saw the cart. "Whoa!"

"I know. We're having fun." I laughed.

Kacie tugged on my shirt, pulling me away from the girls. "Brody, listen. I appreciate all the fun you're having with them, but I'm on a budget. I can't afford all this."

"You don't have to. I can buy my girls school supplies."

"I can't let you do that."

"Kacie, have I ever told you what to do with your money?"

She bit her lip and shook her head.

"Then don't insult me by telling me what to do with mine." I reached over and kissed the end of her nose. "I'm having a blast. Let me do this."

Before she had a chance to argue, I turned back to Lucy and Piper. "All right, Twinkies. Where were we?"

We walked around Target until the cart was completely filled with school supplies, new backpacks, and glitter princess heels. They obviously weren't on the school list, but Lucy's and Piper's eyes sparkled when they saw them. That was all I needed to see.

"Your total is three hundred twelve dollars and forty-one cents," said the cashier.

I heard Kacie gasp quietly, but I didn't bother to look at her as I took my credit card out and swiped it. We'd started toward the exit when a couple of boys tentatively walked up to us.

They looked to be about ten years old and nervous as hell. One of them opened his mouth to talk but shut it before anything came out. The other one nudged him and he started again. "Uh, are you . . . Brody Murphy?"

I took a step away from Kacie and the girls and put my hands on my knees so I was closer to the boys' level. "I am. What's your name?"

"Uh, Cole."

"And you?" I glanced down at his friend, but he didn't say anything. His red hair fell in his face as he stared at me, blinking rapidly behind his black-rimmed glasses.

Cole nudged him. "That's Dylan. Um, can we have your autograph?"

"Of course. What would you like me to sign?"

"Here, take this." A woman, who I assumed was the mother of one or both of them, walked up and handed me a piece of paper and a pen.

"Thanks." I took the paper and ripped it in half neatly. "Cole, you said?" The kid nodded eagerly.

Cole,
Go Wild!
Brody Murphy #30

He grasped the paper in his hand, holding it close to his face as he stared down at it excitedly.

"My man, Dylan." I turned toward the other boy. "If you want me to give you an autograph, you're going to have to say hi."

His eyes were as wide as saucers as he took a deep breath. "Hi," he said in a barely audible voice.

I laughed and ruffled his hair. "Good enough."

Dylan,
Walk on the Wild side!
Brody Murphy #30

"Do you have time for a quick picture?" their mom asked.

"Absolutely," I said.

Both boys turned to face her, and I stood in the middle, squatting slightly. "Smile, Dylan," I said as she clicked the picture.

"So how do you think the Wild will hold up this year? Think you guys will make it to the play-offs? It's a big year for you personally, huh? I'm sure contract years are stressful," Dylan blurted out all at once as he turned to me.

"Wow." I stood up. "For someone who wouldn't say hi a minute ago, you're sure chatty now, huh?"

"He's a sports genius. All he does is read facts and stats." Cole shrugged. "He knows everything."

"Good for you, buddy."

I messed up Dylan's moppy hair again before excusing myself and walking back over to the girls. I silently prayed to all that was holy that Kacie hadn't heard the last part of the redheaded chatterbox's question assault.

"You guys ready to go?" I clapped loudly as I walked up to them.

Kacie gave me a weird smile and my heart sank. I wasn't intentionally lying to her about my contract being up this year, I just didn't want to talk about it now. It weighed on my mind constantly as it was, and knowing that it would be weighing on Kacie's too would kill me.

"Why did those boys want you to sign something?" Piper asked innocently.

"They wanted my autograph. Do you know what an autograph is?" She shook her head.

"I do!" Lucy said excitedly. "It's a piece of paper you write your name on."

"Exactly," I said to her. "They just wanted me to sign my name."

"But why?" Piper still looked confused.

"Girls, Brody plays hockey on TV, so sometimes people see him and ask for his autograph because he's . . . famous." She bit her lip and shrugged as she looked at me, unsure if she'd explained it okay.

I nodded and Piper seemed happy with Kacie's explanation.

We were making our way to my truck when Piper spoke up again. "If you're famous, do you know Selena Gomez?"

"Yeah, can we have her autograph?" Lucy followed.

Kacie looked at me and tried not to laugh at the ego shot her daughters had just given me. "Sorry." She shrugged. "Guess you have to be on the Disney Channel and sing pop music to be cool in their book."

When we got back to Kacie's, the girls wanted to take their new loot to their room and divide it into piles. What can I say? They have OCD like their mom. Sophia and Fred were in the kitchen having coffee with an older couple who were staying at the inn for a few days, so Kacie and I decided to sneak off to her room. We both collapsed on the bed and intertwined our legs while she rested her head on my chest.

"Who knew school shopping could be so exhausting?" I sighed.

Kacie giggled. "Just wait until you see the list for second grade."

"I better start saving now," I joked.

She sat up and looked at me with a pained look in her eyes. "I told you not to buy all that stuff. I could've done it. Not everything you threw in the cart, but the necessities."

"Kacie." I laughed. "I was just kidding. Trust me, I haven't even given it a second thought."

"I know, but . . . I also know hockey players don't get paid like football players, and—"

"Calm down. Do I make twenty million a year like other athletes? No. That's not how hockey is, and I'm fine with it; but I do make well into the seven figures, and I live like a college student, so it all works out."

She rolled her eyes. "You do not live like a college student. I've been to your condo. It's beautiful."

"My mom did all that. If I had decorated it, I'd have patio furniture in my living room. Seriously, though, the condo is really all I've bought. That condo, my two vehicles, and the farm for my parents. If

I retired today, we could live quite comfortably for the rest of our lives. The girls too, and probably *their* girls."

A sweet smile crossed her lips as her head looked down toward the bed. "I like it when you say that."

"Say what?"

"'We,' 'our,' stuff like that. Especially when talking about the future."

"You are my future, Kacie. You're my present *and* my future, and if I could figure out a way to invent a damn time machine, you'd be my past."

The smile that had accented her beautiful mouth just a second before faded. "But what if you have to leave?"

"What are you talking about?"

"Well, your contract and stuff. What if you get traded?"

"You heard that kid, didn't you?"

Dylan. Little ginger bastard.

She nodded. "Why didn't you tell me your contract was up this year?"

"Honestly, I wasn't going to tell you at all because I don't want you to worry about that. You take on everyone's stress as your own, Kacie. You think you have to fix everything, but I didn't want you to think about that. That's for me to worry about. I know how I need to perform to keep my spot on this team, and I plan on doing that every day. No worries, okay?"

"Give me two minutes, and then I promise I won't worry anymore." She pulled her eyebrows together and bit her lip nervously. "But think about it, Brody. What if that happens?"

"What if it does?"

"I can't move, Brody. My whole life is here in Minnesota."

"You won't have to. I told you, I've invested well. Actually, Andy's invested well for me. Before him, my money was in shoeboxes in my bedroom closet. My point is, we'll make whatever it is work, okay?" I gently brushed the side of her face with the backs of my fingers. "If I have to, I'll buy a damn plane to make sure we don't go more than a few days without seeing each other. It'll all work out. Besides, who says I'm getting traded anyway? They don't call me The Wall for nothing, remember?" I winked at her. "Now get over here and park it on my chest."

I hooked my finger in the collar of her hoodie and pulled her toward me, leaving her no choice but to fall on top of me. She tucked herself up under my arm with her head back on my chest where it belonged. We lay like that for a long time, neither of us talking but both of us thinking, most likely about the same thing.

What if I *did* get traded?

13

KACIE

"Well, look what the cat dragged in," Alexa snarled sarcastically when I walked through the doorway at the Twisted Petal. Her arms were folded across her chest and a hard glare was plastered to her face.

"I hear you're mad at me." I pouted, walking over and throwing my arms around my best friend's shoulders.

"Mad? Why would I be mad?" She wiggled out of my grasp and went back to clipping stems at her workstation. "Because I talked to my dear friend—you know, the one who lives four thousand miles away?—and she filled me in on some very interesting happenings that are going on right here in my own town with my best friend and I had no clue? Why would that make me mad?"

Way to keep a secret, Lauren.

"I'm sorry, Lex. Things have been so hectic between my shifts at the hospital, making sure I spend enough time with the girls, and my relationship with Brody—which seems to mainly be a texting relationship now that his season is getting busier . . ." I sighed and plopped myself down in a chair in the corner of her shop. "There just aren't enough hours in the day."

Her face softened and she even let a tiny smile crack her lips. "I hear ya. I don't know how you do it all, girl. Now what's going on with Zach? I really can't believe you didn't tell me. What did Brody say? How is he not in prison for killing him yet?"

"He doesn't know."

Her head flew up and her mouth sprang open. "What?"

My head dropped into my hands. "I know, I know."

"What the fuck are you thinking? Why haven't you told him?"

"I don't know. He's just got so much going on right now with the start of hockey season. He's also really stressed out because it's a contract year." I chewed on the corner of my lip, wondering if I was trying to talk myself into believing what I was saying. "I just don't want to put any more on his plate, ya know?"

Alexa eyed me skeptically. "Mmhmm. So what did the dickhead say? Where's he been all these years?"

"Well, it was a long-drawn-out story, but basically he was battling some pretty big demons. Way bigger than anything I knew about."

Whenever I thought about the conversation Zach and I had in that cafeteria, the way his chin quivered, the sincere regret in his voice as he poured his heart out, I couldn't help but feel bad for him.

"Oh my God. You're going to let him back in, aren't you?"

"Back in where?" I snapped defensively.

"Anywhere!"

"I don't know. He hasn't seen the girls yet, but I think I'm going to let him . . . eventually."

She didn't say anything as she dramatically dropped her pruning shears on the counter and turned to wash her hands in the sink.

"I know you don't agree," I defended, "but it's my decision, and he *is* technically their dad."

She spun around and narrowed her eyes at me. "What did you just call him?"

"You know what I mean."

"Uh, no, I don't. He's a fucking sperm donor, Kacie, not their father. I've been more of a father to those girls than he has."

I looked down at my hands and picked at my dark pink nail polish, distracting myself from making eye contact with her. "I know you have. But . . . what if he's changed? What if he can have some sort of positive role in the girls' lives? Don't they deserve that?"

Alexa tapped her foot against the cold tile, staring a hole right into the top of my head. I could feel it. "I don't know. I have no clue what I would do in your situation. What I *do* know is that you need to be honest with Brody about this." She wiped her hands on her hot-pink-and-black apron and took a step toward me.

"I know."

"I mean it, Kacie. He's the best thing that's happened to you since you had those girls. You don't want to fuck this up because you were too chicken to open your mouth."

"I'm not a chicken; I'm just waiting for the right time. But you're right. I'll tell him tonight."

"Alexa is always right—remember that." She winked at me. "Back to the asshole. What are you going to do, seriously?"

"There's nothing to do right now. I'm just taking it day by day."

"Kacie, be strong. Do not let him near your heart." A worried frown tugged at her eyebrows and twisted up her lips. "Wrap that shit in barbed wire when he's around."

"Lex, don't be dramatic." I laughed. "I'm fine."

"Oh really? You're fine? I seem to remember a time a while back, let's see . . . the girls were probably about four months old. He messed up so bad that I told you if you went back to him, I'd beat the crap out of you. Remember that?" She cocked her head to the side and glared at me. "I still owe you a beating."

I did remember. How could I ever forget that day? It was a normal Saturday morning in late November. The leaves had all fallen from the trees, matted to the ground by the pouring rain. Thanksgiving was the following week and Christmas was just around the corner. It was Lucy and Piper's *first* Christmas and I was beyond excited. I knew they didn't exactly know what was going on, and I'd promised Zach I wouldn't go crazy, but I wanted them to have a few presents each under the tree. We'd been saving money in our trusty savings account, also known as the coffee can in the cabinet above the fridge.

Mom wanted us to come home for Thanksgiving, and that was fine, but I'd also planned for us to have a mini-Thanksgiving the weekend before. I was excited to cook for Zach and the girls and spend the day just being together. Like every other Saturday morning, I let Zach sleep in, waking him for just a second to ask for the debit card. I bundled the girls up and headed out to the grocery store.

Zach and I both made minimum wage, but we made it work. Every week, we bought whatever the girls needed first—diapers, formula, and baby food—and then we stretched the rest.

Admittedly, I probably went a little overboard, but with good reason. We made our way to the checkout and I felt like I was pushing the Grinch's overflowing sled. The cart was piled high with a small turkey, potatoes, and all the fixings to make our first Thanksgiving as a family memorable, not to mention all the regular weekly groceries and Lucy and Piper.

The teenage girl with blue streaks in her hair handed me my debit card back. "I'm sorry, ma'am. Your card was declined."

"Wait. What?" My voice squeaked in confusion.

"Your card, it didn't go through." She shook her head, looking down at her computer screen.

"Can you try it again?" I gave it back to her, my chest growing tight. "I know there's money in there."

"Sure." She took the card back and Lucy started to howl, sick of being strapped in the cart.

"Shh, shh." I tried to calm her while still staring at the cashier. I looked at the line of people standing behind me. An older woman with gray hair looked down at the girls and back at me, smiling sympathetically.

The cashier swiped the card and stared at the screen again, eventually shaking her head. "I'm sorry, it's not going through. Do you have another form of payment?"

"No," I said quietly. An empty feeling grew in the pit of my stomach as I felt my face redden.

She asked me a question, but I didn't hear her over the girls' crying. They were battling each other for the loudest screamer as I was having the most embarrassing moment of my life.

"I'm sorry," I mumbled as I walked off with the empty cart that carried nothing but my two hysterical three-month-olds.

I hurried to my car as quickly as I could, not wanting to see the people who were in line behind me again. As soon as the girls were buckled in, I hurried out of the parking lot and drove home as fast as I could.

"Hey! Wake up!" I sat down on the bed next to Zach.

He groaned and rolled away from me.

"Zach?"

Lifting his head slightly, he squinted at me. "What?"

"Uh, I just tried to go to the grocery store and the debit card was declined. You need to call the bank."

"Why?"

"So they can see what happened. Both of our checks went in yesterday. There should be more than enough money."

"I don't need to call. I know where it is." He lay back down and covered his head with the pillow.

I pulled the pillow off of him. "Zach! Where is it? I need to go to the grocery store. I just wasted two hours!"

"It's gone!" He snatched the pillow back.

"Gone? What do you mean, gone? Where is it?"

"I spent it."

"What?"

"Me and the guys, we went gambling after work last night. I lost."

I shot off the bed and glared down at him. "You gambled away both of our paychecks?"

"Yeah. Sorry."

"You are such an immature ass!" I turned and stormed out of the bedroom. The last thing I wanted to do was dip into the girls' Christmas money, but at this point, I had no choice. I could forget about the turkey and all the sides, but I needed to cover basic groceries for the week. I lifted onto my tippy-toes, grabbed the coffee can from the cabinet, and opened it.

Empty.

What the hell?

I sprinted down the hall and threw the can at Zach, happy when it connected with his head.

"Ow! What the hell, Kacie?" He sat up and rubbed the side of his head.

"You bastard! Where is the girls' Christmas money?"

"Oh. That." He looked down at the bed, avoiding my glare. "I took that too."

"Zach! What the hell! How could you do this?" My throat burned and my voice cracked even though I was trying to stay strong. "It's their first Christmas and now they won't have *any* presents. Nor will we have food for the week. What are we supposed to do?"

"Calm down about Christmas. They don't know what the hell is going on anyway. And there's probably enough food here for the week. We'll be fine." He yawned like he didn't have a care in the world. "Anyway, you should be thanking me. I tried to double it. How much would you have loved me then? Damn blackjack table."

My pulse raced; my heart pounded. I wanted to hit him. I wanted to hit him so bad. How could I be with a person who literally gambled away his kids' food?

I ran to the bedroom and packed two duffel bags. One for me and one for the girls. I had no idea where I was going or how long I would be gone, but it didn't matter at that moment. I just needed to get away.

Zach didn't try to stop me as I left. In fact, I think he went back to sleep.

My mother couldn't know what Zach had done; she'd never let me hear the end of it. I only had one option: Alexa's.

She opened the front door to her house and shook her head.

"Don't say a word," I begged as I walked past her into her house and set the girls in Derek's lap. "Congratulations. It's a girl. Actually, two of them."

He laughed and picked Lucy up, tossing her in the air.

"Dude. He is such an ass," Alexa snarled after I grabbed the bags from the car.

"I know." I sighed. "That's it, Alexa. I mean it. If he doesn't even care about groceries for the girls, there's no hope for the two of us."

"I hope you really mean that this time," she accused, raising an eyebrow at me. "Don't fall for any of his bullshit excuses. You deserve better."

Zach and I were back together before Thanksgiving. He showed up at Alexa's house with apologies and empty promises galore. I was holding strong until he apologized for the twentieth time and asked if we could look at engagement rings before Christmas. I melted and went home with him.

"Earth to Pooks." Alexa's voice rattled in my brain. I was so engrossed in my memory, I hadn't listened to anything she'd been saying this whole time. "You were thinking about it, weren't you? That day?"

I nodded and picked at my nail polish again.

"You were stupid," she said.

My head snapped up and I glared at her.

"It's true." She shrugged. "You were stupid to go back to him and you know that you were, but I believe everything happens for a reason.

If you hadn't gone back that time, who knows what your life would have been like?"

I sniffled and thought back to how hard I'd fought to be a good mom and keep my family together.

"Those girls are lucky to have you, Kacie. And all three of you are lucky to have Brody. Do not fuck this up. Just don't."

14

BRODY

"Hey!" I stood at my counter, cutting up carrots as my mom walked through my front door.

"Hi, honey." She came over and wrapped her arms around me. "How's my boy?"

"Fine. How are you? How was your day?"

My mom's normally bright, cheery face looked gray and tired with dark circles under her eyes. "It was long and exhausting." She sighed. "But I'm glad it's over with." She lifted the lid on the huge silver pot on my stove. "What are you making? It smells delicious."

"Beef stew. Your favorite." I smiled at her. "We have time, though. Do you want to go lie down and take a nap before dinner?"

A slight frown crossed her face as she tilted her head to the side. "No way. I just got here. I'd feel bad."

"It's okay. I was worried you'd beat me home and not be able to get in, so I left as soon as practice ended and didn't shower. I'll do that, take D for a walk, and then we can have some dinner and talk. I went and got all your chick movies; we can pull an all-nighter." I walked over and took her sweater from her, gently rubbing her shoulders as I pushed her toward my guest room. She felt small, weak . . . like if I squeezed too hard, her bones would shatter right in my hands.

"Sounds like fun." She yawned. "I'll try not to sleep long."

"Mom, you had a long day. Rest. I'm not going anywhere." I kissed her on the cheek before she walked down the hall, disappearing into the dark room.

I added the carrots to the pot and hustled off to my room to shower. When I was done, I hooked Diesel up to his leash, peeked in on my mom, who was sleeping soundly, grabbed my cell phone, and left.

Nothing beat Minnesota in early September, especially in the evenings. The air was cool and for a people-watcher like me, it was like hitting the jackpot. Diesel did his business and we parked it on a bench outside my building while I texted Kacie.

Hey, baby. You busy?

K: Hey! Rough day. :(Needed to laugh. I'm at the movie theater with the girls.

Shit.

No problem. I just wanted to say hi. I miss you.

K: I miss you . . . so much. Is your mom there yet? How is she feeling?

Yeah, she got here a while ago. She's napping. Then we're gonna have dinner and hang out.

K: Sounds fun. I'll call you later?

Don't forget. I want to ask you something.

K: Ask me now :)

My palms were sweating. I felt like a nervous, pimple-faced teenager about to ask a girl to prom.

It's not a big deal, really. My first home game is next weekend. Any chance you'd want to take me up on that offer and bring the girls here? Maybe spend the night? All of you?

K: Absolutely!

Really?

Really?

K: Of course! I've been dying to watch you play. The girls have too. Let me just check my schedule and make sure I'm not working. Then we should be good.

Awesome. We'll talk more later. Tell the girls I said hi. Have fun.

K: I will. Love you.

Love you, MORE.

K: ;)

As I tucked my phone in my pocket, Diesel jumped up on the bench and licked my face. "Ready to go inside?"

His ears raised and he tilted his head.

"It's gonna be a long night, D. Lots of chick movies. Don't leave me, okay?"

"Feel better?" I sat up on the edge of my couch and muted the TV when Mom walked into the living room, stretching her arms above her head.

"Much. Thank you." She curled up in the chair across from me.

"Hungry?"

"Starving." She started to get up, but I stopped her. "Sit. I'll get it."

I walked into the kitchen, scooped up two huge bowls of beef stew, and brought them into the living room. "Here." I handed one to her. "Eat, please."

"Stop fussing over me. I'm fine." She smiled and took the bowl from me as I sat down on the couch.

"You're not fine. You're skinny."

"Oh, please." She waved me off. "It's my job to worry about you, not the other way around. Anyway . . ." She sighed. "What's going on with you?"

"What are you talking about?"

"I don't know. You seem . . . distracted."

How do mothers know these things? Was there some sort of alarm system attached to the uterus that let them know when something was going on internally with one of their kids?

"I'm fine, Mom."

"Let's not do that thing where you pretend to be a big, strong man who doesn't like to talk to his mom about his problems. You're my son. I love you. What's going on?"

I sighed. "My first game of the season is a week from tomorrow and I'm stressed about it." I set my bowl on the coffee table and rubbed my temples.

"Brody Murphy, stressed? About a game?" Her eyebrows rose in surprise and her eyes grew wide. "That's a first."

"No, it's not."

"Oh, please! From the time you were eight years old, your dad and I would tell you 'good luck' before a big game and you would say—" She set her bowl down and stood up. Puffing her chest out and marching around the living room, she imitated me. "I don't need luck. I'm Brody Murphy. I got skills."

I laughed and shook my head. "Was I really that much of a punk?"

"Not a punk. Confident. There's a difference." She chuckled and sat back down. "You backed up what you said, Brody. That's all that matters. Now, why are you so nervous about next week?"

"My contract is up at the end of this year and I'm not getting any younger. The pressure to perform is at an all-time high."

"Oh." Concern canceled out her previously playful tone. "I didn't realize this was a contract year."

"Yeah. Growing up in Minnesota, I never imagined playing anywhere else. I love it here, especially now because of Kacie and the girls. The thought of leaving them behind to play somewhere else . . ." I couldn't even finish the sentence.

"Don't think like that. Like you said, you've always been a live-in-the-moment kind of person, and it suits you. Don't worry too much about the future just yet."

"I know, but now I have a reason to worry about my future."

She leaned back in her chair and crossed her arms over her chest. "Look at you," she said, narrowing her eyes and smiling at me.

"What?"

"You are completely smitten, aren't you?"

I nodded. "Beyond."

"Think you'll marry her?"

"I'd marry her tomorrow if I could, but she needs to go slow right now. She's still fighting some demons from her past."

"Stuff with her ex?" she asked cautiously.

"Yep."

"What happened with that anyway?"

"He was an ass. Walked out on her and the girls." I would be thankful every day for the rest of my life that that asshole left; otherwise, I might never have met Kacie. Still, thinking about the way he treated her made my fucking blood boil. "From what she's said, he wasn't all that great to her when they were together."

"That's too bad. Has she seen him at all?" she asked as she picked her bowl up off the coffee table and started eating again.

"Nothing. He literally walked out on them. Left her a damn note. I don't think he's even called once."

"Wow." Her brows pulled together and she tilted her head to the side. "She's one tough cookie, isn't she?"

"That's an understatement."

"Must be. I know women do it every single day, but I can't imagine raising you and Shae on my own, especially as young as she was when he left. And twins?" She shook her head back and forth in disbelief. "Forget it. That's insane."

"Sophia's helped her a lot, but she's stubborn as hell and tries to do as much as she can on her own."

A loud knock on my door echoed throughout my living room.

My mom looked at me with a puzzled expression on her face. "Are you expecting anyone?"

"Nope." I jumped up and went to my door. It was barely halfway open when Viper came barreling through it.

"What's up, ass clown!" He slapped me on the shoulder as he walked past me. "Dude, I just got the number of the hottest blond ever with the *most* amazing tits down in your lobby. She has no idea that I'm going to be fucking the shit out of her in about"—he craned his neck to look at the clock on my oven—"five hours."

"Hi, Lawrence," my mom called out.

Viper's eyes grew huge and his face turned red as he slowly turned toward my living room and peeked around the corner at my mom. His head snapped back at me as he whispered loudly, "Thanks for telling me your mom was here, douche."

"You didn't give me a chance." I laughed, closing my front door and following him into the living room.

"Hi, Mrs. Murphy." Viper walked over and gave her shoulders a quick hug. "Sorry about that."

It was hilarious watching him backtrack like a little kid.

"Want some beef stew, idiot?" I asked, trying to save him from any more embarrassment.

"No thanks. I'm not staying. I actually just stopped by to give you this." He reached in his back pocket. "I found it on the floor in the locker room after you left." He handed me my driver's license.

"Seriously?" I walked over to the counter and grabbed my wallet to put my license in the empty spot where it normally went. "Can't believe I almost lost that."

"Yeah, who's the idiot now?" he teased. "And for the record, I'm not at all shocked that you almost lost it. Your mind is always up north these days."

"We were just talking about Kacie," Mom said. "What do you think of her, Lawrence?"

Viper threw himself on the couch and relaxed with his hands behind his head. " I like her . . . a lot, actually. We just need Loverboy over here to do his job or they're going to be testing out a long-distance relationship." He looked up at me. "You ever been to San Jose? 'Cause you're about to be a Shark. Tony Ingram is having back surgery and he's gonna be out the whole season."

"No shit?"

"Yep, and Louie is looking pretty good at practices. Not to mention he broke up with his girlfriend solely to focus on hockey this year. Collins has been all over him."

Mom's brows drew together and she started wringing her hands, clearly not liking what Viper was saying.

"It'll be fine, Viper. You know there's no comparing me and Louie on the ice. I block twice the shots that cocky little prick does."

"*I* know that and *you* know that, but you need to make sure Collins remembers that." He stood up and wiped his palms on his jeans. "Anyway, I better go. I've interrupted your night long enough."

"You sure?" Mom asked. "We are just about to pop in a movie."

"Oh yeah?" Viper tilted his head back and forth, thinking about her offer. He turned to me. "What did you get?"

"Everything that has Julia Roberts, Meg Ryan, or Reese Witherspoon in it." I rolled my eyes.

"Aw, shit. I'm out." He laughed, waving at my mom as he walked to the door. "Bye, Mrs. M."

"Hey, Lawrence!" Viper stopped when my mom called out his name. He turned to face her and she cocked an eyebrow at him. "Go easy on that girl tonight. Whatever it is you said you were gonna do to her, it sounded painful."

I let out a loud laugh as Viper's face turned redder than it had been when he first realized my mom was in the next room. "I . . . uh . . . okay," he stuttered as he hurried to the door. I watched as he turned the knob and walked backward through it, flipping me off as he went. I blew him a kiss and he was gone.

"All right." I clapped my hands. "Let's get this mushy movie marathon over with."

15

KACIE

Nervously, I looked at the parking lot and then back to my watch for the fiftieth time. Lucy and Piper giggled as they flowed back and forth on the swings, blissfully unaware that their biological father was on his way.

Earlier in the week, he'd asked me if he could see them. I wasn't ready to have a conversation and explain everything to them just yet, but I told him I would bring them to the park, and he could meet us there and watch from afar. The trust issues I had with Zach still occupied most of my headspace, but I had decided to give him a second chance to slowly prove to me that he'd grown.

The slam of a truck door jolted me from my thoughts. I glanced toward the parking lot nonchalantly, thankful my sunglasses shielded my eyes. Zach got out of his car and shoved his hands in his jeans pockets as he slowly walked toward the bench I was sitting on. His eyes were darting around the playground, looking through the sea of kids for Lucy and Piper. When he finally spotted them, he stopped walking and stared. Lucy and Piper held hands and giggled as they slid next to each other down the slide. Once they got to the bottom, they hopped up, ran back around, and flew up the ladder. Zach shook his head and sat down next to me.

"Hey." He still stared at the playground.

"Hey."

"Wow."

"Wow?"

"Them." He motioned to the playground. "They're so . . . big."

"Well, it's been five years." I laughed awkwardly.

His head lowered in shame. "I know. I guess in my mind, I somehow talked myself into thinking that once I left, time just stood still. They wouldn't age, you wouldn't move on. You would all just be there, waiting for me to come back one day, and we could just pick back up where we left off." Finally, his head swept up and looked at me. "That's selfish, I know."

I nodded slowly, staring out at the girls. "A little."

"So . . . there's something I've thought about often. Something I want to ask, but I don't want to make you mad."

My stomach flipped. I didn't feel like reliving the past or having a deep discussion while sitting on a park bench, watching the girls play. "Okay?" I asked nervously.

He sighed and looked up at the park, narrowing his eyes. "What happened . . . after I left?"

I frowned at him. "Um—"

"I know it's a weird request, but I need it. I need to know what happened. I mean, I know you left." He sat back against the bench and crossed his ankle over his knee, still watching the girls play. "I drove by two weeks later. The house was closed up and a 'For Rent' sign was in the living room window."

I didn't know what to say, so I said nothing.

He continued, "I sat in the driveway that night and got plastered. If I remember correctly, I think I even slept in my car."

"What if I had still been there?" I asked quietly, surprising myself.

His head snapped in my direction and I saw him swallow. "I have no idea, Kacie. I like to think I would've wised up, come in the house, and dropped to my knees, begging for forgiveness. You would have wrapped your arms around me and told me it would all be okay. We would've given the girls dinner, bathed them, and put them to bed together. After they fell asleep we would've talked for hours about how to make things better between us, and then we would've gone into our room and made love before falling asleep curled around each other."

My lungs seized up and I had to remind myself to breathe in and out. "That's a lot of would'ves, Zach."

"It is. It's also something we'll never know the answer to, because the truth is, I was a pussy. I was too scared to face my issues and admit my shortcomings to you. I was also weaker than the bottle. It controlled me for a long time. Hell, it *still* controls me. I fight it every single day and I always will."

"Mommy! Look at this leaf!" Lucy ran up to us carrying a bright red leaf the size of her head.

"Wow! Look at that!" I said to her, though I was staring at Zach.

His eyes danced all around her face like he was trying to memorize every feature. He swallowed again and started breathing heavy.

"Who are you?" she asked him innocently.

"Uh. I'm . . . um . . . ," he stuttered, looking back and forth from Lucy to me, unsure of what to say.

"Lucy, this is Mommy's . . . friend, Zach." I smiled.

"Hi." She grinned at him.

His face visibly relaxed a little after my introduction. "Hi, Lucy. Nice to meet you."

She flashed another smile at him before running off with her leaf to find Piper.

He looked at me wide-eyed. "Holy shit."

"What?"

That megawatt smile I remembered from five years ago flashed at me. "She looks just like me."

I stared at him for a second and rolled my eyes. "Trust me, I know. I've been staring at that face every day for six years. That part hasn't been easy."

"She has my smile."

"And your puppy-dog eyes."

I felt him staring at me, but I couldn't bring myself to look at him. Something hung in the air between us. Not quite a spark and not quite nothing. It was history. Good or bad, I shared something with him that I didn't share with any other person on this planet, not even Brody.

"I have to grab something from my car real quick. Be right back." I stood up and walked twenty feet to my Jeep, knowing I needed nothing but air.

I opened my car door and fiddled around in the center console for something to bring back to the bench.

My cell phone!

I grabbed it and noticed the blinking light, signaling a text message.

B: Miss you, MORE.

Oh God. Why did I look at this?

Brody had been calling me "More" since our night on the pier when he told me I was his more. Normally I loved it, but right now, it stung. The guilt built up in me like a volcano. I *technically* wasn't doing anything wrong, but I knew that Brody would lose his mind if he knew where I was right now. Alexa was right. I didn't want to mess this up. I *had* to tell him, just not right now and definitely not through a text message.

I shoved my phone in my pocket and walked back over to the bench. Now, Lucy and Piper were both standing in front of Zach, showing him the leaves they'd collected.

He smiled and held up a yellow leaf as I sat down. "They gave me this one."

Lucy shoved a red leaf in my lap. "Hold that one, Mom. It's for Brody."

"Come on! Let's go get more!" Piper yelled as she scurried away.

We sat in silence for a minute, both of us watching Lucy and Piper collecting leaves under the tree, not wanting to address the white elephant that charged innocently out of Lucy's mouth and stomped right through our playdate.

Zach cleared his throat. "So, none-of-your-business's name is really Brody?"

"Yep," I said softly.

"How long have you guys been together?"

"A few months."

"Is he really a professional hockey player?"

"Yes."

"What team?"

"The Wild. He's the goalie."

"Brody Murphy?" he exclaimed, sitting up straight.

I sighed. "Yep."

"Wow."

I didn't bother asking if that was a good wow or a bad wow. Honestly, I didn't care. It was really awkward sitting on a bench with your children's estranged father, whom you've spent the last five years despising, discussing your new boyfriend, who just happened to be the star goalie of your state's professional hockey team. I felt like I was living in *The Twilight Zone*. All other Mondays would be forever easy compared to this one.

"Do you love him?"

Zach's question bounced around my brain like a pinball for so long, he thought I didn't hear him and he repeated it.

"Do you love him?"

I lifted my head and looked him straight in the eye. "With everything I have."

Zach smiled and nodded. "Good, I'm glad. You deserve to be happy, Kacie. Always have. As long as he's good to the girls, I don't have a problem with it."

What?

"What?" I glared at him.

He held his hands up in front of him. "I didn't mean anything bad by it."

"You said, 'As long as he's good to the girls, I don't have a problem with it.'" I jumped up and spun around to face him. "Where the hell do you get off thinking you have any sort of say in what I do with my life? Or the girls', for that matter?"

He stood up and put his hand on my arm. "Kacie, relax."

"No!" I snatched my arm away from him. "You disappear for *five* years. Then, by some insane twist of fate, we end up working in the same place. You tell me your reasons for leaving and I get it. I'll never fully forget it, but I can forgive it."

"Kacie—"

"But don't think for one second you have any right to tell me what I should and shouldn't do with my life. Nor do you have any say in what I do with the girls. They have been *my* daughters for all that time, and they're staying *my* girls."

"I wasn't trying to tell you what to do—" He stopped talking and looked past me.

I turned to see Lucy and Piper running toward us with their little arms full of leaves. "Look!" they both squealed.

"Wow. That's amazing, girls. You can take them with you if you want, but we have to get going. Mommy has to work in a while." I tried to make my tone as normal as possible.

They both stuck their bottom lips out and pouted.

"Sorry, guys. Come on." I held my hand out and took a step toward the parking lot.

"Bye, Zach." Piper waved as they followed me.

A sad smile crossed his face and he waved one hand at them.

I buckled the girls in their booster seats and climbed into the driver's seat of my Jeep. The engine roared as I turned the key and started backing out of the parking space. Zach and I made eye contact, the tight smile still plastered to his face. He waved once more as I turned the wheel. I turned right onto the little road that passed the park and couldn't stop myself from looking over at him one more time. He sat back down on the bench and played with the yellow leaf from the girls. My heart broke just a little.

Zach was standing at the counter, filling out some paperwork, when I walked into work several hours later. I walked up and leaned on the counter next to him. He looked over at me but didn't say anything as I stared straight ahead.

"When I came home and saw the note . . . I can't even explain how I felt. Words like crushed, gutted, and destroyed come to mind, but they still don't describe how I truly felt. I ran to the bathroom and threw up. That was just one of many times over the next few days."

He sighed but didn't speak.

"I called my mom, absolutely hysterical. I don't even remember what I said or what she said, I just remember crying. Then, all of a sudden, she was there. She was calling the landlord and making arrangements for me to leave. She was packing up boxes, she was doing all the things I should've been doing but couldn't, because I was either sobbing or puking."

"Kacie—"

"Don't," I interrupted. "Don't apologize. I know you're sorry. You've already said that." I finally turned and looked him in the eye. "What I need from you now is for you not to act like I owe you something for all the time you've missed out on. That was your fault, not mine. What's done is done, and I want the girls to know you and to build a relationship with you slowly, but you have *no* right to give me your opinion on what you feel I should do with *my* life."

"Understood." He nodded.

"I mean it, Zach," I continued, not sure my warning had hit home just yet. "I will date who I want, go where I want, and do what I want, and it's none of your business. If you try to make it your business, we'll put a stop to all this and do it the ugly way. Got it?"

"Loud and clear."

"Good. Now if you'll excuse me, I need to clock in." I turned on my heel and walked away, knowing damn well that he was staring at me as I went.

16

BRODY

"What are we looking for again?"

Kacie stood up from behind a pile of boxes and a piece of her hair fell in between her eyes. She blew it out of her face. "A can of clear, sparkly spray paint."

I looked around the garage at the stacks of boxes and odd tools laying around. "You're sure it's in here?"

"Yes. At least, I think it is." She walked in front of me and bent over to make sure it hadn't rolled under the shelf.

Tilting my head to the side, my eyes traveled Kacie's entire backside, then all the way to the floor and back up again. She sighed in frustration and spun around quickly, totally catching me.

"Were you just staring at me?"

"Me? No. Why would I stare at you? You're hideous with your perfect round ass and pouty, pink lips. I mean, come on. Ew."

She stomped her foot and punched me in my arm. "Come on. This is serious."

"What do you need it for again?"

Empty boxes went flying as she started flinging them off the top of the workbench. "For Piper. She lost her first tooth today at school."

"I can't believe this shit. I missed her first day of school the other day and now I missed her losing her first tooth."

"You didn't really miss much with the tooth thing," she disagreed. "The real excitement comes in the morning when she wakes up and realizes that the tooth fairy came to her house. There isn't going to be any excitement, though, if I can't find the damn spray paint."

I ducked as a box narrowly missed hitting me in the head. "Obviously I'm an idiot, but what does spray paint have to do with the tooth fairy anyway?"

"You take the dollar you're going to leave under their pillow and spray it with the glitter spray paint. It's clear so they can still use it if they want, but it's covered in sparkles so they think the tooth fairy really touched it." A tiny smile appeared on her face as she shrugged. "My mom used to do it with me and I wanted to continue the tradition with my girls. I still have all of my glitter dollars. I never spent a single one."

"Wow. Your mom has some pretty awesome ideas."

"She does, but none of it's going to matter if I don't find that damn can." She threw her hands up in the air and turned back to the row of metal shelves that lined the side of the garage.

"What time is it?"

She pulled her phone out of her pocket. "Eight forty-five."

"The hardware store closes at nine, correct?" I grabbed my keys and headed toward the door.

"Yeah, but it's a fifteen-minute drive to town. You'll never make it."

I laughed. "Challenge accepted."

Forty-five minutes later, I walked back into the garage to see Kacie sitting on the floor with a bunch of boxes scattered all around her, none of which appeared to contain spray paint.

"I can't believe you made it!" Kacie jumped up and threw her arms around my neck when she saw the plastic bag filled with glitter spray cans in my hand.

"Barely. I called when I was five minutes away and begged the manager to wait for me. He was grumpy about it until I showed up and he saw it was me." I hugged her back and set the bag on the workbench. "He asked for a picture, but I did him one better and gave him a signed puck. Thank God I always have extras in my truck."

Her eyes softened as she looked at me and gently squeezed my forearm. "Thank you for going to get these. You didn't have to do that."

"Hell yeah, I did. Piper needs glitter dollars." I looked down at the stuff all over the floor. "What the hell do you got going on here?"

"Oh, I found a couple of my old boxes, so I was going through them." She sat back down in the middle of the clutter and I followed suit. "Some pictures, some drawings, old toys, stuff like that."

I reached into a box and pulled out an old crayon drawing of what looked like dogs and cats. "Uh, did you do this?"

"Yeah." Her cheeks turned an adorable shade of pink.

"Wow. This is amazing. I mean, except for the fact that every one of these animals appears to have a penis."

"Shut up." She giggled. "Stop teasing me."

"No, really. You were drawing anatomically correct animals at a very young age. I'm impressed." I turned the paper toward her and pointed to a particularly well-endowed dog in the upper right hand corner. "This guy up here, he's very, uh, gifted in the penis department. His name must be Brody, huh?"

"Gimme that!" She snatched the paper out of my hands and laughed as she put it in another box.

"What's in this one?"

She tried to peek over the top of the box off to the side of me. "Not sure. Haven't gotten that far."

"Let's take a look, shall we?" I pulled another stack of drawings out and set them off to the side. "Well, we have Barbies. Lots of Barbies.

Apparently you don't like blondes, though, because you cut all their hair off and left the brunettes alone." I pushed them off to the side and pulled out a very familiar toy. "I remember this!"

"My View-Master!" she squealed and grabbed it out of my hands. She held it up to her eyes and found the light, frantically pulling the lever on the right down to switch the slide. *"Smurfs!"* Setting it down, she crawled over to the box I was rummaging through. "Are there any other slides in here?"

"Tons." I grabbed the stack of slides and handed them to her. She shoved them in the View-Master, one after another, clicking through to see what they were.

"Wizard of Oz! Lady and the Tramp! Rugrats!"

She set the giant red binocular-looking things in her lap and looked at me, taking a deep, satisfied breath. "I'm over the moon that you found this. I had no idea Mom still had it. I can't wait to show Lucy and Piper."

"You really liked your View-Master, huh? On a scale from one to finding a run-down barn, how excited does this make you?"

She stuck her tongue out at me. "I loved this thing, took it everywhere with me. If any one toy represented my childhood, it was this. I loved that I could just pick it up and immediately be transported somewhere else."

"I had one, but I never played with it. Actually, I think I broke it when I hit it with a hockey stick."

She rolled her eyes at me. "Help me clean this stuff up real quick and let's head in. I have a dollar to spray."

"A dollar?" I asked, surprised. "Just one?"

"Yes, just one. And no, you may not put more under there."

"You know me so well." I leaned over and kissed the tip of her cute, crinkled nose.

The next morning I went downstairs, and Kacie and the girls were already in the kitchen.

"Brody! Look!" Piper squealed when she saw me, waving a glitter dollar around in the air.

"What's that?" I played along.

"My dollar. From the tooth fairy!" She looked down at it like it was the most amazing thing she'd ever seen. "She really came. Can you believe it?"

I took the dollar from her and looked closely at it. "Wow, did you see her?"

Piper shook her head, looking a little disappointed. "No."

"I did!" Lucy bragged.

Kacie turned from the fridge to face her. "You did?"

Lucy nodded furiously. "She had yellow hair and white, sparkly wings and a green dress. She was so pretty."

"That's Tinkerbell, Lucy!" Piper argued.

"No! It was the tooth fairy, Piper!" Lucy's little head shook back and forth in anger as she yelled.

Kacie stepped in between them. "Okay, you two, relax. It's too early in the morning for this, and I haven't had nearly enough coffee yet."

"Hey." I walked over to the fridge and pulled out a mason jar of Sophia's homemade cinnamon applesauce. "Anyone want some of this with me?"

"I do," Piper said.

"No." Lucy scowled.

Kacie looked at her skeptically. "Since when do you not like Gigi's applesauce?"

"I like built apples, Mom, not squished ones," Lucy snarled.

Kacie and I looked at each other for a brief second and tried to hold our laughs in, but we were unsuccessful. Piper joined in shortly after us, and within a minute, Lucy was laughing too. All tension had evaporated from the room, and it turned into the perfect morning.

We all sat together at the island, shoving our faces full with pancakes and cinnamon applesauce, while the girls told stories about their first week at school.

"Brody, does the tooth fairy come to your house a lot?" Lucy asked.

I frowned at her in confusion. "Not since I was a little kid. Why?"

She shoved her hands onto her tiny hips. "Connor Gerjol said if you're a hockey player, your teeth fall out a lot."

Kacie let out a good laugh, trying to cover her mouth with her hands.

"Well, Connor is right, sort of. Hockey players sometimes have missing teeth from getting hit in the face with a puck or a stick, but I'm a goalie. I wear lots of protection when I'm on the ice, so I've never lost any teeth."

Lucy nodded, content with the answer I'd just given her.

"Connor also said you're our dad," Piper added nonchalantly, looking down at her pancakes.

My eyes shot over to Kacie, who sat straight up, her eyes as big as dinner plates.

"Uh . . ." was all she squeaked out.

Lucy and Piper both looked up at their mom, innocently waiting for the answer to a question that had unknowingly just rocked her whole world.

"Brody . . . is . . . uh . . . ," she stammered, looking back and forth from them to me, not sure where to go next.

"It's kind of hard to explain, guys, and we'll be able to tell you a lot more when you're older. The main thing to remember is I love your mom and I love you two a whole lot. If you want to tell people I'm your dad, that's fine by me. Hopefully one day, I will be." I reached over and squeezed Kacie's hand as her face relaxed just a little.

"Okay. Can we go play with those ugly Barbies you brought in from the garage?" Lucy asked.

"Uh, sure," Kacie answered, still reeling.

Lucy and Piper hopped off the stools and disappeared down the hall. Kacie watched to make sure they were out of earshot and spun around to me with tears in her eyes. "Holy shit."

"You okay?"

"Yes. No. I don't know. I always knew that question was coming, but I thought they'd ask where their dad was, not if you were their dad. Oh my God, I froze." She covered her face with her hands and shook it back and forth.

"You did great." I got up and stood behind her, massaging her tense shoulders.

"Brody, I didn't even answer them. You did. If you hadn't been here—"

"But I *was* here, and even if I hadn't been, you would have said something perfect." I wrapped my arms around her shoulders and squeezed tight. "You're a fantastic mom, Kacie. Cut yourself some slack."

She let out a huge sigh and relaxed in my arms. "Thank you."

"For what?"

Spinning on her stool to face me, she looked me straight in the eye. "Thank you for being here today. Thank you for always saying the perfect thing. Thank you for teaching me to relax and not take life too seriously. Thank you for loving me. Thank you for being you."

I studied her face for a second, taking in how insanely in love with that woman I really was. I loved everything about her.

Her captivating green eyes.

Her kissable lips and the way she chewed on them when she was nervous.

The freckles that were sprinkled across her adorable nose.

Even the scar on the corner of her left eye that she got from a bike-riding accident as a kid.

What overwhelmed me about her was that this outside superficial stuff was just that. It was an added bonus. What made Kacie truly special to me was what was inside of her. I loved her for the way she loved me. I loved her for the way she loved her girls. I loved her for the mother she would one day be to my kids, which were somewhere deep inside of her, waiting to be created.

"It's raining out."

She pulled back and narrowed her eyes at me, confused by my response.

I cocked my head toward the front door. "Puddles. Ya wanna?"

A huge grin formed on her face as she realized what I was asking. She hopped off the stool and looked down the hall. "Lucy! Piper! Let's go outside!"

17

KACIE

"Kacie!" my mom called from the kitchen.

I threw the last of my overnight things in my duffel bag and went to see what she needed.

"What's up?"

"Here." She set a cardboard box on the island. "This just came for you."

"For me?" I furrowed my brows, confused. "I didn't order anything."

"Look who it's from." She winked at me.

I looked at the upper left corner of the shipping tag. There was no address; it simply said #30.

A grin broke out across my face as I looked up at my mom. "What did he do now?"

"When it comes to him, anything is possible." She laughed.

God, I missed him. It had only been three days since we'd last seen each other, but it was killing me. I ripped the tape off the box and slowly opened it, revealing a card and three shirt boxes. I opened the envelope, set the tickets on the table, and unfolded the piece of paper inside.

CAN'T WAIT TO SEE MY GIRLS TONIGHT!
#30

"What is it?" Piper poked her head up over the other side of the island.

"It's from Brody. One for each of us." I smiled at her.

"Open it! Open it!" Lucy appeared next to Piper.

"Here. One for you and one for you." I handed each of them a box. They ripped the hunter-green ribbons off of them and tossed them to the ground. Their little hands pried the white cardboard boxes open and they pulled out matching kid-size Minnesota Wild jerseys.

"They look just like Brody's!" Lucy squealed.

"Wow. Very cool! Those will be fun to wear to the game tonight, huh?" I watched their little faces study their jerseys.

"Oh my goodness." Mom covered her mouth with her hand. "Kacie, look at the backs."

I walked over and took the jerseys from the girls as they looked up at me, confused. Both jerseys had the name Murphy stitched across the top and the number fifteen sewn onto them.

"Fifteen?" I frowned and looked at Mom.

She shook her head back and forth, beaming at the overload of cuteness. "Kacie, fifteen plus fifteen . . ."

My heart swelled at yet another gesture from Brody. He had this way of constantly letting me know he was thinking about me, about *us*, even when we weren't together. The best part about him was that he was accidentally romantic. He did these things, gave these simple little gifts, just to put a smile on my face. They meant so much more than he would ever know.

"What's fifteen plus fifteen, Mommy?" Piper asked.

"Thirty, baby. Fifteen plus fifteen equals thirty."

"Like Brody!" Lucy jumped up and down, hugging her present.

◆ ◆ ◆

Still meeting us there?

I waited for Darla to respond to my text.

D: Hell yes. Trying to pick out a shirt that shows the girls off real good.

I laughed and dropped my phone into my purse. Alexa was supposed to go to the game with me, but she got a last-minute funeral order at the flower shop, too large for her assistant to handle. Since Brody gave me four tickets and I didn't want the extra one to go to waste, I asked Darla to go with me. After she handled a quick shift switch at the hospital, we were all set. I told her she'd have to drive herself there and back since the girls and I were spending the night at Brody's, but she didn't seem to mind.

"How much longer?" Lucy whined.

"Just a little bit. Hold your horses." I grinned at them in the rear-view mirror, looking all adorable in their matching jerseys. All three of us, actually. That's what was in my box too—my very own Murphy #30 jersey. I had two others in my closet at home, but those were technically Brody's. I'd confiscated them because they smelled like him and I liked to sleep in them.

A little while later, we pulled into the special parking section of the stadium. I rolled my window down and handed the attendant the special parking pass Brody had included with the tickets.

"Right this way, Miss Jensen. Mr. Murphy requested that we give you his spot."

Of course he did.

He stepped back and waved his arm toward an empty space right up against the building.

The girls and I hopped out of the Jeep and excitedly walked around to the front of the stadium, where we met up with Darla.

"Girls!" she called out when she saw us, running over and scooping them up in one big armful. They both groaned as she squeezed the living daylights out of them. "How exciting is this?" She gave me a quick embrace too.

"It's very exciting," I said. "I've never been to a professional hockey game before."

"Me either." She grinned as we walked inside.

I showed the usher our tickets and he looked up at me with wide eyes.

"Follow me, ma'am." He walked us to our seats, which were up against the glass, right behind the Minnesota Wild's goal.

"Holy shit! Oh, sorry." Darla looked down at Lucy and Piper, who were staring up at her with wide eyes. "I meant shoot. These seats are amazing!"

"Yeah, they are," I said incredulously, looking around the huge arena. "I'm shocked that they give the players seats this good."

Darla shrugged. "I guess they wanna keep their boys happy. I'm not complaining, though. Look at the view we get the whole game." She tilted her head toward the goalie box and wiggled her eyebrows up and down.

I shook my head and chuckled. "You know, I should probably be offended when you say stuff like that, but for some odd reason, I'm not. Come on, girls, let's sit."

Lucy and Piper sat down to the right of me, and Darla sat on my left.

"Mom, can we get popcorn?" Lucy asked.

"Or some ice cream?" Piper followed.

I chuckled. "Guys, we just sat down. Relax."

"Actually, I'm kinda hungry too," Darla added.

I'm not surprised.

"Okay, well, as soon as they start sending the vendors out, we'll grab something."

The words were barely out of my mouth when the stadium, though not completely full yet, erupted in cheers. The Minnesota Wild had emerged from the tunnel and were taking the ice for pregame practice. A sea of hunter-green uniforms scattered all over the ice. I narrowed my eyes and scanned a group of players off to the right, looking for my #30. A loud bang on the glass right in front of me made me jump backward in my seat. I followed a Wild jersey all the way up to Brody's grinning face. He was smiling so big I thought his face might split in half, and his dimples were as deep as I'd ever seen them. His eyes twinkled as he looked at me. He was completely elated to be back on the ice in *his* stadium and have us there watching him. I was bursting at the seams with pride for him.

I grinned back and gave him the thumbs-up sign. Lucy and Piper jumped up and banged on the glass to get his attention. He blew them kisses and winked at me before he pulled his helmet over his face and took his position in the goalie box.

"Why is Brody so fat?" Piper giggled, with Lucy following suit.

"It's all the padding he has to wear to protect himself. He's just regular Brody when he takes it all off."

Darla leaned over and whispered in my ear, "I wouldn't mind seeing him take it all off. By the way, people are staring."

"At what?" I looked around and she was right. People were looking at us and pointing.

"Probably the girl that the hottest hockey player in the NHL just winked at." She laughed. "Oh, girl. You're so clueless."

I sank down in my seat a little bit, praying that the stadium would fill in quickly. My self-consciousness left as quickly as it had come as I watched Brody do what he did best.

Well, one of the things he does best.

His teammates skated by, challenging their goalie with shot after shot, none of which got past Brody. He was amazing, moving quickly and effortlessly. It was like the puck was a magnet to his glove.

He. Never. Missed.

After a few minutes, they all went back into the tunnel so the actual game could start. On their way back, Viper skated by and stopped in front of us. He held his hands up at his ears like horns and stuck his tongue out at the girls. They moved in close to each other and stared back at him, a little frightened. He laughed at their reaction and started to skate away when he noticed Darla sitting with me. He stopped and skated back a few feet, staring directly at her chest. Standing up straight with a cheesy grin on his face, he waved at her and then made a phone with his hand and held it up to his ear, signaling that he wanted her to call him.

"Oh my God," Darla squealed in my ear once he'd skated away. "Who the hell is *that*?"

"That is Viper." I laughed.

"Viper? His name is Viper? Holy crap, that's hot." She fanned herself.

"Actually, his name is Lawrence Finkle."

She frowned at me. "I'm just gonna pretend I never heard that. Is Brody friends with him?"

"Good friends. They hang out together a lot."

"I think I just had a hockeygasm. Can he introduce me? I have to meet him. Tonight." She was practically drooling all over the both of us.

"Sure." I looked at her out of the corner of my eye. "But I have to warn you, he's a pig."

Darla wiggled her eyebrows up and down. "Oink, oink."

I had never really watched hockey before, and I certainly hadn't ever been to a game, so I didn't know what to expect. Let me say this— hockey fans are *crazy*! The guy who sat behind us yelled so loud that Lucy and Piper had to cover their ears. I was just waiting for him to spill one drop of beer on us and I was going to kill him myself.

Wonder if Brody has the connections to get us one of those cute little private rooms up there so we can watch the game in peace and quiet next time.

I also had no idea that hockey was so violent!

The girls had just suckered me out of thirty dollars for popcorn and snow cones, which they set on the ledge of the boards in front of them. All was well for about three minutes until Viper checked one of the Phoenix Coyotes into the glass right in front of us—hard. Their cups went flying toward them, landing in their laps. Red and blue juice splashed everywhere.

"Oh, crap!" I jumped up and glared at Viper, who just grinned and shrugged at me. Darla flagged down a stadium attendant, who brought over paper towels and spray to clean up the floor so their feet wouldn't stick to it.

"Sorry about that," I said to the young man.

"No problem." He smiled. "Your first time here?"

"Yes."

"I can tell. Rookie mistake." He laughed. "Never put anything up on the ledge of the boards unless you want to wear it eventually." He dropped to his knees and sopped up some of the juice while I tried to dry the girls' jerseys.

"Brody Murphy is my dad," Lucy said proudly.

The man's head snapped up to her. "He is?"

"Mmhmm." She nodded.

He looked at me and stood quickly. "I'm so sorry about the 'rookie mistake' comment before. Let me get maintenance down here so they can clean this properly for you and I'll replace your stuff." He turned to Lucy and Piper. "What did you have again?"

While they repeated their order, I looked at Darla, who was laughing hysterically in her seat. As the young man ran off to do . . . whatever, the girls sat back down.

I sat down too and turned to Darla, who had tears in her eyes from laughing. "What the hell just happened?"

"Uh, your girls learned that their soon-to-be father is the king and they are, in fact, princesses."

At intermission, we all decided a bathroom break was necessary. Lucy and Piper giggled and fooled around in the stall while I leaned against the tampon machine, begging them to please hurry.

"I'm not going to let you guys go in there together anymore if you're going to fool around," I warned.

"Liar," Darla called from a stall at the end of the row.

I paid no attention as the door opened and more women filed in.

"*Kacie?*" My head snapped to the left at the sound of my name. Kendall Bauer was standing there with her mouth open. "Hi! It's so good to see you here." She walked over and pulled me into the fakest hug I'd ever had the displeasure of being a part of.

"Hi, Kendall," I said as nicely as I could through clenched teeth.

"We have to stop running into each other in bathrooms like this." She laughed.

My gut reaction was to punch her right in her fake veneers, but I knew the girls would be out any second.

"What are you doing here anyway?" I asked, not caring how snotty I sounded.

She grinned and threw her hands up in the air innocently. "Season ticket holder, remember?"

I walked over and knocked on the stall door that Lucy and Piper were in. "Come on, you two. I want to get back to the game."

"Awww, are your girls in there?" Kendall cooed.

Every hair on my mama-bear back rose. I wouldn't fight her for Brody because I knew there was no competition between the two of us, but if she said one thing in front of my daughters, I would rip her damn head off.

"Yep," I responded as the door opened. The girls came out and walked over to the sink to wash their hands. Darla came out of her stall at the same time and joined them.

Kendall clapped her hands together as she watched Lucy and Piper at the sink. "Oh my, look at their cute little jerseys."

"Brody got these for us," Piper said proudly, whipping around to show Kendall the front of it.

"I have one just like it." Kendall proudly pulled her hair to the side and turned around to reveal her Murphy #30 jersey.

Lucy frowned at her. "Did Brody give you that one?"

I struggled to contain my laugh.

"Uh, no, I bought it. But I am . . . friends with him," she said, putting air quotes around the word *friends*.

"What are you, some hockey groupie?" Darla snarled as she dried her hands.

"Excuse me. I am *not* a hockey groupie." Kendall cocked her hip to the side and crossed her arms over her chest, looking Darla up and down.

"Please, honey. Don't get defensive with me. Your bony ass can't handle it. It's painfully obvious that you're a Murphy reject. The bitterness is rotting on you like spoiled milk." Darla tossed her paper towel in the trash. "I can smell it from miles away. There are plenty of other men on the team; go find one. Brody is spoken for."

Kendall's mouth fell open, and her tarantula eyes, cloaked in too much mascara, grew wide.

"What's the matter, Princess? Cat got your tongue? That's probably best for both of us." She waved Kendall toward the doorway. "Go on now. Shoo, shoo."

Kendall glared at me like she was looking for me to defend her, but I just tipped my head to the side and grinned at her. "I'll be sure to tell Brody you said hello. You can say what you want about being friends, but I know for a fact you haven't spoken to him in months."

Kendall narrowed her eyes at me and huffed toward the bathroom door. She opened it and turned to say something to me one more time, but I didn't give her the chance.

"Be sure to give Blaire my best and tell her I'm really sorry how things have worked out for her," I sneered.

The door closed behind her and that was that. I turned to Darla and clutched my chest. "Oh my God, I thought I was going to die of a heart attack just now. I've been trying so hard to stand up for myself lately. I'm shaking, but holy crap, that was exciting."

Darla laughed at me and took the girls' hands. "Come on, Bambi. Let's take your wobbly legs back to our seats."

18

BRODY

After we put our first Wild win in the books for the season—and my first shutout—I was ready for a quick shower and a day off with my girls. Coach Collins gave us a good talk in the locker room after the game, and on the way out the door, he patted my shoulder and nodded at me.

"Good game tonight, Murphy."

"Thanks, Coach." I nodded back.

There were always a few autograph seekers or kids straggling around in the hallway after the game, hoping for pictures or whatever. I scanned through the crowd, trying to find Kacie. We hadn't really agreed to meet up after the game, and I supposed she could've left and just gone straight to my house. I squinted against the lights and saw three Minnesota Wild jerseys halfway up the concourse.

One big one and two little ones. My girls.

Before I went to them, I happily made my way through the sea of waiting kids, signing autographs and taking pictures. When the crowd cleared, I looked up the hallway, and Kacie was propped against the wall, smiling at me. Piper and Lucy were sitting on the ground using each other as crutches, clearly done with all things hockey related.

I walked over but stopped before I got to Kacie and leaned on the wall just like she was. "Hey, hot mama. You waiting on anyone special?"

She cocked an eyebrow and sighed, looking past me. "Just this hunky hockey player who winked at me during the game tonight."

"Mom, that was Brody!" Lucy giggled.

"How are you guys? Did you have fun?" I bent down and scooped them up, one in each arm.

Piper squeezed my cheeks with her little hands. "We had so much fun. Bobby was our waiter and he kept going and getting us everything we wanted."

I paused and glanced at Kacie. "Waiter?"

She laughed. "A very nice stadium attendant who came running every time these two knuckleheads raised their hands."

"His name was Bobby? I'll have to look him up and say thanks. Anyway, who's ready for a sleepover at my house?"

Lucy and Piper both raised their hands. "Me!" they hollered.

"Me too!" said Kacie, throwing her arm up in the air.

I set the girls down and hooked my finger in the collar of Kacie's jersey. "Get over here." I pulled her forward and planted a big kiss on her lips. I easily could have devoured her right there, but I knew she would be uncomfortable with a major make-out session in front of the girls. I pulled back and leaned my forehead against hers. "I've been dying to do that since I first saw you sitting in that seat. Thanks for coming today."

She peeked up at me from under her long lashes. "Thanks for inviting us. And giving us your parking space. And those seats were amazing."

I pulled away and started to walk up the ramp, grabbing Kacie's hand. "They better be. They cost a fortune."

Kacie's eyes lit up. "I knew they didn't give the players seats that good!"

"No way!" I laughed. "Those are top-of-the-line, premium money seats. I was lucky enough to buy them like five years ago, and I'll never give them up as long as I'm on this team."

My eyes slid over to Kacie when the last part of that sentence stupidly tumbled out of my mouth. We had both been purposely not bringing up my contract *at all*. Just the hint that I could ever play for another team was stressful on both of us. Thankfully, she smiled at me and that was it.

"Mom, who was the lady with the bony ass in the bathroom that was mean to you?" Lucy asked.

"What?" My gaze frantically went back and forth between Kacie and the girls.

"First of all, don't say *bony ass*. Second of all"—Kacie looked from Lucy to me—"it was Kendall."

I ran my fingers through my hair and sighed. "You've gotta be kidding."

"Relax. It was fine." Kacie gently squeezed my hand. "She was her usual charming self, but Darla really gave it to her. Then it was my turn. I wasn't quite as good as Darla, but for once I didn't freeze. Proud of me?"

"Always." I leaned over and kissed her cheek as we got to the parking lot that led to the players' vehicles.

I opened the doors for them and stepped back. "You know I haven't talked to her, right? I wouldn't lie to you. Ever."

For just a brief second, Kacie's face fell into sadness and her eyes looked at the ground. "I know you wouldn't. I totally believe you; that's why I'm not worried about it. I'll follow you to your house." She planted a small kiss on my lips as she walked by.

By the time we got home, the girls had perked back up and were excited for a fun night. They fell out of Kacie's Jeep and yelled all the way to the elevator, listening to their echoes in the parking garage.

We walked into my house and Diesel damn near stroked out from all the excitement of the girls being there. As soon as we were in the door, I ordered a couple of pizzas since it was already late.

"What time are you leaving tomorrow?" I asked Kacie.

"Not sure. We don't have anything planned, but the girls do have school Monday, so I didn't want to leave too late." She walked over and grabbed her purse off the counter.

"Sounds good. Wanna have breakfast at Scooter Joe's?"

Her face lit up. "Yes! I miss Joe. The girls will love it there."

"What is this?" I asked as she put two twenty-dollar bills in my hand. "For dinner."

"Hell no. Are you nuts?" I tried to give her the money back, but she wouldn't take it. "I'm not taking money from you."

"Yes, you are, or I'll be mad." She crossed her arms and put her nose up in the air dramatically.

"I don't need the money, Kacie."

"I know you don't, but that's not the point. You got us tickets, parking, and enough souvenirs to last a lifetime." She pointed to the stack of T-shirts, mini hockey sticks, pucks, and Brody Murphy bobblehead dolls on my counter. "I need to pay my own way."

"Fine, fine. I don't want to spend my time arguing with you. Just know that you'll get it back," I promised. "Anyway, change of subject. Did you guys really have fun tonight?"

"We had a really good time. It was great watching you out there. My favorite part, though, was watching you after the game."

I motioned for her to follow me into the living room. "After the game?"

"Yeah." She sat down on the couch with me and snuggled into my side. "In the hallway outside the locker room. With all those kids around you, talking to you, taking pictures. You were in your glory."

She was right. That was one of my favorite parts of this job. It's definitely good for the ego to come out of the locker room after the game to a group of cheering fans, even if you lost.

"I love that part."

"I can tell." She smiled sweetly. "Tell me about it. How amazing does that feel?"

"Before I knew how it felt to be the player, I knew how it felt to be that kid. One of my favorite childhood memories: April 18, 1999, Madison Square Garden with my dad. We flew there just to see Wayne Gretzky's last game. My dad bought me a Gretzky jersey that we probably couldn't afford and insisted that we stay after to get his autograph." She laid her head on my chest and sighed. "Am I boring you?"

"No way." She rubbed my inner thigh. "I love it when you talk about your childhood. Keep going."

"You keep rubbing my thigh like that and my brain is going to seize up."

"Sorry." She giggled, moving her hand to my stomach. "Continue, please."

I propped my feet up on my coffee table. "We waited for over an hour. There were so many people there. I remember biting my nails down to stubs, worried that he was going to send the rest of us away, but he didn't. He signed every paper, picture, and jersey people put in front of him. When it was my turn, my dad told him I was a hockey player too. Gretzky probably heard that from every dad who brought his kid up to him. Anyway, he acted interested, like it wasn't the millionth time he'd heard it. He looked me right in the eye and said, 'Remember, kid, you miss one hundred percent of the shots you don't take.'"

"Wow. Powerful."

"I know. That moment changed my life. Hockey was no longer just a hobby to me, it was a way of life. It was a goal. I wanted to be Wayne Gretzky when I grew up. Then I fell in love with being a goalie instead, but I'll never forget that moment as long as I live."

"Mommy, what's this?" Lucy ran up to us and handed her mom a condom.

Kacie sat straight up and stared down at the square in her hand. "Uh, where was this?"

"In our room. In the drawer."

Kacie looked over at me in a panic.

"Have you ever eaten ribs, Lucy?" I asked.

She frowned and nodded.

"You know how your hands get all messy and they give you those little wet towelettes to clean up with after? That's what that is."

"Ooooh, okay." Lucy turned and ran back down the hall, very excited to tell her sister she was wrong. "I told you it wasn't candy, Piper."

My head fell back against the couch. "Holy shit. Is parenting always this stressful? Are you constantly lying?"

"Pretty much." She took my hand and flipped it over, placing the condom on my palm before she lay back down. "Except don't think of it as lying to them, think of it as protecting them. They don't need to know what a condom is right now; there's lots of time for that." She sat up quickly and spun to face me, her eyes hooded by her frowning brows. "Why was that in the guest room?"

"It was in there from the last time you were here. Remember?"

"Yeah, but we used that one."

"When I grabbed that one, I put a couple extras in the drawer." I cocked my head to the side. "Kacie, whatever you're thinking right now, stop. Since the minute I walked into the inn during that storm, there's been no one *but* you. Period."

Her shoulders sank and she looked down at her lap, playing with her fingers. "I'm sorry. Every once in a while, I have these panic moments that you're going to get bored of the girlfriend-and-her-kids thing and want out."

"Bored?" I laughed at the irony. "Life with you and the Twinkies is far from boring. My life before you guys was boring. I played hockey, worked out, and hung out with Viper and Andy. You and the girls give my life excitement. Don't ever think otherwise."

"Deal." She looked down the hall and leaned in to kiss me. What started off as a sweet kiss quickly jumped to the next level when Kacie slipped her tongue in my mouth. I put my hand on the back of her head and pulled her in tight, kissing her deep. As our tongues moved and teased together, Kacie's hand started rubbing my inner thigh again. I cupped her face with my hands and sat up a little straighter. My cock pressed tight against the seam of my Nike pants—and there was a knock at the door. Kacie jumped back and wiped her mouth, looking over toward the door.

I groaned. "Pizza."

"I'll get it." She grinned, looking down at the obvious bulge in my pants. "We don't want to scare the poor delivery guy."

After dinner, we took the girls into the guest room together and tucked them in.

Kacie sat on the side of the bed, rubbing Piper's arm. "In the morning, we're going to go to this little café around the corner and have breakfast, okay? Does that sound like fun?"

Lucy's eyes lit up. "Do they have blueberry muffins there?"

"They have all kinds of muffins and scones and treats." I bent down and kissed her cheek. "And the best cinnamon rolls ever. They're as big as your head. You'll love it there."

"Can we bring Diesel?" Piper sounded worried.

I laughed. "Sure, we'll sit outside under the heaters. Diesel gets to eat all the crumbs off the ground. He likes it there too."

Kacie got up and walked to the door. "Good night, girls. I love you." She reached over and turned the light switch off.

"Love you, Mommy," they sang in unison.

"Night, Twinkies." I started to follow Kacie out.

"I love you, Brody," Lucy called out into the dark.

"Me too," Piper added.

I stopped in my tracks and leaned back against the door frame, closing my eyes and pulling my hand up over my heart. My chest ached.

Holy shit.

Before I responded, I had to clear my throat to get rid of the basketball-size lump those two little girls had unknowingly just put in it. "I love you guys too. So much."

As Kacie reached past me to shut the door, I noticed a tear fall onto her cheek.

"Come here." She took my hand and pulled me into the living room. "I want to talk to you about something."

We sat down on the couch and she pulled her leg up, turning to face me.

"What's going on? Are you okay?" I asked.

Her eyes moved around my face, but she wouldn't meet my stare. "I'm fine, but I've been meaning to tell you something." She took a deep breath and let it out slowly. "My first day at the hospital—"

"Mommy! Mommy!" Lucy and Piper yelled, running down the hall toward us. Lucy clutched the collar of her pajamas and Piper dived into Kacie's lap. "It's dark in there; we don't like it."

"Dark?" Kacie frowned at them. "You want me to leave the light on?"

"No. There are weird noises. We don't want to sleep in there." Lucy shook her head back and forth.

"You've only been in there for like two minutes." Kacie chuckled. "Let's try again."

"No, Mom. Pleeeeeeeease," Piper whined. "Can we sleep out here with you?"

"Um . . ." Kacie stalled.

"I have an idea!" I jumped up.

An hour later the girls—and Diesel—were sound asleep on my living room floor under a canopy of couch cushions and blankets that were pinned to bar stools with stacks of books. Kacie and I lay on either side of them with our heads propped up on our hands, facing each other.

"I can't believe you made them a fort," she whispered across them, her soft eyes grinning at me.

"It's been a long time since I've made one." I looked up at my design. "I did a pretty damn good job."

"You certainly did."

"Anyway, what were you gonna say before they came in?"

Kacie looked down at the girls and back up at me. "It can wait. No big deal."

"You sure?"

"Absolutely." She sighed. "Tonight was fun."

"It was fun. I'm hoping you guys coming here wasn't a one-time thing?"

Her lips pulled up into a tiny smile. "More like a once-a-month thing."

I'd had such a fantastic night with Kacie and the girls. I didn't want to make her mad and push her boundaries, but we hadn't seen each other in days and I couldn't stop thinking about the way she'd kissed me on the couch.

"Interested in ending this night the fun way?"

Raising one sexy eyebrow, she turned her head slightly. "What way is that?"

I motioned toward my bedroom door. "In there."

She chewed on the corner of her lip and looked down at Lucy and Piper. "You think it's safe? Think they'd hear us?"

A playful smirk tugged at the corner of my mouth as I looked her straight in the eye. "I can be quiet. Can you?"

I backed out of the fort and walked around to Kacie's side, taking her hands and pulling her up off the floor. As soon as she stood up, I cupped the side of her face with one hand and tilted it up to me. I studied her beautiful greens for a quick second before I had to taste her. I took my time kissing and sucking her full lips. She kept trying to hurry me along, but I knew it was going to be several days before I saw her again, and I wanted to enjoy every single second with her tonight. She put her hands on my chest and kept kissing me as she pushed me backward toward my bedroom.

I let her.

Once inside, she turned to quietly close the bedroom door. Diesel appeared in the doorway, eager to go to bed in my room where he normally slept.

"Sorry, bud. Park it out there for a while," I said as Kacie closed the door in his face.

She turned to face me, her back pressed up against the door. I slid my hand around behind her and clicked the lock securely.

Kacie looked up at me, frowning nervously. "What if they need me?"

"Then they'll knock." I swiftly bent down and claimed her mouth again, picking up right where we'd left off. My hands slowly traveled the length of her back and slid over her hips. I cupped her ass and lifted, pinning her between me and the bedroom door as she wrapped her legs around my waist. Dragging my tongue along her neck, I pushed my erection into her. A small moan escaped her as she grabbed my shirt with her hands and yanked it over my head. I picked her up off the wall and walked backward to my bed, sitting on the edge with her straddling me.

The time away from each other had clearly started affecting Kacie too. Our clothes weren't even off yet and she was already grinding herself on me.

"Holy shit, Brody. Hurry. I need you," she moaned, tossing her shirt on the floor.

"Hey, that was my job," I teased, kissing my way down her chest.

She whined, "If you don't touch me soon, I'm going to explode—and not in the way I want to."

I slowly took her bra off and massaged her breasts for a second before pushing them together and bringing her nipple to my mouth. She fisted her hands in my hair and ground harder as I took turns licking and sucking each nipple. I stood her up just long enough to unbutton her jeans and slide them off of her. My pants weren't halfway down my legs when she was pushing my shoulders back and climbing on top of me again. I could feel how warm she was even through her panties.

"Wow." I laughed. "I don't think I've ever seen you so needy. I kinda like it."

"Less talking, more touching, Murphy."

I had no idea why, but when she called me Murphy, it really got my motor running. Considering I was already sitting at the starting line when she said it right then, I went from zero to sixty.

Quickly leaning over to my nightstand, I pulled out a condom and lifted her just high enough to put it on. I grabbed the side of her lace panties and looked up at her. "Sorry," I growled, pulling hard until they ripped right off.

I pressed my palm against her belly and used my thumb to test how wet she was. "Fuck. You're wet already."

"I haven't seen you in days. There was probably a puddle under my chair at the stadium." She pushed my hand away and positioned herself over me. Watching her face twist in pleasure as she slowly slid all the way down my cock was one of the most erotic things I'd ever seen.

She put her hands on my chest, balancing herself as she slowly started lifting up and down, riding me at a deliciously torturous pace. I was so close to blowing that I had to resort to ol' trusty to take me away for a couple of seconds.

Polar bears. Ice skates. Pizza. Dog leash.

Fuck. It wasn't working and she was grinding into me even faster.

I dug my fingers into her hips and pulled down, thrusting up into her just as hard as she was into me. Her pussy pulsed tight around me and I could tell she was close too.

"Come for me, Kacie," I groaned, plunging deep into her. "Come all over me."

"Shit. Brody!" she squeaked, trying so hard to be quiet. "Oh God. Yes!"

As bad as I wanted to watch her unfolding right on top of me, no amount of words were going to stop my own release at that point. I squeezed her hips tight and pumped into her one more time, grinding my teeth so I didn't wake the girls—or the neighbors.

"Jesus, Kacie. Fuck." I came so hard, I thought I might lose consciousness. Pushing myself into her slowly a couple more times, I started the descent back to planet Earth. After a second, Kacie rolled off me and lay flat on her back next to me.

"Oh my God," she whispered, still slightly out of breath.

"I second that."

"You think we woke them?" She turned on her side and leaned on her hand. The way her breast rolled on top of the other one almost made me hard again.

"No. I think we were fairly quiet, considering."

She blinked a couple of times and frowned at me. "Considering what?"

"Considering that I came so hard, if I didn't have a condom on, you'd already be pregnant with quadruplets." I got up off the bed and went into my bathroom to get rid of the condom. I grabbed a T-shirt from my closet and tossed it to Kacie while I pulled my pants up. I'd forgotten that my cell phone was in my pocket and pulled it out to set it on my nightstand, noticing I had a text.

I opened my phone and laughed.

"What?" Kacie asked as her head popped up through the T-shirt. Without saying a word, I turned my phone to show her the text from Viper.

V: Dude, you still thinking Joe's for breakfast? I'm meeting you there and I'm bringing Kacie's friend Darla. She's sleeping over. One time was not enough with that crazy, flexible bitch.

19

KACIE

"Stop!" Darla walked into work, and I held my hand up before she could say a word. "Before you say anything, Viper is Brody's best friend, and I do not want to hear any stories that you would not tell your mother, got it?"

"I have been dying to talk to you!" She was practically shaking with excitement.

It had been two days since the game and she still couldn't wipe the ridiculous grin off her face. Brody, the girls, and I had breakfast with her and Viper the next morning, but she couldn't exactly gossip in front of them, and I knew she wanted to give me all the disgusting details about her night with him.

"I know you have, but please don't give me too much, okay?" I begged.

She tossed her jacket in her cubby and spun around to face me. "Did you know his dick is pierced?"

I groaned and sank into my chair, covering my face with my hands. "Like that. That's too much."

Darla let out a hearty laugh. "Oh, my dear Kacie, that's only the beginning."

I spent the last hour of my shift following Maureen from room to room, performing all the procedures she'd allow, no matter how big or small. When I wasn't with Maureen, I was dodging Darla and her wicked stories.

Four o'clock rolled around and I was done. Darla was sitting at the desk, updating a chart and munching on some Cheetos.

"So, still no details, but are you gonna see him again?" I asked carefully.

"Not sure." She spun the chair to face me, licking her orange fingers. "He wants to, but he might be a little *too* spunky for me. I like a good lay every once in a while, but he was tossing me around the room and doing me on every piece of furniture he could find."

I closed my eyes and shook my head, trying to dump out the mental pictures I was having.

She stood up and rolled her shoulders, stretching her back out. "I think I pulled a muscle and I've been sleeping for two days straight."

"Okay. On that note, I'm out of here." I tossed my hoodie on and grabbed my lunch bag. "See you tomorrow?"

"I'll be getting off just about the time you come in. What are you up to tonight?"

"One of my best friends has been home from Italy for a week, but I've been so busy with Brody and everything else, I haven't even seen her yet; I'm having dinner with her and my other girlfriend."

"Sounds like fun. Have a cocktail for me." She waved.

I said good-bye to a few other nurses I'd become friendly with and was almost to the door when I heard my name being called. I spun around and saw Zach jogging toward me. "Hey." He grinned when he caught up with me.

"Hi."

"I've been meaning to give you something." He dug around in his coat pocket and handed me a piece of paper.

"What's this?" I asked, unfolding it.

"My cell number."

"Oh." My head snapped up. "Why do I need this?"

"I don't know." He shrugged. "Just in case . . . the girls, you . . . whatever. I don't know."

"Okay. Well, I'm late for dinner. I'll talk to you later." I smiled and rushed out into the parking lot.

Traffic sucked. By the time I got to the restaurant, Alexa and Lauren were already sitting down.

"Sorry I'm late," I said, sliding around the table to hug Lauren. "You look fantastic! I'm so excited to see you."

"Me too!" Lauren squeezed me tight. I didn't realize how much I'd really missed her until she was right in front of me.

"What's up, asshole?" I winked at Alexa as I sat down.

"You tell him yet?" she responded in a snotty tone.

"Oh my God, could we please sit and have dinner and then we'll talk about all that?" I glared at her.

She pursed her lips together and turned toward Lauren. "That means no."

Lauren gasped and her mouth fell open. "You *still* haven't told him?"

I dropped my head in my hands and shook it back and forth. "I know, I know. I tried. I really did, but then we got interrupted by the girls and he made them a fort and I didn't want to ruin the mood."

"What are you waiting for?" Lauren asked.

Alexa scoffed, "The girls to graduate high school."

"Stop it." I narrowed my eyes at her. "I'm going to tell him. I feel absolutely awful about it, but he's had so much going on lately, I don't want to stress him out any more."

The waitress brought over spinach-avocado dip, which they must have ordered before I got there. Lauren smiled and popped a chip in her mouth as the waitress walked away. "What's going on with him?"

I finally took my hoodie off and put it on the back of my chair. "Well, his contract is up this season, so the pressure is on to play well. Obviously if he knew this was going on, it would mess with his head. Also, his mom just had her scans and they haven't gotten the results yet. He hasn't said it out loud, but I know he's freaked out about it."

"That's understandable." She took another bite and reached over, smacking Alexa's arm. "Cut her some slack, Lex."

"I understand that he's got a lot going on. I even think it's slightly adorable that Kacie loves him so much she doesn't want to make it worse." She sighed. "I'm just worried. I don't see this ending well."

"It'll be fine." Lauren waved Alexa off. "These two are so crazy in love with each other, Brody will totally understand why she waited. And then they'll ride off into the sunset on a Zamboni."

"Yeah, well, hopefully Kacie is on that Zamboni with Brody instead of sitting in the penalty box, crying."

My stomach hurt, and Alexa's jokes about Brody leaving me were *not* helping. I wasn't lying when I said I felt awful about not telling him. I felt beyond awful, but I really didn't want to stress him out.

"Stop it!" Lauren slugged Alexa in the arm again.

"Listen," Alexa warned her, "if you don't stop hitting me, I'm going to hit you back—pregnant or not."

Wait, what?

"What?" I exclaimed.

Lauren shrugged and grinned at me. "Surprise!"

"Oh my God, Lauren! How could you not tell me?" I jumped up and rushed to her side of the table to hug her again. "Congratulations!"

"How could she not tell you? That's a good question coming from you, huh?" Alexa teased sarcastically.

"Listen." I spun toward her, unable to hold my frustration in anymore. "I get that you don't agree with the way I've handled this situation, but seriously . . . kiss my ass." Tears welled up in my eyes and my voice started cracking, but I didn't care. "You have no idea what I've been going through. None. Zach walked out all those years ago and I never expected to see him again—ever. Then on my first day of work, boom! There he was, in my face. Things with Brody had *just* started getting serious, and selfishly, I didn't want to mess anything up. Hell, I didn't even know if it was worth it to say anything because I had no idea if I'd ever see Zach again after that day." Lauren reached for my hand and squeezed it, but I didn't stop. "I have two kids, I'm trying to finish my degree and keep my still new relationship alive, all while juggling this huge pimple on the face of my past that is my ex. Stop looking down your nose at me, damn it! You have no idea how hard this has been for me." At that point, tears were spilling out of my eyes and people were staring.

Alexa's cheeks flushed as she sat frozen, staring at me with her mouth open. She blinked a few times and shook her head back and forth slowly. "Kacie, I am so sorry. I didn't mean to upset you."

"Just . . . forget it." I wiped my cheeks with the backs of my hands and bent down and hugged Lauren. "I'm sorry, Lauren, but I have to go. I'm beyond exhausted and need a break. Call me tomorrow. Maybe we can have lunch before you leave?"

Lauren stood up and hugged me so tight I almost started sobbing right there in her arms, but I just needed to keep it together long enough to get to my car. "It's okay, Kacie. I understand."

I pulled back and cupped my friend's face. "I really am so happy for you. You're going to be a great mom. Tell Tommy I said congrats."

I grabbed my hoodie and left without saying good-bye to Alexa. By the time I got to my car, I was in a full-on sob. It felt good and awful at the same time.

20

BRODY

"Hello?"

"Hey, Son."

"Dad?" My dad never called me. I hardly recognized his voice. "What's up?"

"Nothing. Just wanted to call my champ and say hi."

Champ? He hasn't called me that in years.

Instantly I was ten years old again . . .

"Hey, Champ. I can't make your tournament this weekend, but good luck."

"Heard you played great tonight, Champ. Sorry I missed it."

When it came to my father, calling me Champ was a way to soften whatever blow was coming.

"Hi," I said cautiously. "Everything okay?"

"Everything is great. What are your plans this coming weekend?"

"Uh, we're home this weekend. I have a game Friday, but then just practice Saturday morning. Probably heading to Kacie's after. Why?"

He hesitated. "Saturday after practice, can you head up here for a while before you go to her house?"

I didn't like the tone in his voice. Not even a little.

"Dad, what's going on?"

"Nothing. Mom and I just have a few things to talk about with you and Shae."

Dad, Mom, me, and Shae? SHIT! Her scans were a couple of weeks ago. No, no, no, no.

"Dad, is this about Mom's scans?"

"No. Mom is okay; we just need to talk to you guys." He sounded tired.

Exhausted. Stressed.

"Fuck that, Dad. I'm coming now."

"Brody, that's not necess—"

I hung up on him, grabbed Diesel's leash, and out the door we went.

I wouldn't say I had an out-of-body experience, but when I pulled onto the long dirt driveway at my parents' farm, I didn't remember any of the drive from my house to theirs. My heart raced the whole way there with the worst scenarios playing over and over in my head. If her cancer was back again, I would not break down at their house. I would remain strong. She beat it once; she could do it again. We would do it together. What if Dad was sick this time? Fuck. He's her rock. Should I retire early? It wasn't like I couldn't afford it, but could I live without hockey?

I marched up to the house and through the front door as Diesel sprinted around back to find something to play with.

Closing the front door quietly, I listened for voices or crying. Nada. That was good, right?

"Brody?" Mom called out as I walked into the kitchen. She came right over and embraced me. "You didn't have to come up here tonight."

"Dad never calls me. What's going on?"

Mom's eyes shifted over to my dad, who was sitting at the kitchen table, looking ten years older than he had the last time I saw him. He was staring down at the large oak table, picking at the fingernails on his weathered hands.

"Come. Sit down." She went over and pulled a chair out for me.

I groaned and stubbornly followed my mom over to the table, sitting across from my dad.

Mom cleared her throat while Dad looked everywhere except at me.

Looking back and forth between the two of them, it became apparent that neither of them wanted to talk. "Will someone please tell me what the hell is going on?" I barked, causing my mom to jump slightly.

"Honey, it's really no big deal." My mom tried to reassure me with a fake smile, but I was growing increasingly more pissed off with each second that passed.

"Great. Fine. Please fill me in on this 'no big deal,' then."

Once again, Mom looked at Dad. He met her glance this time. She reached over and put her hand on his as she looked back at me. "Brody, your dad and I are getting divorced."

For a moment, there was absolute silence.

I sighed and ran my hands through my hair. "Not funny. What's really going on?"

Dad glanced at Mom, who never stopped looking at me. Her eyes were wide, her mouth slightly open in surprise. "We're not kidding, Brody. We've separated."

I pulled my hands up over my mouth and looked back and forth between the two of them, waiting for someone to tell me they were joking.

When no one said anything, my pulse started to race. "When? How? Why?"

"It just happened, Son," my dad mumbled.

"Ending a thirty-year marriage doesn't just happen, Dad. Cut the crap. Why are you guys doing this?"

Mom looked down at the table and back up at my dad as if she was waiting for him to explain himself.

I lowered my eyebrows and glared at my father. "Is this your fault? Did you cheat on her? Not that I would be surprised. You were a shitty father, you're probably an even shittier husband."

"Now you calm the hell down," my father ordered, pointing at me from across the table. "I know this can't be easy for you, but it's even harder for us."

"Let's all just calm down, please." My mom rested her hand on top of mine. "Brody, your dad didn't cheat on me, nor is this his fault. It's no one's fault. We've both been feeling this way for quite a while, but we were waiting for Shae to finish up her education and for both of you to be secure and independent before we made any final decisions." She quietly looked down at her hands. She was spinning her wedding ring around and around, something she always did when she was nervous.

"I can't believe this." I rubbed my eyes with my palms. "It's been *thirty years*. After thirty years, you're just going to give up on each other?"

Neither of them responded.

They just sat there, wallowing in the failure of their marriage.

"What about counseling? I'll pay for the best marriage counselor in the country."

My dad looked at my mom, but she just shook her head.

"How about a vacation? What if you guys went to Hawaii for a week—a month? Maybe you just need to reconnect?"

"Brody, your offers are all very sweet, but they're not necessary." She looked at my dad, who gave her a tight smile. "We've talked about this at length. We're okay with it. We've even hired the same lawyer and settled everything already. We're content with our decision."

I couldn't believe what I'd just heard. My eyes were wide, darting back and forth between the two of them. "How long have you known you were doing this?"

"A year."

"*A year?*" I exclaimed, jumping up from the table. "You guys just celebrated your thirtieth anniversary in May. Shae and I threw you a surprise party, for fuck's sake!"

"Brody," my dad warned.

"I know." Mom covered her face with her hands. "We were mortified the whole time, but we had no idea. What were we supposed to do? Announce the split in front of all our family and friends?"

"I don't know." I sighed, pacing the kitchen. "This can't be the end, though. It just can't. I know you two still love each other."

My mom looked at me with tears in her eyes. "I can't imagine how hard this must be for you, Brody. I can't begin to imagine."

"No. You can't. I've gone my whole life with my parents together and loving each other. Once I hit adulthood, I felt pretty secure that you two were a forever thing." I frowned at both of them. "I swear I think it would have been easier to find this out at seven than at twenty-seven."

"We're so sorry, Brody." My mom cried softly.

"When Dad called, I thought something showed up in one of your scans. I'm obviously relieved that's not the case, but this is equally as shocking." Opening the back door, I whistled loudly for Diesel.

"What are you doing?" Mom's eyes looked sad, worried.

Diesel trotted through the back door and we headed toward the front of the house. "I gotta go. I need to think."

"Brody, wait!" Mom hurried after me. "It's so late. Why don't you just stay here tonight?"

I opened the front door and turned to face my mom. Dad had followed her out of the kitchen and had his hand resting on her shoulder, rubbing her arm lovingly. I stared at his hand for a second longer than I should have, wondering what the hell happened and where everything had gone wrong. I looked her straight in the eye. "Not a chance," I said coolly and slammed the door.

By the time I'd started my truck, Mom had looked out the living room window three times. Knowing her, I'm sure she was hoping

I would turn the truck off and head back inside. I probably should have. She and Dad didn't deserve the way I'd treated them, but I was beyond pissed.

I felt duped. I felt betrayed.

Flooring the gas and spitting up gravel as I sped off, I fishtailed out of the driveway onto the road, but I wasn't heading home.

After the week I'd had, I felt out of control. I'd played like shit the last two games, and now my parents dropped the bomb that they were getting divorced. Tonight, I needed the one constant in my life.

My compass.

My anchor.

My more.

I headed straight for Kacie's house.

21

KACIE

Lucy and Piper wrapped their tiny arms around my neck and squeezed as hard as they could. I groaned playfully as they cut off my air supply.

"I'm going to hug you so hard your guts are going to spill out!" Piper giggled.

"Noooo!" cried Lucy, pulling back. "Leave Mommy's guts alone. She needs those."

I laughed heartily. "My guts are okay, Lucy. I promise. Now, how much do I love you guys?"

"More than all the stars in the sky and all the waves in the sea," they recited in unison.

"You got that right!" I kissed each of their foreheads and tucked them into bed. "See you in the morning. Love you both!"

"Love you, Mom!" they called out as I flipped on their night-light and pulled the door shut.

After my miserable meeting with Alexa and Lauren, I was mentally exhausted. I should have been ready to crash, but for some reason I wasn't ready to sleep yet. Normally, once the girls went to bed at night, my life was a bore. Now that Brody's season had started and he was traveling more and more, I would sometimes go a whole week without seeing him. I missed him so much, sometimes it physically hurt. We hadn't talked all day, and it was unlike him not to call me as soon as the girls were tucked into bed, so I shot him a quick text.

Hope you had a good day today. Call me later! :)

Tucking my phone in my back pocket, I snuck off to the kitchen to pour myself a bowl of cereal. Fred and my mom were snuggled up on the couch watching TV. I took my bowl into the living room and plopped down next to them.

"Whatcha watching?" I shoveled a bite of Lucky Charms into my mouth.

"*Chopped.*" Mom sighed. "Though I'm fading fast."

Fred looked down at her. "Me too. I have to get up early in the morning and change the oil on your truck."

"Awww!" I grinned at them. "Cooking shows and oil changes. You two are so romantic."

"Someone is feisty tonight," Fred joked as he picked up a small throw pillow and tossed it at me, narrowly missing my cereal bowl.

"I know! I had coffee at work today, way later than I usually do. I'm wired." I threw the pillow back at them. "And now you two losers are going to go to bed and I'm stuck here all alone with the *Chopped* contestants."

My mom giggled as she leaned over and kissed my cheek. "Sorry, baby girl. See you in the morning."

Fred stood up and my mom followed, walking him to the back door.

He wrapped his arms around her and pulled her in for a tight squeeze. She lifted her chin, angling her mouth to line up with his. He tilted his head to the side and looked her straight in the eyes. "I love you."

Her cheeks puffed out as she smiled. "I love you too."

He pressed his mouth against hers passionately and I started making fake gagging noises.

They pulled apart and grinned at me like a couple of proud teenagers as I brought my hands to my throat and pretended to pass out.

Slightly dramatic, yes, but I was having fun teasing them tonight. Fred delivered one more peck and disappeared out the back door. Mom turned and rolled her eyes at me. "You're a pill."

"I know." I giggled. "But you know I really love you two. And I love you *together*."

A sweet smile slid across my mom's face. "Want me to hang with you tonight?"

"Nah, I'm good. I'm just waiting for Brody to text me back and then I'll hit the sack." I returned her smile. "Thank you, though."

Mom blew me a kiss and walked down the hall to our apartment. I heard the door close behind her as I pulled my phone out of my pocket to see if Brody had answered. Nothing.

My show was over and I had just finished up my cereal and put my bowl in the kitchen sink when I thought I heard a quiet knock on the front door. Pausing, I listened again. Another knock. I raced through the hallway, excited at the thought of another surprise visit from Brody. Maybe more pier sex?

Whipping the front door open, I stopped dead in my tracks. "I was hoping it was—" I blinked, not sure if I was really seeing what I was seeing. "Zach?"

"Hey!" A lazy grin tugged at the corner of his mouth. "Are the girls awake?"

Confused, I slowly shook my head back and forth. "No, they're in bed."

"Aw, crap. I really wanted to see them again. They're cute."

I took a step closer to him and sniffed. "Have you been drinking?"

"Oh yeah," he slurred. "It was so good too. I forgot how fucking good it tastes."

Oh shit.

"Listen . . ." I stepped out onto the front porch and closed the door quietly behind me, praying my mom hadn't heard him. "What can I do for you? Is there someone I can call? A sponsor maybe?"

"No, fuck that." He waved the idea off. "He's an asshole. Always bossing me around and never letting me have any fun."

"Zach," I said calmly, sitting on the swing, "I know this isn't what you want. You've worked so hard to stay sober all this time."

"One thousand one hundred and seventy-five days!" he yelled, thrusting his fist into the air.

"Shhh!" I hissed. "Come sit down. What's going on?"

"Nothing is going on. I just liked sitting with you at the park and I wanted to see you again."

I frowned at him. "You saw me at work today, remember?"

"Yeah, but there you're always busy with patients and preoccupied."

"Zach, you're not making any sense. Really, who can I call to help you?"

"No one!" he snapped. "I have no one, remember? My mom is dead, my dad is dead, Tara got married and moved away from me. I have *no one!*"

I cringed at how loudly he was yelling. "Shhh, it's okay. Come sit down."

He staggered over and dropped down on the swing so hard I was worried the bolts were going to fly right out of the ceiling. "Talk to me. What brought this on?" I asked.

"You. Them." He sniffed, leaning forward and resting his elbows on his knees.

"What?" I searched his face, looking for any clue as to what he was talking about. His blond curls peeked out from under his baseball cap as the muscles in his biceps flexed over and over. He was extremely agitated and I had no idea why.

"You, but mainly them. That day at the park." The muscle at the corner of his jaw was popping as he clenched it in between sentences. "It was remarkable watching them. They are people, *real* little people, with opinions and personalities and thoughts. You've formed them into these tiny beings that are amazing to watch and I . . . I had nothing to do with any of it. I've missed *so* much, their whole lives, really. So much time gone that I can never get back. And then there's you."

Oh no.

He turned his head and captured me in his gaze like a wounded animal. My heart was racing and a small part of me felt very nervous sitting here with him. Unsafe. I barely knew him anymore and I had no idea what he was capable of, especially in this state.

"Me?" I asked, barely audible.

"I never stopped loving you, Kacie. After all these years, I've thought about you constantly, compared every woman I've been with to you, wondered what you were doing every second."

Oh God, no.

"All this time, did you think about me at all?"

"Um . . ."

"You didn't." He stood up and angrily marched to the edge of the porch, raising his hands above his head and gripping the trim. Looking out across the property, he continued, "I don't blame you, though. I wouldn't have thought about me either. I was awful to you, and you did absolutely nothing to deserve it."

I stared down at my hands, which were folded in my lap to keep from shaking, too scared to respond. The fear of saying the wrong thing and setting him off gripped me like a vise.

"Sorry is a stupid word," he mumbled, though I was unsure if he was talking to me or to himself.

Keeping my head down, I peeked up at him with just my eyes.

"Think about it," he continued into the air. "You say it when you bump into someone in the grocery store or when you're late for a doctor's appointment. How the fuck can that word possibly be the only one in the English language appropriate to say to the ex-girlfriend that you royally screwed over? How do you apologize for the biggest mistake of your life?" After a minute, Zach walked back over and sat down next to me again, pulling my hands into his. "I'm sorry, Kacie. I'm so, so sorry. I'll gladly say it to you every day for the rest of my life. I wish more than anything I could take back that day, take back that stupid moment when I decided you guys would be better off without me. Who knows? That may have been the case, but I wasn't better off without you. You were my life and I threw you away. All of you."

What the hell was I supposed to say to that? I would never know what my life would have been like had he stuck around, and honestly, I didn't want to know. I was happy where I was, proud of what I'd been able to accomplish as a single mom. My hands were shaking in his as I thought about what to say back, how to follow that up. Before I could form a coherent thought, headlights appeared at the end of the driveway.

We both looked up, squinting our eyes at the approaching lights.

"Who is that?" Zach asked, not letting go of my hands.

As the car got closer, I realized it wasn't a car at all, but a truck. A big black pickup truck.

Brody.

Fuck. Fuck, fuck, fuck.

I pulled my hands back quickly as the truck screeched to a stop. I'd barely made my way to the end of the porch when Brody came walking purposefully up the steps. "What's going on?" he questioned, looking from me to Zach.

"Nothing, baby. Let's go inside and talk." I put my hands on his chest, hoping to slow him down, but he walked right through me.

"Brody Murphy!" Zach grinned as he walked over with his hand out. "Nice to meet you. I'm Zach, Lucy and Piper's dad."

The world moved in slow motion as I watched the realization of what Zach had just slurred reach Brody's brain. His head slowly turned to look down at me. His normally crisp green eyes were filled with anger. Intense, seething anger. I could only imagine what he thought he just saw as his chest heaved under my hand.

I cupped the sides of his face, trying to get him to look *at* me instead of through me. "Listen to me, this is not what you think it is. Let's go inside and talk. Please."

"Don't leave me hanging, bro." Zach laughed, motioning toward his still-outstretched hand.

Brody was looking at me, but his mind was somewhere else. When Zach laughed, Brody's eye twitched and that was it. I grabbed a fistful of his sweatshirt and pulled back as hard as I could, but I was too late.

Brody reeled back and swung with his right arm as hard as I'd ever seen anyone hit another person. It happened so fast, Zach didn't even see it coming. He was still smiling when Brody's fist connected with his jaw, making the most horrific crunching sound. Zach stumbled back, holding the left side of his face. His hat was askew and he was obviously disoriented and in severe pain, but that didn't stop Brody from lunging for him again. He grabbed a handful of Zach's shirt and pulled him forward, hard.

"What the fuck are you doing here, dickhead?" Brody roared through clenched teeth.

"Whoa, whoa!" Zach threw his hands up in front of himself. "Calm down."

"Fuck you!" Brody snapped, punching Zach even harder than before, this time with his left fist. After another fierce collision, Zach covered his head with his hands, either in pain or self-defense, and wobbled his way over to the railing.

"Brody! Brody, stop!" I screamed. I tried wrapping my arms around his core and pulling him off of Zach, but I would've had better luck trying to move the Empire State Building. I barely got out of the way when Brody reared back and punched Zach once more, sending him flying over the porch railing and onto the grass down below.

Brody walked over and stood at the railing, glaring down at Zach. Blood droplets fell from his knuckles onto the porch, but it didn't seem to faze him one bit.

"I'll ask you again. What the fuck are you doing here?"

After he rolled around in the grass for a minute, Zach sat up and held each side of his jaw, which I was sure was broken—probably in more than one place. "I came to talk to Kacie about the girls," he mumbled, opening his mouth as little as possible.

"The girls? You have no goddamn business discussing anything about those girls."

"The fuck I don't. I'm their father."

Brody's eyes grew wide and I thought he might jump the railing and kill Zach right there on the lawn. "Their father? What the fuck do you know about being their father? *I'm* their father! You're a deadbeat sperm donor—Kacie's big fucking mistake in life. The hell if I'm going to let her make the same mistake twice. Now, get the hell out of here."

Zach narrowed his eyes at me. "He doesn't know, does he?"

"Know what?" Brody growled.

I sighed, pulling my shaking hands up to my face. Alexa was right, I should've told him a long time ago. This was so much worse than I had ever imagined it could be. My stomach cramped like I was going to throw up.

"Know *what*?" he roared again, causing me to flinch.

22

BRODY

"Know *what*?" Kacie flinched as I demanded an answer for the second time.

"We work at the hospital together," Zach said through clenched teeth, still holding on to the side of his head.

"You *what*?" I yelled at Kacie, pretending it was her who told me and not Zach.

Her hands fell from her face just enough for me to see her tear-filled eyes. "We work together." She pulled her hands all the way down and reached for me, but I stepped back. "But not really. He's an EMT, so we don't see each other every day, just occasionally. I had no idea he worked there, Brody. I saw him my first day and—"

"Your *first* day?" I shouted. "That was *weeks* ago!"

What. The. Fuck.

The front door to the house flew open and Sophia stepped out onto the porch. "What's going on out here? I can hear yelling all the way from my bedroom." Her eyes panned the front yard and stopped suddenly on Zach. "What are *you* doing here?"

Zach didn't answer her; he just looked down at his lap.

"Brody, let me explain." Kacie ignored her mom as her chin trembled and tears poured from her eyes.

Normally when I saw Kacie cry, I would walk through walls of fire to make her stop, but right now I just couldn't. She'd put those damn walls up and needed to get out from behind them on her own.

I was seething.

"Wait," Zach interrupted. "Before you do, I'm gonna go."

"I would say that's a good idea." Sophia walked to the edge of the porch and crossed her arms across her chest.

He wiped some blood from the corner of his mouth with the back of his hand, reached over to grab his hat, and stood up slowly. I stared a hole through him as he walked to his truck, thankful that he was at least smart enough not to say a word to me or Kacie.

When he opened his driver's door, Kacie called after him, "Zach! Wait!" She looked from him to me. "He's drunk, Brody. He can't drive."

"He drove himself over here, didn't he? He can drive his ass home," I snapped.

"I had no idea he was coming. He just showed up here," she defended. "Please, let me just drive him home, and then we can talk and I'll tell you everything."

"Drive him home?" I pointed toward Zach. "Not a chance in hell."

"Please. You can follow us and then give me a ride back," she begged.

I sighed and ran my hands through my hair in frustration. "Fine. There's no fucking way he's getting in a car with you, though. You drive his car; he rides with me."

She opened her mouth to argue and I cut her off. "That's the only option, Kacie."

She nodded and turned toward the porch. "Mom, will you—"

Sophia waved her off. "I've got them. Go."

"I'm not riding in a car with him," Zach argued as Kacie walked up to him and held her hand out for the keys.

"Please." She sniffed. "If you want to make things better, please make this easy on me."

Zach looked from her to me and back again. "Fine," he grunted, dropping the keys in her hand. "I live in the Meadowbrook Apartments on Maple. Do you know where that is?"

She nodded and sat down in his truck, turning to watch as he walked back to my truck. I hopped up into my driver's seat and rested my wrists on the steering wheel, watching her. She pulled her eyebrows in tight and looked at me with sad eyes. More than anything, I wanted to go over, pull her into my arms, and take away her misery, but she had caused mine and I was pissed the fuck off.

"In the back, D." I watched as Diesel woke up and gingerly crawled into the backseat, still half-asleep.

Zach opened the truck door while I looked out my window, worried that if I met his deadbeat eyes, I'd pull him out of the truck and beat the shit out of him again. My hand throbbed as I wrapped it around the steering wheel, and the thought crossed my mind that it might be broken. I couldn't get it checked out and I couldn't complain. Not this season.

He climbed up and sat down. Before I even put the truck in reverse, he tried talking.

"Listen—"

"No. You listen," I interrupted, finally looking straight at him. "I'm going to explain how this ride is going to go. You're not going to talk to me and I'm not going to talk to you. Regardless of why you're back or what the fuck has been going on, we're *not* friends and we'll never *be* friends. And talking about Kacie is so fucking far off-limits that if I feel you even *thinking* about her, I'll put your head through my goddamn windshield."

He stared straight ahead and didn't say another word while we followed Kacie the whole way to his apartment. I put my truck in park and he opened the door immediately. Once his feet were on the ground, he turned to me. "Kacie didn't invite me over tonight. She didn't even know I was coming. I got in my truck and drove there, so if you want to be mad at someone for that, be mad at me." He paused and winced, holding the side of his jaw. "Also, I didn't fight you back because, aside from being blindsided, I probably deserve a broken jaw for all the pain I've caused her over the years. Even so, I'm not going to apologize because I do want back in Lucy and Piper's life in some capacity."

"You don't deserve to be in their lives," I seethed.

He tilted his head to the side slightly and nodded. "You're probably right about that, but when I watched them play at the park, it hit me how much I'd truly missed. I'm not going to let them slip through my fingers again."

"They didn't slip through your fingers, asshole. You threw them away. I picked them up, cleaned them off, and have been there for them since the day I met them. Don't be dumb enough to think this is going to be an easy road for you," I warned as he backed up and shut the door.

I watched as he walked over and took his keys from Kacie. He stopped and said something to her, but she just shook her head and walked back to my truck. She slid into the passenger seat and dropped her face into her hands, crying quietly. Peeking at her out of the corner of my eye as I pulled out of the parking space, my heart wrenched. It physically hurt me to resist touching her.

My fingers tingled. I wanted to run them through her hair and pull her into my lap. I wanted to tell her it would all be okay and we'd get through this, but I didn't even know what the hell we were getting through yet. Then, Zach's words from before he walked away replayed in my head.

When the fuck did he watch them play at a park?

I didn't speak one word to Kacie on the way home. She just cried. We pulled up the long driveway to the inn and I saw Sophia sitting on the front porch swing with Fred next to her. Kacie jumped out of the truck and came around to my side, waiting for me to follow her.

I rolled my window down. "I'm leaving."

Her mouth flew open and she took a step back as new tears started falling from her eyes. "You're not coming in?"

"No." I looked straight out the front window, my fingers tapping on my dashboard. "I'm too angry. I can't talk to you right now."

"Brody," she sobbed, "please. I need you."

My eyes shot toward her. "You know what? I needed *you* tonight. I just came from my parents' house, found out they're divorcing. I'm crushed."

Her eyes grew wide as her hands clutched her throat.

I continued, "You know where I wanted to go when I was crushed? Here. To you. Only to be completely fucking gutted when I find out that you've been lying to me for God knows how long. So, yes, I'm leaving. I need to think—about my parents, about you, about all of this. I'll be in touch."

I rolled up my window and started to pull out of the driveway. Against my better judgment, I checked my rearview just in time to see Sophia running off the porch toward Kacie, who had dropped to her knees and was sobbing right there in the grass.

Fucking gutted.

Part of me felt like an ass for leaving her like that, and part of me knew it was for the best. I had so many questions for her about Zach and what the hell had been going on the last couple of weeks, but it wouldn't have done either of us any good if I'd asked those questions now. Most likely I would have said something I'd regret, or punched something else, and I couldn't afford for my hand to get any more swollen.

A couple of miles from her house, I pulled over and took out my phone to text Andy.

Hey, bro, you home?

A: Yep. Folding laundry, living the dream. What's up?

Can I come by?

A: Sure. It's late. Everything okay?

Not even close.

"You broke his jaw?" Andy leaned forward on his couch, propping his elbows on his knees, and rubbed his temples.

I shrugged. "I don't know for sure, but something cracked. Very well could have been my hand. I'm gonna grab some ice."

A minute later, I walked back to his living room, and he was still sitting in the same position. "I couldn't help it," I defended. "First, I saw him holding her hand—that was bad enough. Then, when he introduced himself as Lucy and Piper's dad, I lost it. I don't even know how many times I hit him. He went over the railing."

Andy's head sprang up. "You punched him over a railing?"

I nodded and groaned, gently putting the baggie of ice on the top of my hand.

"Fuck." He stood up and started pacing the living room. "You know if he presses charges, you're screwed. It's a contract year, Brody. How could you do this?" He walked back and forth with his hands on his hips.

"I told you. I snapped." I crossed my ankles on his coffee table.

"Yeah. Tell that to Collins."

Fuck.

It was days like this when I wished I had a normal nine-to-five desk job. My boss wouldn't give a shit what I did outside of working hours, and I could just fucking call in sick tomorrow.

"I'll talk to Collins. Don't worry."

He spun around and raised his eyebrows at me. "You'll do no such fucking thing."

"I won't?"

"No. You won't. You'll wait and see what happens. There's a chance this dickwad might not call the police."

"Why the fuck wouldn't he?"

"Think about it, Brody. We don't know the story of why he's back and what's going on with him. For all you know, he's got a boner for Kacie and wants her back. Getting her boyfriend arrested certainly isn't going to make her run back into his arms."

"First of all, did you just say *boner*?" I stared up at him in disgust. "What are you, thirteen? Second of all, don't ever talk about Zach's dick and Kacie in the same sentence again."

He stopped pacing and sat on the chair across from me. "You gonna call her?"

"I don't know. Eventually, yes. I just don't know when." I exhaled.

"Is this a deal breaker for you?" he asked carefully.

I stared off into space for a few seconds, thinking about his question. I would take a thousand broken hands if the knot in my stomach whenever he said her name would disappear for five minutes. "I can't control where that asshole wanders around the planet, so if he showed back up in her life, that's not her fault. But why didn't she tell me?" I searched Andy's face for answers. "Is she in love with him again?"

"Whoa." He shook his head vigorously. "I seriously doubt that. Don't go jumping to crazy conclusions."

"I don't even know what to think anymore, about anything . . ."

"What about your parents? What happened there?"

The ache in my chest flared up again. The only silver lining to the Zach bullshit was that for a couple of hours, it took my mind off what was going on with my mom and dad.

"I have no idea what went wrong. They basically just said they grew apart and these things happen."

"I'm really sorry about that. I can't even imagine how weird it must be to be going through this *now*." He interlocked his fingers and tucked them behind his head. "You think they'll work it out?"

"Who knows? Supposedly they're using the same lawyer and have everything all sorted out already."

"Jesus, that's one hell of an amicable split. Blaire and I can't even agree on what date we officially separated." He huffed. "Does Shae know?"

"Nope, they're telling her this weekend."

As sad as I was for myself, my heart was completely broken for Shae. She had no idea what was coming her way. Shae was without a doubt the most romantic human being on the planet. She was constantly watching sappy movies, setting her friends up on blind dates, and writing poetry about love. She was so in love with love that she had become a wedding planner—a damn good one too. This was going to completely crush her.

At least we'd have that part in common.

23

KACIE

"Hey." My bedroom door cracked open just enough for my mom to stick her head in.

I sat up and yawned. "Morning. Are the girls already up?"

"Yeah. I fed them and their backpacks are ready to go. Want me to put them on the bus?"

"No." I sighed. "I'll do it. I called in; I'm not going to work today."

The corner of her mouth turned down. "No call from Brody, huh?"

I couldn't speak past the lump in my throat, so I just shook my head. Fresh tears started to build in my eyes, though I had no idea how, since I'd cried enough to fill the lake out back.

"Okay, honey. We'll see you in a little bit." She closed my door and I turned to my right, staring at my cell phone on the nightstand. I was scared to look at it. So many scenarios ran through my head.

Brody could have texted to say we were done.

He could have texted to say he was coming over and we would work through this.

He might not have texted at all.

I took a deep breath and grabbed it.

Nothing.

Shit.

Now came the question of what I should do. Do I turn into a teenager and text the crap out of him, begging for forgiveness, or do I have confidence in our relationship and give him space?

Screw that. I didn't have enough confidence to tell him about Zach in the first place; now was the time to fight.

> Hey, I know last night was crazy and you're confused and mad at me. I'm mad at me too. First of all, I'm so sorry about your parents. I can't imagine how that must have felt to show up at my house looking for comfort to instead see Zach here. Last night was the worst night of my life. It was way worse than when Zach left because when he left, I was already dead inside. The day I met you, I came back to life. I'm madly in love with you and will forever regret the colossal mistake I made of not telling you sooner. Please give me a chance to explain.

I hit "Send" on the longest—and most important—text of my life.

Staring at that phone all morning, praying for a response, wasn't going to do me any good. I jumped up and took a quick shower before walking Lucy and Piper down to the bus.

The smell of burning leaves permeated the air and the crisp morning chilled me just a little bit. The girls and I held hands as we walked down to the edge of the driveway, leaves crunching under our feet. The bus came quickly and they hopped on, blowing kisses at me out the window. I waved until I couldn't see the bus anymore, desperate to put on a happy face for them when in reality, all I was thinking about was the cell phone in my back pocket.

I was halfway up the driveway when it vibrated.

It was a text! From . . . Lauren.

L: Hey, chicky. I'm leaving tomorrow. Can I stop by this morning and visit for a little bit or are you working?

Thank God I called in. I can't let her go back to Italy like that.

No, I called in sick. Please come over. I owe you the biggest apology ever.

L: You owe me nothing. I'll be there soon.

I had two mason jars, filled with ice and raspberry tea, ready to go just a bit later when I heard a loud knock. As excited as I was to see Lauren, part of me really hoped it would be Brody on the other side of the door instead. No such luck.

I barely had the door open and Lauren was pushing through it, throwing her arms around me. "I'm so sorry for the way dinner went last night. That's not at all what I had in mind."

Exhaling, I hugged her back and rested my head on her shoulder. "Me too. I shouldn't have run out like that, but I couldn't take the guilt from Alexa anymore."

"I'm sorry too," Alexa said quietly, stepping up behind Lauren with her hands shoved in her hoodie as she stared at the ground.

Seeing Alexa look so sad, combined with my already fragile mindset . . . I couldn't stay mad at her. Not letting go of Lauren, I sighed and held my arm up for Alexa to join in on the hug.

"I'm so sorry for being such a bitch, Kacie," Alexa said into Lauren's hair. "You're right. I have no idea how hard this has been for you. I'm such an asshole."

I didn't respond, but I squeezed her hand.

"Come in. Let's sit." I finally pulled away, grabbing Lauren's hand too, and led them to the back of the house. They followed me into the kitchen as I grabbed another mason jar from the cabinet. I poured another glass of tea and sat down across from them.

"So, when are you due?" I asked Lauren.

Her full red lips spread into a wide smile. "March. We got pregnant the minute we got to Italy."

"Aw, a spring baby. I'm so excited for you. How has Tommy been?"

Lauren laughed and rolled her eyes. "Well, I was never very blessed in the boob department, but they were the first things to gain weight. Now as much as he wants to play with them, they hurt too much for him to touch."

"I remember those days," I groaned. "They hurt so bad, I couldn't even sleep on my stomach. How are you feeling otherwise?" I asked.

"Okay. For a while I was nauseated all the time. I threw up every time Tommy cooked bacon, which is a problem because he tries to incorporate it into every meal."

I leaned forward, not wanting any wandering guests to hear me. "Have you been constipated at all?"

Alexa's face twisted in disgust as her eyes darted back and forth between Lauren and me. "This is gross. You two are making my decision of never having kids easier and easier to swallow."

"Oh, stop it." I tilted my head at her skeptically. "You'll have kids."

"No way." She took a sip of tea. "Derek and I already decided it's not our thing. We're totally fine just being the cool aunt and uncle our whole lives. We're too selfish for kids."

"I guarantee you'll change your mind." I nodded at her.

"Not a chance." She laughed. "That's why I'm friends with you two baby factories. I get any weird baby urges out with your kids and then go home to my clean, non-toy-filled house and drink copious amounts of wine while having sex with my husband in the middle of the living room floor."

"Sounds like the night I got pregnant," Lauren sighed, causing Alexa and me to roar with laughter.

"So what about you, Kacie? Would you have more kids with Brody?" Alexa asked.

The sound of his name was a punch to the gut. While the memory of last night's events hadn't left my mind, I had been able to push them aside long enough to chat with my friends for a while. But when Alexa innocently mentioned his name, it all came flooding back. My eyes dropped down to my hands. I wasn't sure how to answer her question. I didn't even know if I would ever see him again, let alone be lucky enough to have him father my kids.

"Kacie?" Lauren looked nervously at me and then Alexa.

My head swept up and I brushed tears from the corner of my eye.

Lauren's eyes widened and her mouth dropped. "What happened?" She reached over and gently rubbed my arm.

A shaky sigh escaped me as I looked at her, but not Alexa. I could not handle any judgmental glares right now. "Zach was here last night. He showed up drunk."

Alexa leaned forward as her eyes bulged from her head. "Zach?"

"Yep. We sat on the porch for a few minutes while he rambled on and on about missing the girls and me and all this other weird crap." I rubbed my eyes with my hands, thoroughly exhausted. "Anyway, while we were sitting there, Brody drove up the driveway. Apparently he was at his parents' and they told him they were divorcing. He was upset, so he came here and found . . ." I choked on a sob before I could finish the sentence.

They both sat perfectly still, their eyes large as they hung on my every word. My heart raced and my body shook from retelling the events of the night before.

I cleared my throat and continued, "He found Zach and me on the front porch. Needless to say, he flipped."

"Did he hit him?" Alexa asked.

"More than once. I think he broke his jaw." I dropped my head into my hands.

Lauren smacked the table hard with her hands. "Shut up! He did not!"

I peeked at her through my fingers. "He absolutely did. Brody punched him so hard, he flew over the railing and landed on the lawn."

They both gasped.

"I . . . what . . . how . . . ," Lauren stuttered. "I don't even know where to begin."

"Zach didn't fight back; he just wanted to leave. I told Brody that he was too drunk, so I'd drive him home."

"Whoa," Alexa exclaimed softly. "You drove Zach home? Did Brody stuff him in the trunk first?"

I shook my head as I got up and grabbed a bag of pretzels out of the pantry.

"Pretzels?" Alexa stared at the bag as I sat back down. "It's nine o'clock in the morning."

I shrugged, shoving a pretzel in my mouth. "Shut up. I'm stress eating."

"Finish the story. What else happened?" Lauren reached over and grabbed a handful of pretzels.

"Brody argued, naturally, and then said the only way that was happening was if Zach rode with him and I drove Zach's car." I took a deep, cleansing breath. "So that's what we did. After I parked Zach's car, I hurried back to Brody's truck and lost it. I cried the whole way home. We pulled in the driveway and I hopped out, thinking he was right behind me, but he said he was leaving." My voice cracked. "He said he needed to think and process and whatever, so . . . he left. I haven't talked to him since."

"Have you reached out to him?" asked Lauren.

"Yeah, I sent him a text this morning, asking him to let me explain. Nothing yet." I picked up my phone and glanced down at the tiny envelope in the top right corner, silently begging it to light up.

"Wow." Alexa sounded shocked.

"I know, I know. You were right." I glared at her. "I don't want to hear about it, okay?"

"Kacie, I'm not trying to be right, nor am I throwing anything in your face. I just feel bad that all this happened to you. I'm so sorry." She reached across the island and squeezed my hand.

I let her.

I needed it.

After a couple of hours of the girls telling me it would be okay and Lauren and me trying to gross out Alexa with pregnancy details, it was time for them to go. "When will I see you again? Not till summer?" I whined at Lauren. She got to the front door and turned to face me, grabbing my hands and swinging them back and forth. "Yeah." She sighed. "We come back for good in June. Next time you see me, I'll be the mommy of a three-month-old. God, how weird does that sound?"

"Very weird, but amazing." I pulled her in for a long, tight hug. I didn't want to let go. Selfishly, I wanted to move her into my house so she could always be there to tell me everything would be okay. She was so good at that.

She stepped back and cupped my face with her hands. "Chin up. Brody's a wise man; he'll come around. You'll probably have a huge rock on your finger next time I see you."

I gave her a small smile. "Cross your fingers for me."

"I'll cross my fingers and my toes. Hell, I'll cross my legs. I'm already knocked up, what does it matter now?" Lauren laughed.

"I'm not good with words like she is." Alexa tilted her head toward Lauren and rolled her eyes. "But I love you. Hang in there. Call me if you need me. I'm only a few miles away."

"Bragger." Lauren narrowed her eyes at Alexa.

"I love both of you. Now go." I opened the front door. "Lauren, have a safe flight tomorrow. Give Tommy a hug for me."

"Will do, love."

They left and I closed the door, turning and leaning against it. I was about to give in to the nasty feeling in the pit of my stomach again when my back pocket vibrated.

A text.

From Brody!

B: Hey. I'm definitely confused and pretty pissed. I need some space to think. I'm heading out of town with the team tonight but will be back in a few days. I'll call you. In the meantime, I'd appreciate if you didn't hang out at the park with Zach.

Shit. The park. How did he know about that?

My stomach flipped and I suddenly felt worse than I had two minutes before.

I understand. I love you. I love you so much. Please don't forget that.

I waited and waited, staring at my phone.

He never answered.

24

BRODY

"What the fuck?" Viper skated up to me as the burgundy jerseys from the Colorado Avalanche all clumped together, high-fiving and celebrating their goal against me.

Without making eye contact with him, I lifted my helmet up and rested it on top of my head. The Colorado fans cheered and banged on the glass, some of them even flipping me off, as I set my stick on the net. It took every drop of strength within me not to flip them off in return. My eyes panned over to Coach Collins, who was pacing the bench with his arms folded across the chest of his cheap-ass suit, glaring at me.

Calm down, Collins. It's one fucking goal.

"You're playing like shit tonight. Get it together," Viper snarled at me when he realized I wasn't going to answer him. Now I wanted to flip him off too. I took a swig from my Gatorade bottle and pulled my helmet back on.

Four more times the Avalanche players piled in together and congratulated each other.

Four more times Collins glared at me.

After the game, I put my head down and tried to ignore the taunting fans as I skated off the ice.

"Fuck you, Murphy!"

"Don't look like an MVP to me!"

We'd lost 5–2 and it was my fault. I get the whole "Win as a team, lose as a team" bullshit, but this was all on me. It was my job to block that little black puck from making its way across the line and sounding the alarm, but I failed tonight.

Five times I failed.

I hated that fucking alarm, especially when it came from my goal. That spinning red light and annoying horn signaled failure to me. I'd heard it more times tonight than all the other games this season combined.

Big deal.

It was one game.

One game that, at the end of the season, wouldn't matter.

I'm lying.

That game did matter. They all mattered. More times than I could count, a team lost a play-off spot with one game. Sometimes one fucking goal in your *whole entire season* made the difference between being on the ice for play-offs and sitting at home and watching them on TV.

When I got to the locker room, Collins was already in there, standing by my locker.

"You okay?" he mumbled as I walked up.

"I'm fine," I lied, not wanting to tell my coach that my world had collapsed in more ways than one over the last few days.

He nodded and scanned the bustling locker room. "Just an off night or what?"

"Yeah," I snapped, looking him in the eye. "I had a rough night. Sorry."

"You want to go up for interviews?"

"No. Not tonight."

He patted me on the shoulder and walked off.

The *last* thing I needed was a bunch of bloodthirsty sports reporters asking me the same questions over and over, wanting to know why I'd missed so many shots. Who the hell even knew the answer to that?

I pulled my jersey over my head and started the process of taking my pads off. Louie glanced at me out of the corner of his eye before he turned the TV in the locker room on and flipped the channel to the postgame interview. It was no secret I'd played badly tonight. It was also no secret I was pissed off at myself about it. Normally, I was the jokester after the games, but tonight, I didn't want to talk to anyone.

Well, except for one person, but I wasn't ready to talk to her just yet.

I sat on the bench and sighed, leaning forward on my elbows and resting my head in my hands. It was bad enough that I could hear the interview; I didn't want to see it too. The reporters started firing out questions about me right away.

"Coach, are you worried about how Murphy played tonight?"

"No," he responded. "It is what it is. We're all human. It's his first bad game all season. Everyone is entitled to a couple."

"Coach, Coach!" another reporter shouted out. "This is a contract year for Murphy. Is that having an effect on his abilities?"

Collins exhaled loudly into the microphone. "It *is* a contract year. Is it having an effect on him? Who knows? I can't answer that. I'm sure it's stressful to know that your every move is being watched and weighed by the front office, but he's tough. He can handle it."

"Coach Collins, sources close to Murphy say that there are some personal relationship things that could be affecting the way he played tonight. Do you know anything about that?"

My head snapped up to the TV.

Fucking vultures.

I could feel every guy in the room staring at the back of my head.

"Listen. You know what? He doesn't talk to me about things like that, and he doesn't owe it to me either. He's here to do a job and he does it damn well. Did he have a rough night? Yes. Will he bounce back tomorrow? Yes. Do I think his personal life has anything to do with it? No. Even if it did, it's none of my—or anyone else's—business. That's all for tonight." He pushed the microphone away from his face and stood up from the table looking as pissed as I'd ever seen him. He lost his cool just as much as the next guy, but almost never on camera and certainly not during an interview.

Collins stormed through the locker room without making eye contact with anyone—especially me.

"That was rough." Viper sat down next to me, sweat dripping from his temples. "You all right?"

"Fine." I slammed my skates into my bag.

"You don't look fine."

"Okay, I'm not fine."

"Anything you want to talk about?" he asked carefully.

I sat up and stared straight ahead. "I don't want any advice," I warned.

"Done. Lay it on me."

"He's back, her ex. For weeks apparently, but she didn't tell me." I sighed.

"Interesting."

"That's all? Interesting?" I gawked at him.

"You didn't want my advice." He shrugged. "So I'm listening."

"If I were to ask for your advice, what would it be?"

"Easy. Kick his ass. She's your woman; fight for her."

"I did. I think I broke his jaw."

His head whipped around to look at me as he clapped my shoulder, hard. "Nice! Attaboy! So why didn't she tell you?"

"I don't know. I'm assuming she didn't want me to be mad?"

"Wait a second." He stood and tossed his own skates in his bag. "What the fuck do you mean you don't know why she lied? Didn't you ask her?"

"I was mad. I left. Haven't talked to her since."

His mouth hung open as he pulled his brows in tight, frowning at me. "What are you? An idiot? What if there's a perfectly good reason why she didn't tell you? What if you, being the stubborn asshole that you are, are sitting here stewing about it while that douchebag is comforting her and mending her broken heart?"

"I told her I'd call her when we got back."

"Moron, we're on a road trip. How long do you think it would take for him to weasel his way back in? Hopefully not literally?"

"She wouldn't do that. Not with him." I shook my head, blowing him off.

"Why the hell not? You're not talking to her. She's heartbroken. She's going to be looking for some sort of shoulder to lean on."

I felt sick to my stomach.

Viper was right . . . and that wasn't something I could say often.

I got back to the hotel room after my shitty game and checked my phone before I took a shower. I had four missed calls—three from my mom, which I wasn't in the mood to return, and one from Shae.

I didn't have to think twice about whether or not I was going to return my sister's call, even though I was nervous as hell to do so. Had Mom and Dad talked to her yet? Did she know? If she didn't, could I act normal, like nothing was wrong? I didn't want to be the one to break her heart.

"Hey, kiddo." I tried my best to sound cheerful when she answered the phone.

"Brody!" she blurted out when she answered. "What the hell is going on with Mom and Dad?"

I sighed. "They told you, huh?"

"Yeah. They called me this morning claiming they wanted me to find out from them, not you."

"How nice of them," I said sarcastically as I stretched out across the hotel bed.

"What happened with them? They won't tell me anything." Her voice was quiet, sad. She sounded how I felt.

"I don't know. They didn't say much to me either." I rubbed my temples with my fingers. "I wasn't there long, though. I kinda stormed out."

"Mom told me. She's most upset about that, of all things," she said in disbelief.

"Did they tell you how long they've known about this?"

"Yeah," she yelled. "A whole fucking year! What the hell? This is such crap, Brody. We have to do something."

"Shae, what can we do?" I understood how she felt. She was reacting the same way I did the other night when I was determined to fix them.

"I don't know," she whined. "Lock them in a room together until they decide to drop all this?"

"Unfortunately, life doesn't work like that."

"I'm mad, Brody, and hurt and confused and . . . mad."

I took a deep breath and let it out slowly. "I'm mad too, kiddo. I just don't know who to be mad *at*."

25

KACIE

I started my morning, just as I had the previous few days, by sending a text to Brody that he most likely wouldn't respond to.

> Your silence is killing me. I miss you so much I ache. Please call me. XO

Three days without a text or phone call from him was complete torture. Every time my cell phone made a noise, my heart leaped into my throat. I'd even started praying the house phone would ring, though I didn't think he had that number. There was an ache inside of me that even a phone call couldn't heal. I had texted him a few times just to say "I love you," always without a response.

I'd just about finished my externship hours and was pretty sure that Maureen was going to pass me. Apparently she was grumpy to all of her students; it was just her personality. Darla assured me that if I was hired on at the hospital and she saw me as a coworker and not just a student, she'd actually be quite pleasant to work with.

Whatever.

There was a better chance of Viper marrying a nun than of me applying at that hospital. I would miss working with Darla, though. As close as we'd become, I knew we'd still see each other often.

"Look at how far you've come," Darla said proudly.

"I know! I'm almost like a real nurse, huh?"

"You are a real nurse, Kacie. It's in your heart."

"It is, but I think I've made a decision." I sat down next to her at the desk. "I think I'm going to apply somewhere doing labor and delivery."

She tilted her head slightly and raised her eyebrows. "Really?"

"Yeah." I shrugged. "I've been talking to my girlfriend from Italy a lot about her pregnancy and I realized that's where my passion is. Helping women who are pregnant or in labor, that's what I want to do. And don't even get me started on holding those teeny-tiny babies. It's like heaven."

Darla stuck her finger in her mouth and proceeded to make a gagging noise. "You can have it. All those whiny, complaining women who act like they are the first ones on the planet to have a kid. No, thanks. I'll stick with my middle-of-the-night drunks, broken bones, and God knows what else here in the ER."

"Well, we're just going to have to meet up often to swap stories, then." I smiled at her.

"Definitely." She smirked at me. "Maybe we can go on a double date sometime."

"Ooooh. Double date? Who's the lucky guy?"

She batted her eyes at me as a devilish grin spread across her face. "Let's just say he has a giant snake."

Realization washed over me, and my mouth fell open. "Viper? I thought you said that was a one-time thing?"

"It was supposed to be." She shrugged. "But he texted me and I couldn't stay away. That boy can lick the bark off a tree."

"Okay, okay. I get it." I scrunched my eyes closed and held my hands up, not wanting to hear any more. "For what it's worth, I'm glad you're happy. And I would love to go on a double date, assuming . . ."

"You'll still be together," Darla said softly, reaching over and putting her arm around me. "He's just angry. He'll get over this. You guys will be just fine. Want me to ask Viper to tell him to call you?"

"Sure." I laughed. "Maybe Viper can pass him a note in homeroom to meet me in the science lab after the assembly. I appreciate it, but no thanks. I got myself into this, I'll get myself out."

"Speaking of getting themselves in and out of trouble . . ." I looked up at her as she nodded down the hallway. I followed her gaze and saw Zach walking toward us.

"Hey, guys." He waved as he walked up. "Kacie, can I talk to you?"

I nodded and offered him a polite smile. "Sure." I turned toward Darla and whispered quietly, "I'll be right back. Cover for me, okay?"

"You got it," Darla said as I followed Zach down the hall to a waiting area.

We sat across from each other in itchy sage-green hospital chairs with wooden arms. It was uncomfortable but private. He leaned forward with his elbows on his knees, his chin resting on his folded hands. Yellow and purple bruises stained his cheeks.

"You okay?" I asked, leaning to the side to get a better view of his face.

"Yeah. I had an X-ray. Not broken, thank God."

"I'm . . . uh . . . sorry about that," I stammered, not sure the apology was fitting coming from me. I wasn't sure that he deserved an apology, period.

"Don't. Please don't apologize. It just makes this harder." Before he started speaking again, he sighed. "Listen, Kacie. I have no idea what to say except *I'm* sorry. I've been replaying the other night in my head over and over and I can't figure out why I did what I did."

"First things first—why did you drink?" I searched his face, looking for a sincere answer.

"Honestly?" He looked up at me. "I don't know. Something about hanging with the girls at the park just set me off. I was sitting around feeling sorry for myself when my friend Brett called. Before I knew it, we were in a bar and I was throwing back rum and Cokes like I just came in from the desert."

I studied his face as he stared down at his hands, clearly ashamed.

"What does this mean? Ya know, for your sobriety?" I asked, genuinely concerned.

"I'm still taking everything day by day. I'm just going to check in more often with my sponsor, and instead of going to meetings a couple of times a week, I'm going to go every day for a while. I'm not worried about that part. I'm worried about the damage I did . . . to you."

"Yeah, that part sucked, but it wasn't completely your fault." I took a deep breath. "Had I told Brody that you were back and we'd talked, he wouldn't have reacted the way he did."

"It wasn't your fault I got drunk and came over uninvited." He shook his head.

"That's true. It's over and done with, though; nothing either of us can do about it. Now I just have to try and figure out how to fix things with him."

"That's actually why I wanted to talk to you," he said slowly. His eyes caught mine and my stomach sank.

"That first time I saw you here, at work, I felt like there was a reason we were put together at the same hospital at the same time. I mean, what are the odds? Out of all the hospitals in our area, out of all the departments you could have been placed in, out of all the shifts between the two of us . . . we ended up in the same room at the exact same time."

"I would call that dumb luck on your part. From my end, it was terrifying." I didn't mean to sound like a total bitch, but I was being honest.

"I realize that. For me, it seemed like maybe a second chance at what I'd missed out on five years ago."

I started to roll my eyes and he reached forward and grabbed my hands. "Hear me out. Time has gone on and, as one pissed-off hockey player reminded me, I threw you and the girls away. I didn't miss out on anything."

When had Brody told him that? Ugh. That damn truck ride.

"That's right, you did," I said quietly.

"That's my point. I've always, in my head, twisted everything to feel like I was a victim of my disease. I'm not. And the decisions I made during the height of my addiction were just that—my decisions. I have to own them and that's what I plan on doing, starting now." He let go of my hand and sat back in the chair. "Life is about choices. Every day we make them. From things as minor as what we should eat for breakfast to major things like if we should leave our family today. Well, I made a bad choice. I tell myself that I left to protect you guys, and I suppose in some ways, that's true. But mostly, I left because I was selfish."

"Where are you going with all this?" My eyes were damp with tears. I was sick of him rehashing our past every time we saw each other. I just wanted to be happy again.

"I've made another choice and I pray to God it's finally the right one. I've been selfish my whole life when it comes to you, so for once I'm doing the exact opposite. I'm going to walk away, again. Except this time, it really *is* for you and the girls."

My mind raced in a hundred different directions.

He's walking away *again*? We'd just gotten to the point where I could be in the same room with him and not want to kill him. I'd been thinking about how I'd tell Lucy and Piper their real dad was back and wanted to see them. And now he wanted to go?

"I don't understand." I blinked and my eyes darted around his face.

"Selfishly, I would give anything for another chance with you, but I can see that your life was pretty awesome before I came barging back into it. Me being around has caused you nothing but stress, so I'm going to disappear. The girls didn't know who I was, so it's no loss to them. You seem really into Brody, and he's obviously very into you and protective of my daughters. I really couldn't ask for any better for them or you."

I dropped my head into my hands and rubbed my eyes, desperately trying to digest all that he'd just said to me. My own dad had taken off when I was ten years old and I hadn't seen or heard from him since. When I was in high school, I often wondered how different my life would've been if he'd stuck around. Naturally, I wanted a better life for Lucy and Piper than I'd had, and if that meant asking their biological father not to walk away, so be it.

"Kacie?" he questioned quietly after a minute.

My head snapped up to face him and I took a deep breath. "I don't want you to go."

He pulled his brows in tight and cocked his head to the side. "You don't?"

"No. I don't. I never imagined myself saying this, but we lost you once, Zach. I don't want to lose you again. You've been through a lot and you're right, you made some shitty decisions. But you've shown me more change in the weeks we've been in contact than in the whole three years we were together before."

A shy smile spread across his face and he looked down, fidgeting with his phone.

"You were right about one thing, though," I continued. "Romantically, there's *no* chance for us. My heart belongs to Brody and it *always* will."

"I understand." He nodded.

"I'm going to try like hell to get things back on track with him, and in time we'll see about introducing you to Lucy and Piper. Like I said a few weeks ago, though, my trust for you is pretty broken. It's going to take a *long* time and a lot of work to fix. And no more drinking. Period. That's a deal breaker."

"As long as it takes. You're in charge. And you have my word about the drinking. I'll never touch the stuff again." He smiled slowly as his shoulders relaxed.

Relief rolled across his posture and I was jealous. I could only feel that kind of relief with contact from one person right now, and he wanted nothing to do with me.

26

BRODY

Diesel's cold nose pressed against my cheek, waking me out of a sound sleep.

"Morning, buddy. You gotta piss?" I asked without opening my eyes.

I lifted the pillow and shoved my head under it, trying to block out the sunlight.

We'd gotten back really late the night before from our road trip and I had come home and collapsed. My body and my brain were exhausted. I was playing like shit and thinking about Kacie nonstop, but I couldn't bring myself to call her. Not yet.

She wasn't the only one trying to reach me. My mom had called me so many times, I was surprised she hadn't sent out a search party for me yet.

My phone rang again and I knew that I couldn't ignore her much longer.

"Hello, Mom," I said flatly as I answered.

"Brody! How are you?" She sounded relieved.

"Fine."

"That's good." She tried hard to sound like everything was normal. "I've been worried about you. You haven't been returning my calls."

"I know." I took a deep breath and held it for a second. "Listen, Mom. I owe you an apology for the way I stormed out the other night."

"Stop right there. I know what you're going to say and I don't want you to say it. You don't owe me any apologies."

"Yes, I do," I argued.

"No. There's no handbook to life, Brody. No rules on how you're supposed to handle situations," she said softly. "You were given news that was upsetting and you reacted. You're allowed to react. I didn't expect you to be happy about our divorce."

"I know, Mom, but I shouldn't have flown off the handle the way I did."

"It's okay. Really," she assured me.

"So, how are you with all this, Mom? Really?" I wanted to get her opinion on things without my dad sitting next to us.

She paused for a second and I was worried that I'd pissed her off. "I'm good, Brody." She sounded perkier than I was prepared for. "I'm actually totally at peace with it. It's for the best, it really is."

"Seriously?" I exclaimed. "I just don't get that. Thirty years, Mom."

"I know how long I've been married. Things have just changed. It's no one's fault. We just have to learn to roll with the punches."

She was sounding a little happier about her current situation than I would have been, though she had already known about this for a year. Apparently she'd adjusted well.

"Is Dad around?"

"Uh, yeah. I think he's out in the workshop. Let me take him the phone."

A few seconds later, I heard scratching on the phone—like someone was holding it against their shirt—muffled talking, and then my father's gruff voice.

"Hello?"

"Hey, Dad."

"Hey, Son. How are you?"

"Pretty shitty. How are you?"

"Hanging in there." He'd shown almost no emotion as far back as I could remember. I don't know why I thought now would be different.

"I wanted to talk to you for a minute and tell you that I'm sorry for the way I left the other night. That whole conversation with you and Mom was a shock, but I shouldn't have freaked out the way I did." I took a deep breath and swallowed my pride. "I'm most sorry for accusing you of cheating on Mom and calling you a bad dad. It was reprehensible and I'm so sorry."

"Water under the bridge, Son. Don't sweat it." I could hear light hammering in the background and Dad's AM radio station. That workshop was the best thing that ever happened to him. He spent hours and hours out there.

"I'd feel a lot better if you'd call me an asshole or something."

"Fine. It's water under the bridge, asshole." Dad laughed. "Really, don't give it a second thought."

There were unanswered questions I had from the other night, and I don't know why, but they just started flying out of my mouth. "So what happened, Dad? Where did this all come from?"

A hefty sigh filled the phone line. "Honestly, I don't know. One night last summer, she made my favorite: barbecued pork sandwiches. We were two bites in and she told me she wanted a divorce."

What?

"Wait. This wasn't a mutual thing?" I was shocked by what he'd just said.

"Far from it, Brody. I love your mother. Love her just as much today as the day I married her, probably more."

"So what the hell? Why aren't you fighting her on this?"

"She's made her decision, Brody. I can either be mad about it and push her away completely, or I can accept it and still have a best friend."

"So you're just gonna give up?" I was getting pissed again. If he still loved her, he needed to grow a set and fight.

"I don't look at it as giving up, Son. I look at it as . . . she's unhappy. I love her so much, I'm willing to let her go and be happy."

I didn't respond. I let what Dad said roll around inside my brain for a minute. All these years I thought my father was a simple, cold man. He *was* simple, but he was far from cold. Turns out he was so in love with my mom, even after thirty years, that he was willing to sacrifice his own happiness for hers. From that point on, I would never look at my dad the same way again. He was the most selfless, humble man I would ever know in my whole life, and I'd never felt like I had more in common with him than at that exact moment.

I hung up with my parents, still feeling annoyed and unsettled, but we weren't getting anywhere and it was pointless to continue. I didn't want to think about my mom and dad's situation anymore. The only problem was that if I wasn't thinking about that, I was thinking about Kacie.

It'd been six days since I'd heard her voice. Six days since I'd driven away and left her crying on the grass. Six days since I was sure I could kill someone with just my fists.

Like clockwork, my cell phone chirped. Kacie had texted me every single morning at the same time and they were getting harder and harder to ignore.

K: Are you done with me?

My chest tightened with the thought of how shitty she must be feeling to send *that* text. I was angry and needed some space but didn't want her feeling like that. I had to send her something back.

We'll talk soon. I miss you.

It wasn't much, but it was all I could give up at that moment. There were so many things running through my head to say to her, none of which I wanted to share over a text message.

I dragged myself out of bed and tossed on a baseball hat.

"Come on, D. Let's go."

Diesel perked his head up at my call and dived off my bed, sprinting to the front door as he heard the jingling of the metal leash.

The last week had easily been the worst of my life. First I thought there was something wrong with my mom's cancer scans. I find out those are fine, but less than an hour later find out my parents are divorcing. You would think at twenty-seven years old, I would be able to process their separation logically, but my world crashed with that news. And a couple of hours after *that*, I find out the one person I thought I could go to for comfort had been lying to me for weeks. I just didn't know what to do. Everything was spinning out of control and my one true constant—hockey—was suffering because of it. We lost three out of five games on the road and I knew my teammates were looking to me for guidance. Collins had asked me twice if there was anything going on that he needed to know about, but I continued lying. There was a home game tonight and I was bound and determined to play like myself.

I hurried Diesel along so that I could scarf down some breakfast and head to the stadium early to work out. The workout would distract me, and hopefully it would score some extra credit with Collins.

One quick text that I'd been meaning to send and I was off . . .

A few hours later, I finished up a light workout before the game and was feeling charged, despite my rough morning at home. The good vibes coming from the crowd when we took the ice were a huge jolt to my already pumping adrenaline. It probably helped that we were playing the Vancouver Canucks, one of our biggest rivals. They were in the Pacific Division, and we were in the Central, so it wasn't a division rivalry, more of a personal one between teams. For some reason, more blood was shed on the ice when we played them than with any team in the whole league. We looked for reasons to fight each other, and I didn't expect this game to be any different.

The first period was exciting but nerve-racking. The score bounced back and forth. First, Viper scored a goal for us; then they scored against me. Then Big Mike scored for us and they scored again almost immediately.

We were skating off the ice for intermission after the first period and I got cut off by Edgar Shepard, one of the biggest assholes in all of professional hockey. He stood a couple of inches taller than me with a shiny bald head. A huge scar went from one side of his cheek to the other, a souvenir from where he got sliced up by a skate years ago. He also had a loud mouth and no skills on the ice—a terrible combination. We had jarred with each other before, so him spouting off was nothing new.

"Sorry, Murphy. Did I get in your way?" he sneered as he skated right in front of me, almost making me fall flat on my ass.

"Fuck off, Shepard," I bit out, continuing past him.

After a quick team talk from Collins, we all went back out with renewed determination. I took my spot on the ice and started cleaning the crease. It was always too slick after the Zamboni made its run during intermission.

Players from both teams were scattering about and taking their places when Shepard skated behind my net.

"What's with you, Murphy? You've been playing like shit for days. Getting old?"

I ignored him, determined not to let him get to me. The game was close and it was obvious he was attempting to rattle me to gain an edge.

The second period was brutal, fast-paced, and intense. There were three fistfights, and Viper sat in the penalty box nearly the entire time. Despite all the shenanigans, the score didn't change. Still tied 2–2.

We took the ice at the beginning of the third period and I rolled my eyes as Shepard skated my way again. He skidded to a stop about three feet from me and grinned, without saying a word.

"What do you want?" I snarled, still refusing to make eye contact with him.

"Jensen? Is that Kacie's last name?"

My skin tingled with adrenaline as my head snapped toward him. I clenched my jaw and lifted my helmet up so I could look him straight in the eyes.

"I don't know what the fuck this game of yours is, Shepard, but you just took it to a whole other level. Back the fuck off."

His eyes widened while he continued grinning at me, enjoying my anger. "Whoa! Did I hit a nerve? Relax, Murph. I was just asking a simple question in case I wanted to look her up. Ya know, since you two are done and all . . ."

Breathe. He's just trying to get under your skin.

I laughed, trying my hardest to look amused by his threat. "Regardless of whether we're done or not, she's way too classy to give your dumb ass the time of day. I would say good luck, but it wouldn't help anyway."

"That's too bad." He skated closer, leaning in. "I heard that hot little cunt of hers is worth all sorts of trouble."

I. Lost. My. Fucking. Mind.

I dropped my gloves on the ice and lunged at him, grabbing the collar of his jersey and pushing him backward. He fell back hard, his helmet slamming against the ice. I climbed on top of him and started punching as hard as my restrictive pads would let me.

Left. Right. Left. Right.

I lost track of how many times I hit him.

Blood splattered the ice next to his face as he wrapped his hands around my throat and tried to push me off.

"That's enough, you two!" It felt like a dozen arms wrapped around me, pulling me off of him. Two refs and most of my teammates were standing around as I stood up, my chest heaving. Fans were banging on the glass as his team skated up behind him screaming at me, but I was so zoned in on getting my hands on him again that I didn't even hear what they were saying. He got up off the ice with help from Pekarske, their center, and wiped his mouth, smearing blood across his cheek. He looked up at me and grinned again, now missing a front tooth.

"Both of you, off the ice!" the ref shouted.

Viper skated up next to me. "What the fuck are you doing?"

"Back off," I roared, staring straight ahead.

"Dude, you just got a game misconduct penalty. Now you're out the rest of this game and maybe the next. What the fuck were you thinking?"

"Get away from me!" I pushed his chest back, sick of him yelling in my ear.

I skated over to my bench and past Collins, whose red face stared out at the ice as he gritted his teeth. "Louie, get in there," he yelled as I made my way to the locker room, where I watched the rest of the game by myself.

My team lost 4–2, but I lost a hell of a lot more.

27

KACIE

"What is he *doing*?" I yelled into the stillness of the living room. I watched in horror as Brody climbed on top of a guy from the opposing team and started punching him. There wasn't even a play near them at the time.

"Oh my God, this isn't good." My mom pulled her hands up over her mouth.

"Wait," I squeaked, slightly panicked. "It's normal, right? There are always fights in hockey."

"Not like this." Fred shook his head. "Goalies very rarely fight. They are off-limits. And the game wasn't even going on. Something else happened here."

Brody was relentless, hitting the guy over and over. Viper and a couple of other guys I didn't recognize rushed over with the refs and pulled Brody off of him. The other guy stood up and had blood all over his face.

"Did he just smile at Brody?" I asked incredulously.

"I think so." Fred scratched his head, frowning at the TV.

"What is going on down there?" one of the TV announcers asked.

"I'm not sure, but we were still in intermission. Something must have set Murphy off," responded the other man.

"You know, Bill, that's par for the course with Brody Murphy lately. He's been a little off the whole season, but particularly this last week. That stunt he just pulled will most likely get him suspended for at least one game, maybe more."

Suspended?

The ref said something to both men and pointed off the ice. Brody turned and started skating away with Viper following right behind him.

"Wait. Did he just push Viper?" My eyes widened.

"He did." My mom still stood with her hands cupped against her cheeks. "What is going on with him?"

Once he was off the ice and out of sight, I sat on the couch and dropped my head into my hands. "What should I do?"

She sat down and put her arm around me. "What can you do, honey? Unfortunately, nothing."

"I just . . . I wish he would talk to me." Tears stung my eyes as I searched my mom's face for answers. "I haven't spoken to him in days. How can he just turn it off like that?"

Mom bit her lip as her eyes danced nervously around the room like a couple of jumping beans.

"Mom?"

She closed her eyes and let out a big sigh. "I'm not supposed to tell you this, but I can't let you sit there and think he's just forgotten all about you. He texted me . . . this morning."

Every nerve ending in my body tingled with a combination of fear and excitement. "What? When?"

"Earlier this morning. They got back into town late last night. It was brief and we didn't get into anything about Zach, but he desperately wanted to know how you were and said he missed the girls."

For the first time in nearly a week, my heart was filled with hope instead of utter soul-crushing sadness.

He texted. It wasn't to me, but he texted. That must mean he still cares, right?

"What did you say?" I fought hard to swallow the huge lump in my throat.

"I said that you were miserable but hanging in there. I said that you were incredibly sorry, and I said that the girls missed their Brody, all three of you." She reached over and squeezed my hand.

My heart raced so fast that I had to remind myself to slow down and take deep breaths. "Did he respond?"

"He just said he missed you guys too. I didn't want to ask him a lot of questions or push him, so I left it at that."

I took a full, shaky breath. "Thank you," I whispered to my mom, "for telling me. I know you weren't supposed to, but I'm so glad you did. I might actually be able to sleep tonight for the first time in days."

I kissed her on the cheek and hurried off to my room.

I threw myself on my bed and grabbed my cell phone.

Okay, Kacie. Calm down.

Brody texted my mom under the assumption that she would be discreet and not tell me. I couldn't reward her for telling me by ratting her out, so I had to think really hard about what to say to him. I considered leaving it as it was and going to bed, but given what I saw at his game and what he was probably going through right that second, I needed to reach out.

Hey. Saw your game tonight. I hope you're okay. Please call me. We don't have to talk about what happened. I just need to know you're okay. I love you.

I knew he wouldn't respond; his game wasn't over yet. Even if it was, I wasn't confident that he would, but knowing that the game was still going on gave me an excuse to cling to. I curled up in bed and turned the light off.

My eyes snapped open to nothing but darkness. Everything was black, but I knew I'd heard my phone beep. Squinting in the dark at the bright screen, I blinked several times, waiting for the text to come into focus. It was from an unknown number.

UNKNOWN: Kacie, it's Viper. Call me ASAP. Brody got arrested.

My eyes still weren't completely focused when I read his next text with the number. I dialed, pretty sure I got it right. It started ringing, and I glanced at the clock on my nightstand. Just after three o'clock in the morning.

"Hello?" a gruff voice answered.

"Viper? It's Kacie. What the hell is going on?"

"Dude. I don't know." He sounded out of breath. "He played like complete shit tonight, so I figured he'd want to go straight home and sleep it off, right? Well, after the game, he tells me he wants to go blow off some steam at the bar. Fine. We're sitting there having a drink; everything is great. I go to the bathroom, come back, and he's in some fucking barroom brawl with like four guys. Next thing I know, the cops were there and he got cuffed."

"Oh my God."

"You have to come, Kacie. He's fucking spiraling. I don't know how to get through to him."

"Text me the address of the station. I'm on my way."

I threw a hoodie over my head, put my flip-flops on, and wrote my mom a quick note in case I wasn't back in time to put the girls on the bus.

An hour and a half later, my hands were shaking as I circled the same city block for the eighth time, trying to find a parking space.

I finally found one and parallel parked like a pro for the first time in my entire life. I grabbed my phone from my purse and texted Viper.

I'm here. Where are you?

A loud knock on my driver's-side window nearly made me scream out loud.

"Jesus!" I yelled, glaring at Viper's grinning face, which was pressed up against the glass. "You scared the shit out of me."

He laughed. "I was sitting on the stairs. I watched you circle the block a million times, thought maybe Stevie Wonder was driving the car."

"Not funny." I rolled my eyes, trying not to laugh at him.

The crisp autumn air slapped me in the face as I hopped out of the Jeep. It was a little surreal that two hours before I was sound asleep in my bed at home, and now I was in a city police station to help bail my boyfriend out of jail.

"Okay." I slammed my car door. "I've never bailed anyone out before. How does this work?"

"I already went in and talked to them. He's in a holding cell in the basement." He fell in step beside me as we made our way to the building. "We go in, pay the bail, and sign him out. Then I hold him down while you slap some sense into him."

"I have an idea." I narrowed my eyes at him. "Think any of those cops are hockey fans?"

After Viper turned on the athletic charm and promised to hang around signing autographs for a while, a fresh-faced, nice officer led me downstairs to the holding area. There were two cells. The one on the right held a few passed-out frat boys who'd clearly had too much to drink, evidenced by the putrid smell of vomit that assaulted my nose as I walked by.

To my left was the other cell, and in it, sitting on a cement bench, was Brody. He was leaning forward with his elbows resting on his knees, his head in his hands. I stood for a second, staring at the loose curls on top of his head. I was overcome with love for him and guilt for the part I'd played in his internal torment.

I took a deep breath and mustered up every ounce of courage I had. "Hey," I said softly.

His head snapped up at the sound of my voice and his eyes widened when he saw me. Standing up quickly, he wiped his hands on his jeans and took a couple of steps closer. "Kacie? What are you doing here? How did you know?"

A sympathetic smile tugged at my lips. "Viper texted me and I got here as fast as I could."

"You didn't have to drive all this way." He shook his head back and forth slowly. "Viper could've gotten me out."

"I know that, but this actually worked out better." I crossed my arms across my chest.

He raised his eyebrows and looked around the cell. "It did?"

"Yep." I took a step forward and wrapped my hands around the bars. "He's upstairs entertaining the officers, with strict instructions not to pay the bail until he gets the 'all clear' text from me."

"Huh?"

"You can't run from me in there. You can't ignore my texts. You have no choice but to hear me out."

A smile threatened to tug at his mouth. "Resourceful little thing, aren't you?"

"Desperate times call for desperate measures." I took a deep breath, exhaling slowly. "Brody, I love you. I love you so much. You walked into my life almost five months ago and have completely changed it. You've changed *me* for the better. You've made me relax—a little—and taught me to live life less timidly. Every once in a while, though, the scared, overanalyzing girl in me still rears her ugly head and stands at the edge of that damn catastrophe cliff."

He frowned at me, scratching his cheek. "The what?"

"Never mind." I shook my head quickly. "It's something Lauren talked about; it's not important. My point is when I went to the hospital for the first time a few weeks ago, I never in a million years expected to see Zach there. I never expected to see him again in my whole life."

The sides of Brody's jaw twitched at the mention of Zach's name, but I didn't stop. It was now or never, and I wasn't about to walk away and leave anything on the table.

"Should I have come straight home and told you? Yes. Would that have been the rational thing for a girlfriend to do? Yes. Did I do that? No." My voice started to shake, but I cleared my throat, determined to regain my composure and get through this. "It was our last week before you started practice and things had *just* settled down from the whole Kendall-Blaire fiasco. I chickened out. Selfishly, I just wanted to keep things as smooth as possible between us."

His eyes softened and he opened his mouth to talk, but I wasn't done yet.

"I'm a mama bear, Brody, quick to assume I always know what's best and slow to admit when I'm wrong. But I admit it: I was wrong. I was wrong for not telling you sooner, but I was *not* wrong for lying to you. I never lied to you; I just made a poor judgment in my timing." I swiped a tear from my cheek.

He walked up to the bars and stood inches from me. "You're not the only one who made a mistake, Kacie."

My heart stopped beating and I held my breath.

Oh God. Is he telling me good-bye?

"Pushing you away this past week was *my* mistake. Whether I understand your reasoning or not, I can't tell you how bad I wish we would've had this conversation right away. It's my fault that we didn't."

"I wish we would've too." I sniffed and rested my forehead against the bars as the tears ran freely down my cheeks. "Can we be done with all this, please? I really need to hug you right now and these damn bars are in my way."

"I'm not done," he said cautiously.

"Oh." Deflation washed over me.

"I've actually done a lot of thinking this week, and let me tell you, being inside my brain is a crazy place to be lately." He laughed in such a foreign, nervous way that goose bumps covered my skin and my stomach flipped. "I talked to my parents this morning, trying desperately to figure out a way to convince them to give it one more try. Then I started thinking . . . I'm a total hypocrite."

"A hypocrite?"

"Yeah, think about it. My parents are separating. I'm twenty-seven and fucking devastated about it. I would give anything, pay anything, do anything for them to give it one more try. What if it wasn't their own stupidity but a person who had come in between them? How would I feel about that person? I would hate them for the rest of my life, assuming I didn't spend it in prison for killing them."

The tiny hairs on the back of my neck stood up. "What are you saying, Brody?"

"I love your girls, Kacie. I can only pray that the way I feel about them is the way I'll feel about my own kids one day. The last thing in the world I would ever want is for them to hate me or resent me in ten years because they think I came in between their mom and dad." He blinked as the rims of his eyes grew red. "As sick as it makes me to say it, I think I'm going to step back and let you figure this out with him first."

My mouth fell open as I let go of the bars. "Are you serious?" I asked, struggling for a full breath.

"I am." He pressed his lips together and swallowed hard.

As quickly as the confusion took over my body, it evaporated, leaving anger in its wake. I stepped back and started pacing the length of the cell as I scratched my head. I didn't look at Brody, but I knew his eyes were following me. I could feel them.

"Kacie, talk to me," he uttered slowly.

I spun on my heel to face him. "Do you love me?"

His head jerked back in surprise and he licked his lips. "Yeah. That's why I'm doing this."

"No." I took a step toward the bars. "Do you *really* love me?"

"Yes," he responded firmly.

"Then screw you."

"What?"

"Screw you."

"No, I heard you. I just don't get it."

"Do you know why Zach left me?" I cocked my hip to the side and crossed my arms across my chest.

He rolled his eyes. "I have no idea."

"He was dealing with some major substance abuse. I had no idea it was as bad as it was, so he thought he'd do me a favor and leave. Ya know, for my and the girls' sake," I said sarcastically. "Then yesterday, he told me he'd decided to leave—again—for me and the girls. I told him I didn't want him to."

His eyebrows shot up at my news. "You did?"

"Yep, you heard me. I told him not to go, that we would give it time and see about introducing him to the girls eventually. I also told him there was no chance of us being together again—ever. You see, I'm twenty-four years old. I've been a single parent for five years. In that time, I've managed to all but finish my nursing degree, help my mom run an inn, and fall in love with the most amazing man. The same man who now thinks *he* knows what's best for me and should walk away."

"Kacie—"

"Nope. I'm not done," I interrupted. "I've made a decision. From now until forever, *I'm* going to be the one who gets to decide what's best for Kacie and her girls. If you're no longer in love with me and think it's best we separate, that's one thing. But please don't think for a second you're doing me any favors by turning your back and walking out on me."

Brody walked right up to the bars and rested his head against them, staring at me.

"I *need* you, Brody. I would give up everything in my life, with the exception of Lucy and Piper, to have you by my side—forever. I don't care about money or celebrity status or any of that crap. I just need *you*. If you get traded, I'll move tomorrow. If you get hurt and can't play anymore, I'll work two jobs to support us."

Neither of us spoke for a minute. We just stood there, staring at each other with tears in our eyes.

"I need you too, Kacie. I just don't want the girls to hate me."

"Hate you?" That thought was ridiculous to me, but it was a real fear of his. "They think you're Superman, Brody. There's a lot they won't understand now, but as they get older, they'll get it."

"And what if *that's* when they blame me?" he asked. "When they get older?"

"Then together, we'll sit them down and give them as much truth as they can handle." I stepped closer to the bars and looked up at him. "The key word in that sentence is *together*. Now, let's get you out of there and go home—together."

"Dude, if you don't marry her today, I will," a familiar voice called out.

My head snapped to the left to see Viper and the same officer who'd brought me down there standing at the bottom of the stairs. "Sorry." He shrugged. "You guys are taking forever and I'm fucking starving. I figure if you haven't made up yet, I'll drop you off at home and you can fuck it out while I go get pizza."

The cop took out his keys and started our way with Viper right behind him.

"Holy shit! Viperrrrr!" one of the drunk guys in the other cell yelled out as Viper walked past them.

"What up, dudes?" Viper waved, stopping to shake their hands through the cell bars.

I stepped back, allowing the officer access to the lock. Brody was watching Viper and the guys with an impassive look on his face. The jingling of the keys in the lock pulled his attention away from them and he stared right at me.

Through me.

The cell door swung open, but Brody didn't budge. He kept his eyes glued to mine but turned his head just a hint toward the officer. "He's gonna be a minute, right?"

The cop turned and looked at Viper, who was high-fiving and chatting with the now wide-awake group. "Looks like it."

A smirk started at the corner of Brody's mouth and rose to his eyes as he reached out and grabbed the collar of my hoodie. He pulled me into a bear hug and squeezed tight. "Then close the door and give us a minute too."

I buried my face in his shirt and let go of all the pent-up emotion from the last several days. I sobbed and sobbed, overwhelmingly relieved that he wasn't walking away from me. From us.

28

BRODY

Suspensions fucking suck. There's no other way to say it, they just do.

The fight during the game earned me a game misconduct penalty, which forced me to sit out not only the game I was kicked out of, but the next game too. Rather than appeal the decision and go in front of the commissioner, Collins and I decided it was still early enough in the season for me to just serve out the suspension, pay the fine, and move on. Well, move on from the league's perspective, but I was far from done with trouble.

Due to my little testosterone outburst in the bar, and my resulting arrest, the Wild suspended me two extra games. The only good thing to come from that arrest was Collins hauling my ass into his office for a long talk the next afternoon. I explained everything that had been going on, without making excuses for my performances.

"Murphy, I plucked you right out of college because there was something special about you. You're a hell of a hockey player, but it's more than just that. You were a crazy, immature kid who has grown into a remarkable man right in front of me. I would like to think I had something to do with that, but we both know I can't take the credit." He leaned forward and rested his elbows on his desk, pulling his hands up to his mouth. "You've had some stuff going on in your personal life, I get that. Take these few days off and get your head screwed on straight."

I looked down at the ground and nodded, fidgeting uncomfortably in my chair like I was a kid in the principal's office. "Have you heard any trade whispers in the front office?"

My chest was tight with anticipation of his next sentence. I didn't really want the answer, but I had to ask the question.

"No. Nothing. And believe me, I've had my people listening."

I exhaled a deep breath and stood up to leave. Collins followed me to the door.

"Hang in there, kid. This is just a small bump in the very long road of your career." He patted my shoulder as I opened the door.

"See you later, Coach." I waved.

"Wait. I have to know . . . the bar fight. Why did it start?"

"Viper was in the bathroom and I was sitting there drinking my beer, not bothering anybody, but still pretty wound up from the fight and the game. Guy started telling everyone I was a goalie because I didn't know how to throw a punch." I shrugged. "He poked me in the back, so I proved him wrong. Then I proved him wrong again. Then again."

"Wait a minute." Collins frowned in confusion. "Viper wasn't arrested, but his knuckles are all banged up. How did he get involved?"

I tried to hide my grin unsuccessfully. "He came out of the bathroom and I was fighting like four guys. I remember him yelling my name, asking who he should hit first. I didn't answer, so he just started swinging."

Collins sighed and shook his head. "You two are like *Dumb and Dumber* on ice skates. Go. We'll talk in a couple of days."

I opened the door to my truck and looked across to the passenger seat as I climbed up.

Kacie jumped as her eyes snapped open.

"Sorry. Were you sleeping?"

She pushed her arms out in front of her and stretched her neck side to side. "I must have dozed."

"I feel bad that you're so tired today. It's my fault."

"Eh." She winked at me. "You're worth it."

"So," I sighed. "What's the plan for today?"

Please don't say you're going home. Please don't say you're going home.

"Well, I should probably go home." She craned her neck to look at the time on my dashboard. "Mom put the girls on the bus for me, but I need a shower desperately."

"I don't know . . ." My eyes lazily traveled the length of her body and back up to her face. "You look pretty hot in your pink pajama pants with little yellow ducks on them."

She reached across and swatted my arm. "Shut up. I was in a rush to save my boyfriend from the clink. Anyway, about this going-home thing, do you wanna come with me?"

"I do. Really bad."

A lazy smile crawled across her lips. "I was hoping you'd say that. We're gonna have to drive separately. My car is still here, remember?"

"No problem. I'll follow you." I peeked at her out of the corner of my eye and squeezed her hand. "It's usually a good view from back there."

She looked at me and raised a playful eyebrow. "Your back end isn't so bad either, Murphy."

We drove to my house in silence, content with just holding hands and being together again.

I pulled into my garage and parked in the space next to her Jeep. She didn't make any immediate move for the handle, not that I was in a rush to get rid of her.

"So, I was thinking . . ." She paused.

Uh-oh.

"How about we go to my house, I get cleaned up and get Lucy and Piper settled in—"

"Sounds good," I interrupted.

"And *then*," she continued, pretending not to hear me, "I was thinking we drive out to your parents' place so you can talk to them."

"No." I shook my head adamantly. "I'm not in the mood for that shit today."

"Brody, hear me out." She put her hand on my forearm, rubbing it gently with her thumb. "They're still your parents whether they're together or not, and you love them just as much as you did last week before you found this out. I think you'll feel better if you just talk to them, especially your mom. I can tell from what you told me about your phone conversation you're mostly mad at *her*."

How does she always know this shit?

I clamped my jaws together and stared straight ahead at the concrete wall in front of my truck.

"Knowing what I know about your mom, she's losing her mind right now over you not talking to her. I'm actually surprised after your game last night that she wasn't sitting in the hallway outside your condo this morning." She giggled.

I shot her a *not funny* glare and her smile disappeared.

"Sorry. Too soon." She covered her mouth, trying to muffle her laugh.

"Fine. You're . . ." I paused.

"Right?"

"No. Not right," I said sarcastically, "but not completely wrong either."

"Good. I win." She leaned over and kissed me on the cheek quickly before hopping out of the car and running to hers.

We put the girls in bed that night and it was hard to walk away. I just wanted to hang out in their room with them and watch as they fell asleep.

The closer we got to my parents' house, the stronger my urge became to turn my truck around and go the other direction.

I didn't want to go there.

I didn't want to talk to them.

I didn't want to see them.

"You nervous?" Kacie's sweet voice pulled me back to reality.

"No," I answered flatly.

"Well, you're something. You've been sighing over and over out of your nose like a dragon for the last thirty miles."

I glanced her way quickly and lifted her hand to my lips, kissing the top of it. "I just don't know what to say to them. I think they're stupid."

She chuckled. "Don't say *that*."

Ten minutes later, we were walking up the steps of my parents' front porch.

"Deep breath. I love you." Kacie smiled at me as I knocked on the door.

The door cracked open and my mom took an instinctive step back, clutching the collar of her robe. "Brody?" Her voice was shaky as she looked from me to Kacie and back again. "What are you doing here? Is everything all right?"

"Not really, Mom." I sighed.

"Here. Come in," she ordered, opening the door all the way.

I walked past and turned around as she pulled Kacie in for a quick hug. "Hi, honey. How are you?"

"I'm okay. Brody told me the news." She rubbed my mom's arm gently. "How are *you*?"

Mom pulled her robe closed and crossed her arms over her chest. "Divorce sucks, but we're dealing with it the best we can. I know this is new to you guys, but we've had a year to get used to the idea."

I had to fight the urge to roll my eyes. Every time they mentioned that they'd known about this separation for a year and hadn't bothered telling us, it just pissed me off more. It wasn't fair to me and it wasn't fair to Shae.

"Can we go sit?" I asked gruffly.

Mom's eyes widened and she swallowed hard. "Sure. Of course. Come on."

She walked past me to the family room and flipped the light on. Kacie grabbed my hand and tugged on it gently, trying to get my attention.

"Relax," she whispered, smiling at me.

We walked into the family room and Kacie and I sat together on the couch while my mom disappeared into the kitchen.

"Can we just go?" I begged Kacie. "This is dumb. I don't want to talk to my parents about my feelings."

"You'll feel better when this is over. Shhh."

I pulled my brows in and looked down at her. "Did you just shush me?"

"Yes. I love you. Shhh," she whispered again. I couldn't help but smile at her. She was adorable.

Mom came back in the room carrying four water bottles and set them on the coffee table. "I brought these, unless you'd rather I made coffee or tea?"

"No, no. Don't go to any trouble." Kacie waved her off. "This is great. Thank you."

"I called your dad down. He'll be here in a second." Her neck was red and splotchy and her voice shook when she spoke. Normally, my mom was calm and cool and in charge of every situation. I felt bad that I was making her so nervous; I needed to find a way to relax the room.

"So I got arrested last night," I blurted out as my mom eased into her chair.

Her mouth fell open as Kacie dropped her head in her hands and sighed.

"You what?" my mom exclaimed.

"What?" I shrugged. "It's true. Figured you'd want to hear it from me before you read it in the paper."

"Read about what in the paper?" my dad asked as he walked into the room.

Mom pursed her lips and looked from me to Dad as he sat down in the chair next to her. "Your son got arrested."

His head whipped over to me. "Again? For what now?"

I rolled my eyes. "You say that like I've been arrested a million times."

"You want to know how many times I've been arrested in my life?" Dad pulled his glasses down his nose and looked over them at me, raising his eyebrows. "Zero. What was this one for?"

"I got in a fight."

"We saw that. They can't arrest you for fighting on the ice, though, can they?" asked my mom.

"No. I got into another one *after* that one."

Mom sat up straight in her chair. "You got into two fights in one night?"

I nodded.

Maybe this wasn't the best icebreaker.

Mom reached out and grabbed a water bottle off the coffee table. "Well, what happened? Fill us in."

"I had a rough game and wasn't in the mood to go home, so me and Viper went to the bar. We were drinking a couple of beers and talking about the game. Everything was fine. He had to take a leak and as soon as he left, some prick started in on me about being a shitty goalie and how I was a goalie because I didn't know how to fight." I shrugged. "I ignored him for a while and then . . . he poked me in the back with his pool cue."

"Uh-oh," my dad said under his breath.

"Exactly!" I pointed at him. "Needless to say, that was all I needed. Next thing I know, I'm rolling around on the ground with a bunch of guys, and then I'm being handcuffed."

"What happens now?" Mom asked.

"Nothing. They'll plead it down. I'll probably end up on probation, *if* it even goes that far."

My mom let out a heavy breath. "Oh, Brody. What brought all this on?"

"My life has been a little stressful, Mom. I've been wound pretty tight." I glared at her, sounding more sarcastic than I meant to.

She recoiled like a scorned child, slumping her shoulders and looking down at her hands as she sat back in her chair.

"Listen." I sighed. "That's why I came up here, or was forced here, or whatever." I looked down at Kacie, who nodded proudly at me. "Things with us haven't been great the last week and I just wanted to get it all out, I guess. I don't know."

"I'm so sorry this is rattling you like it is." My mom sniffled. "I wish there were something I could do to take this pain away for you. I just don't know how to make it better."

"I'm just pissed, Mom. I don't understand why you guys are giving up."

"Brody, here's the thing . . . it's not your relationship to understand," she said softly. "Your father and I didn't wake up and just decide this last week. We've been growing apart for a while. We're different people now. He still loves me and I still love him, just not in the same way."

"There's really nothing that can be done? That's just it?" I sounded desperate, looking back and forth between the two of them.

"That's it, Son," my dad spoke up. "Your mom is right. We have nothing bad to say about each other and we'll always be friends."

"You're just starting this process, honey, this mourning process," my mom followed.

"Mourning?" I asked.

"Yeah. You're mourning the loss of what you thought things would be like, the life you *thought* you would have. You grew up with this idea of how your life would be when you were older, and I'm sure it didn't include having your parents separate." Her wise words and soothing tone made me relax for the first time in a week. "This is going to take some getting used to, but eventually you'll realize you're not losing either of us. Just the idea of us."

She was right. I'd always figured one day I'd bring my kids to this house to have picnics and sleepovers with their grandparents, together. This was just going to take some getting used to.

I felt defeated.

Deflated.

Exhausted.

"But if *you guys* can't make it work, how is there any hope for any-one else?" I resigned, waving my imaginary white flag.

"Honey, just like I said, the relationship between your dad and me isn't for *you* to understand; your relationship with Kacie isn't for *me* to understand. Hell, I shouldn't even be offering advice, but I can tell you what I've learned along the way. If you guys want to be together, you're going to have to roll up your sleeves and put in the work. Forever. Peo-ple stand in front of an officiant and say 'I do,' but that shouldn't mean 'I'm done' when it comes to putting time and effort to grow their rela-tionship." She looked at my dad and a sad smile appeared on her lips. "I wish I could go back in time and take my own advice."

An hour later, Kacie and I were in the car on the way home and she was quiet. Really quiet.

"What are you thinking?"

She sighed. "Just kinda going over in my head what your mom was talking about."

"What part?"

"All of it, but mostly the part when she said that no two families are the same and they come in all shapes, sizes, and colors. It really hit home for me." Nervously, she looked down and started playing with her hands. "Especially the part when she said that sometimes what people want at twenty-five years old isn't the same thing they want at fifty."

I looked back and forth from her to the road. "What are you trying to say?"

She shook her head at me. "No. No. Nothing about us, nothing about us at all. I'm just thinking. Do you think that people can sometimes want something different at twenty-five than what they thought they wanted at twenty? Like Zach?"

I clenched my jaw and dug my fingers into the steering wheel.

"Think about it, Brody. The fact of the matter is he's here and he seems different. I feel like I owe it to the girls to at least give them a shot at having a meaningful relationship with him."

"You owe him nothing," I said sternly.

"Okay, you're right. I don't *owe* him anything, but I'm thinking about it from Lucy and Piper's perspective. I don't want them to grow up and ask where their dad is someday and I have to tell them that he came back but I wouldn't let him see them."

"What if he wants *you* back?"

"Not possible," she insisted. "I have the sexiest, sweetest, most amazing boyfriend on the planet who's not afraid to kick his ass if he gets out of line."

"You can say that again—about the ass-kicking part."

"We want to move forward as a couple, right?"

"Right," I agreed.

"Then I need your blessing on this."

"Why?"

"Brody! Because! I love the way you protect the girls and me with the fierceness of a lion protecting his cubs, but you can't kick his ass every time he comes to the house to see them."

I took a deep breath and exhaled like a dragon again. "When were you at the park with him? We never talked about that."

Her eyes dropped to her lap again. "He wanted to see the girls, but I wasn't comfortable with introducing them to him, especially since you didn't know yet, so I told him I would bring them to the park to play and he could watch from a distance. We were only together about fifteen minutes or so."

"Hm."

"What does that mean?"

"That's actually not as bad as I was picturing," I admitted.

"What were you picturing?"

"I don't know." I shrugged. "The two of you having a picnic and pushing them on the swings together."

"Oh God," she scoffed. "Not even close. You're the one I want to do those things with. Not him."

"But—"

"Stop but-ing me and stop assuming that just because he's back, I'm going to run off with him. You're what I want, Brody. I want you now. I want you in ten years. I want you in fifty years. Now, let's roll up our sleeves and work on this shit." She winked at me.

We pulled up to a stoplight and I used the driving break to my advantage, leaning over and kissing my girl. She grinned at me with that crinkly nose that brings me to my knees. I couldn't imagine spending thirty years with her and then just giving up. If I was lucky enough to one day persuade her to marry me, I was holding on tight and never letting go.

29
KACIE

"Why am I so nervous?" Brody asked, pacing the kitchen like an expectant father.

I laughed. "Because they're six and Lord knows what's going to come out of their mouths."

Today was the day.

Today was *the* day.

We were sitting the girls down and telling them about Zach. I was nervous, but excited to get the weight off my shoulders and move on. I had no idea what to expect from them when I told them. They were only six years old, after all.

"So what are you going to say?" He sat down at the kitchen island, nervously tapping his thumb on the counter.

"I'm going to keep it simple. They're still pretty little, so just the basics." I sat down across from him and held his hand, steadying it. "As they get older, they're going to have more questions, and we can get into detail then. For now, less is more."

"Yeah. Okay." He sighed.

"Are you sure you want to do this tonight?"

It was Halloween and Brody had suggested that it would be a good night for us all to put the past behind us and take the girls trick-or-treating. I called Zach and suggested it. He was overwhelmed with my offer and thanked me profusely.

"Yes. Let's just rip that Band-Aid off." He nodded.

"By the way, I'm dying to see these costumes you have for them," I said excitedly.

A devilish grin slowly rolled across Brody's lips as he cocked an eyebrow at me.

"Okay. *That* face makes me even more curious than I already was."

A couple of weeks ago, Brody had asked if he could be in charge of the girls' Halloween costumes. He said he had a plan and the girls were in on it too, but they didn't want me to know. As a mom, Halloween costume selection was a very big deal, but I threw caution to the wind and let him have this one.

"I'm so surprised that they haven't told you. I really thought they would."

"Me too. I was kind of counting on it, actually." I rolled my eyes.

My heart pounded as the front door swung open. Mom and Fred had gone for a walk and had agreed to pick up the girls from the bus stop on the way back. I heard their giggling in the foyer and looked at Brody. His eyes were practically bulging out of his head.

"That's them!" he whispered.

"I know. Relax." I walked to the other side of the island where he was sitting and wrapped my arms around his shoulders. "We got this."

He reached up and squeezed my hands. "Sleeves up, Jensen."

Brody and I had been saying that to each other for a couple of weeks now, ever since his mom had said it to us. It'd become a little thing we said to each other when we were nervous about doing something. I kissed the side of his head and took a deep breath as Lucy and Piper came running around the corner.

"Mom!" Lucy squealed, jumping into my arms.

Piper dropped her backpack and sat at the island, propping her chin on her hand. "Can we have a snack?"

"Yes, in just a minute, okay?" I set Lucy down in the chair next to Piper and sat across from them. "We want to talk to you for a minute."

My mom kissed my cheek as she passed through the kitchen. "Good luck," she whispered in my ear.

I gave her a tight smile and looked at Lucy and Piper. Their little faces stared back at me, blinking innocently. In twenty years, they probably wouldn't remember the conversation we were about to have, but I would never forget it. All of our lives were about to change, forever.

"So . . ." I took a deep breath, preparing myself. "Remember a few weeks ago when you said that there was a little boy at school who said Brody was your daddy?"

They both nodded.

"And remember how we told you that you could tell anybody you wanted that Brody was your daddy?"

"Yes, like we told the man at the hockey game," Piper stated proudly.

"Exactly," I answered. "Well, it wasn't completely true."

They both frowned in confusion.

"You guys know that I love Brody, right?"

They nodded again.

"Well, before I loved Brody, I loved another man . . . a long time ago. His name was Zach."

Lucy's eyes lit up. "The man from the park!" she exclaimed.

I flashed Brody a quick glance, thankful that he was so focused on the girls the park comment didn't seem to bother him at all. "Yes, the man from the park. Like I said, a long time ago we loved each other. And we loved each other *so* much, we made you guys."

Brody looked down at the table and took a deep breath.

"So Zach is our dad?" Lucy's little face twisted with such confusion as to where she'd come from; it made my chest ache.

"Yes, honey. Zach is your real daddy." I swallowed the lump in my throat that formed instantly as those words left my mouth.

"But I want Brody to be my daddy." Piper's chin started to quiver.

"I know you do, but—"

"Brody kills all the spiders and he's really good at tying our shoes, Mom. He should be our daddy."

"Listen," Brody interrupted. "Just because I'm not technically your daddy doesn't mean I'm going anywhere. I'll still be here to kill all the spiders and tie your shoes and build your forts. Forever and ever, okay?"

"Pinkie swear?" Piper asked quietly, holding her tiny pinkie finger in the air.

"How about we change it to Twinkie swear?" Brody grinned. "It'll be our own secret way to promise each other something."

"Yay!" Lucy clapped.

"And yes, I Twinkie swear. Forever." They wrapped pinkies and Twinkie swore before Brody cleared his throat and continued, "Think about it. How cool is this? You guys get one mommy and two daddies! You're the luckiest kids ever!"

Lucy searched Brody's face adoringly, thinking about what he'd just said.

Piper, on the other hand, wasn't affected as deeply. "Mom, can we have a snack now?"

I'd agonized over telling them about Zach for days, and the whole conversation was over in five minutes flat. They hopped off their stools and each grabbed an apple out of the fridge before they ran down the hall.

I puffed out my cheeks as I exhaled. "Wow. That was interesting."

"'Interesting' is an understatement." Brody patted the stool next to him, signaling for me to move around the island and sit next to him.

I walked over and sat, immediately leaning into him and resting my head on his arm. "I'm so sorry about that."

He played with a strand of my hair but didn't respond.

"I wanted you here and I know you wanted to *be* here, but I'm sorry you had to hear it like that, ya know?"

"Don't sweat it. They're little. It's hard to explain all of this without freaking them out and giving them way more science than they're ready for." He laughed. "As they get older, they're going to ask questions, but it won't matter. They'll already love me way more than they love him anyway."

I sat up and grinned at him. "Duh. How could they not?"

He tucked a piece of hair behind my ear and smiled at me, showcasing those adorable dimples.

"I love you, Murphy."

"I love you, *More*."

Brody quickly pulled his phone out and looked at the screen. "What time is what's-his-name coming over?"

I rolled my eyes at him. "Trick-or-treating starts at four o'clock. He said he'd be here at quarter till, so any minute?"

"Shit!" He jumped off the stool. "I gotta help the girls put their costumes on." He walked over to the backpack he'd brought and took out two sets of black sweatpants and sweatshirts and handed them to me. "Can you take these in there and ask them to put them on? I'll help with the rest."

"Black sweats?" I cocked my head to the side. "You guys have me totally thrown off."

"Good." He handed me the sweats and smacked my ass as I headed down the hall.

The girls giggled and tortured me the whole time I got them dressed, laughing about how funny it was that I didn't know what their costumes were. I tried asking questions and digging around for clues, but they just covered their mouths and grinned at each other.

They followed along behind me as I walked back out to the kitchen. "Okay, they have on their—" I stopped dead in my tracks with the girls bumping right into me. Zach stood on one end of the kitchen, leaning against the counter. Brody sat at the island with his hands folded in front of his mouth.

"Hi," I said nervously.

"Hi." Zach smiled and waved. "Brody let me in."

"Well, the evening is starting off on the right foot already. At least he let you in the door." I laughed, trying to ease the tension in the room.

Zach offered up a fake laugh and Brody cracked a smile.

I considered that a win.

Lucy called out, "Hi, Zach."

"Uh, you should probably call him . . . what should they call you?" I stuttered.

Zach shrugged. "Whatever you guys are comfortable with. Really."

"Brody's our dad and we call him Brody." Piper skipped around the island.

Holy crap, now I was worried Zach was going to be offended. Was it always going to be that way? Me freaking out and on edge that someone was going to have hurt feelings?

"So call me Zach. I'm cool with that," he said.

"Brody, we're ready for our costumes," Lucy tugged on his shirt.

Brody's face softened. "You are?" He looked down at Lucy. "Well, come on, then." He stood up and started out of the kitchen.

"Where are you going?" I asked as they followed along behind him.

"I didn't trust you not to snoop, so I left them in my truck." He laughed on his way out the door.

Zach and I stood in the kitchen awkwardly, not making eye contact with each other.

"He really loves them," he finally said.

"He does. A lot."

"I can tell. They're lucky to have him."

I nodded in agreement. "Very lucky."

"I'm lucky too." He sighed.

"How so?"

"That you invited me here to be part of this tonight. I really appreciate it."

"Don't thank me; it was Brody's idea."

His eyebrows shot up. "It was?"

I nodded again. "He thinks that we need to try and move forward."

"Wow." He looked at the ground and shook his head slowly. "I'm impressed."

I heard the front door swing open again and turned toward the hall, excited to see what Brody had cooked up.

"Mommy! Come here!" Lucy called from the foyer.

I looked at Zach and shrugged. "Guess it's the moment of truth." I walked up front with Zach following behind.

When I got to the foyer, I pulled my hands up to my mouth, trying to contain my laugh. Standing at the front door, side by side, were Lucy and Piper in the cutest Twinkie costumes I'd ever seen. "What in the world? Where did you find those?"

Brody looked down at the girls proudly. "I had them made. Aren't they perfect?"

"We're cute!" Lucy clapped.

"Do you want to bite us?" Piper asked, giggling.

"You guys look *so* cute!" I pulled my phone out of my pocket and aimed it at them. "Smile! Brody, get in there with them for one." He walked up behind them and squatted down in the middle. "Say 'Happy Halloween.'" They smiled and I clicked away.

"Want me to take one of the four of you?" Zach asked, holding out his hand for the phone.

"Really?" I asked. "You wouldn't mind?"

"Of course not." He took the phone from me. "Hop in there."

I walked up behind the girls and squatted next to Brody, who wrapped his arm around my waist. That moment was incredibly surreal to me. Overwhelming even. As my past was taking a picture of my present, a calm wrapped its arms around me and I just knew things would be okay. Brody and Zach were acting like champs around each other and the girls had handled the news perfectly. Could life get any better?

"We better get going, Twinkies," Brody said excitedly. "There's a lot of candy out there to claim."

"Wait, one more pic. Zach, you wanna take one with Lucy and Piper?"

Zach nervously rolled his top lip in between his teeth. "I would love it, if you guys wouldn't mind." He pointed to Brody and me.

I took my phone from him and stepped around front.

"Have at it." Brody stepped to the side.

After the picture of Zach and the girls, Lucy jumped up and down. "We need one of all of us, Mommy! One more!"

I looked up at Brody and bit my lip nervously before glancing over at Zach, who had shoved his hands in his pockets and seemed beyond uncomfortable with the prospect.

"Uh . . ." I stalled, trying to decide how to deal with the awkward situation.

"Come on." Brody walked over behind the girls again. "I have long arms. I'll try and get everyone in. Let's go."

Zach looked at me and shrugged as a small smile cracked his lips. *Why the hell not?*

I squeezed in between Zach and Brody.

We snapped a few more pictures and were out the door.

Two hours of walking door to door and the adults were complaining more than the kids.

"Do they always have this much energy?" Zach yawned.

"Unfortunately, yes." I laughed. "They never stop moving. They're going to have enough candy to last them until next Halloween." Zach shook his head as they ran past us to the next house.

"Not after the candy tax," Brody joked.

Zach turned and frowned at him. "Candy tax?"

"Yeah. Once the kids go to bed, the parents get to raid the bags and pick out their favorites as a tax for walking all night."

Zach threw his head back and laughed. "I think I'm gonna like the candy tax."

Lucy and Piper looked up, saying something to the older man who had just dropped candy in their bags. As they waved good-bye and ran down the sidewalk toward us, I stopped them. "What were you saying to that man?"

"Oh!" Lucy shrugged. "He asked if that was Brody Murphy on the sidewalk and we told him yes, that we have two dads and Brody is one of them." She grinned.

"You told him that?" I blurted out.

"Yeah, lots of people asked about Brody and we told all of them that he was one of our two dads," Piper said proudly. "Come on, Lucy!" They linked hands and sprinted off for the next house.

Brody, Zach, and I stood frozen on the sidewalk with our mouths open.

"Did she just tell people—" Zach stopped halfway through his sentence and looked at Brody and me.

"I believe she did." Brody laughed hard. Zach and I followed suit.

"Oh my God," I said as my laughter died down. "I'm so sorry. People are going to think you and Zach are . . ."

He grinned and shook his head, chuckling. "Andy's going to have a good time explaining this one to the tabloids on Monday."

EPILOGUE
BRODY

Today is June twenty-fourth.

Two months ago today, my team was knocked out of the play-offs by the fucking Chicago Blackhawks, once again. Despite my rough start to the season, I ended it with more wins and more saves than any other season in my career.

Yesterday, Andy called and told me he had a contract offer for me, but he wouldn't tell me from what team. I had no idea if I was still going to be Minnesota Wild's goalie next year or a Florida Panther. He didn't want to tell me over the phone, so I was going in to his office to meet with him.

Today is also Kacie's birthday. She's turning twenty-five years old. She's the most mature and selfless twenty-five-year-old on the planet. When I scroll through Facebook, most of the girls I went to high school with are still pretending to be drunk airheads to impress a guy or posting stupid selfies of themselves in their bathrooms. Kacie has been a single mom for years, though she doesn't call herself that anymore. Between me and Zach, who has been spending more and more time with the girls lately, she's anything but alone. She passed her exams with flying colors and has been working in the labor and delivery unit of Rogers Memorial Hospital since shortly after she graduated. She worked three twelve-hour shifts a week, and while that's been a huge adjustment for us, we'd gotten good at going with the flow.

And thank God for that, because I had no idea what was going to happen at this meeting with Andy. He told me to come by at nine o'clock. I looked at my phone. 9:12 a.m.

I was stalling. I really didn't want to hear that the Wild was letting me go, and the last thing in the whole world I wanted to do was give Kacie that news on her birthday. But we'd promised each other: no more withholding information. And we hadn't. Not so much as a blip on the radar in the eight months since our Hell Week, as she called it.

Before I rolled out of bed and dragged myself to Andy's office, I shot my girl a text.

Morning, Jensen.

Diesel hopped up and curled into my side, giving me another excuse not to get out of bed yet.

K: Good morning to you, Murphy.

Listen, I was thinking . . . I've got a lot of errands to run around here. I'm probably gonna come up tomorrow instead of today, okay?

I laughed out loud in my bedroom. "Holy shit, D. She's going to be so pissed." A second later, my phone beeped.

K: Really? Today? You have to run errands today?

Yeah. I'd like to get them over with. Why? Did you have something going on?

K: Ummmm . . .

I couldn't let her suffer any more.

Just kidding. I'm coming up. Of course I wouldn't miss my girl's birthday! Happy birthday, baby.

K: You jerk! I thought you really forgot!

Not only did I not forget, I already planned out our evening and asked your mom to babysit.

I didn't like lying to her, but I had been working too long on her surprise and I wanted her to think we were going out tonight after we all took her to dinner.

K: You did? Where are we going?

Can't tell you that. It's a surprise.

K: What should I wear?

You still have that blue dress that you wore to the charity banquet last year?

K: No, but I can borrow it from Lauren again. We're going somewhere that formal, huh?

Nope. We're going somewhere totally casual, you just look smoking hot in that dress.

K: You're a pain in the ass.

The biggest. I'll be up in a few hours.

K: Okay. Can't wait to see you. I love you.

I love you, MORE.

"Well, look who decided to show up." Ellie smiled at me as the elevator doors opened. "And only an hour and a half late."

"Sorry." I grinned back. "Is he in there?"

She rolled her eyes and shook her head. "Yep. Go ahead in."

The door to Andy's office creaked as I opened it. He looked up from his computer and leaned back in his chair when he saw me, clamping his hands behind his head.

"I know, I know. Shut up." I threw myself down on the leather couch across the room from him.

"I didn't say shit." He chuckled.

"No, but I could feel you thinking it."

"I'm actually impressed." He looked at his watch. "I figured I probably wouldn't see you before noon."

"I'm heading up to Kacie's after this." I picked a football up off of his coffee table and flipped onto my back, tossing it straight up in the air. "Stop fucking around. Give me the news."

He stood up and grabbed a paper off his desk.

"Before I give this to you"—he sat down across from me—"I want you to know how proud I am of you. You ended with an amazing year, even with that rocky start. This is a fair deal that I think you should seriously consider."

My heart started beating as fast as I could ever remember it beating in my whole life.

I'll take less money; I don't care about that. Please be the Wild. Please be the Wild.

He set the paper down on the table in front of me and sat back again. I grabbed it off the table, searching through the legal bullshit, looking for a city and a team name.

MINNESOTA WILD

Yes!

I jumped up off the couch and fist pumped the air as every muscle in my body contracted at the same time with excitement. I vaulted over the coffee table and landed in Andy's lap, bear hugging him.

"First of all, get off me, this is weird. Second, I'm assuming you're happy with that offer?"

"I didn't look at the offer." I hugged just his head. "It's in Minnesota, that's enough for me."

"You should probably look at the offer, Brody."

I stood up and climbed back over the coffee table to my side. Picking up the offer, I squinted as I scanned it quickly, this time looking for a dollar sign and a time period.

There it is.

"What the fuck?" I dropped the paper on the table and stared at Andy incredulously.

He grinned at me and nodded. "You're reading that right. They're offering you seven million a year for six years. A forty-two-million-dollar contract. That's a franchise record for a goalie, Brody. I think you should take it."

"Take it?" I yelled, jumping up again. "I want to hump it."

"Well, Ellie doesn't want to clean anything gross out of the fax machine, so keep your dick in your pants, okay?"

"Dude." I shoved my fingers in my hair and left them there as I paced his office. "This is fucking huge."

"It's beyond fucking huge. After the way you kicked all kinds of ass the second half of the season, I knew they would offer to keep you here. I didn't expect that number, though." He took a pen out of his pocket and tossed it on the table. "Whenever you're ready, bro. Sign away."

I was facing the bookshelves in the far corner of his office with my hands still locked on top of my head.

"What are you thinking about?" he asked.

I spun around slowly to face him. "Kacie. I can't wait to tell her. She's gonna fucking flip."

He tilted his head to the side. "Dude, you've had it bad for that girl for a year now. You gonna marry her or what?"

Nothing short of the building falling down around us at that very moment would have stopped the grin that slid across my face. "Funny you should mention that . . ."

KACIE

"Did you guys have fun tonight?" I ran my fingers through the tiny blond strands of Lucy's hair that fell across her forehead.

She beamed and nodded excitedly.

"We've never been to that place before. It was fun, huh?" I said to them, looking over at Brody, who was sitting on a chair on the other side of their bed. They had their own beds but insisted on sleeping together still.

"It was really fun," Lucy said. "Can we go back again?"

"Sure," I answered.

"Tomorrow?" she asked.

"I don't know about tomorrow." I laughed. "But we'll definitely have dinner there again soon, okay?"

"I liked it when they sang 'Happy Birthday' to you and made you wear a cowboy hat." Piper giggled.

"And then they made you ride that stick horse," Lucy yelled, hopping out of bed and galloping around the room.

"That was my favorite part too." Brody held his hand up and high-fived her as she skipped by him. Then he looked at me and winked. "I never wanted to be a stick horse so bad in my whole life."

I raised my eyebrows and gave him the warning look, trying not to laugh. "Come on, Lucy, back in bed. It's late."

Lucy climbed back into bed and snuggled up as close as she could to Piper.

"How much do I love you guys?" I followed Brody to the door.

"More than all the stars in the sky and the waves in the sea," they sang together.

"And how much do I love you?" Brody asked them before leaning in close to me and whispering, "Listen to this."

"More than all the zeros in your new contract." Piper giggled.

I smacked him on the arm. "You're terrible."

"I taught it to them at dinner when you were talking to your mom. Pretty awesome, huh?"

"Go." I pushed him down the hall. "Good night, girls."

"Night, Twinkies!" he called over me.

"Night, Mom! Night, Brody!"

"I'm exhausted," I whined, collapsing onto the couch in the family room.

"No, no. You're not gonna lay there and fall asleep." Brody grabbed my hands and tried to pull me back up. "I still have to give you your present. Come on. Up."

"Where are we going?"

"Outside."

"Outside? Can't you bring it here? I'm tired." I laughed.

"Who's the pain in the ass now?" he teased, leading me toward the front door. "Let's go."

We walked out the front door and he grabbed my hand, pulling me down the stairs and to the right, around the side of the house.

"Uh, last time you led me this way, I lost a tank top." I giggled, again trying not to step on anything.

He turned back to me. "Keep walking, birthday girl."

We got to the back of the house and started our way down the hill when a light up ahead caught my eye. I squinted through the darkness and realized it wasn't a light, but a row of lanterns on the pier.

Our pier.

"What did you do?" I squeezed his hand and grinned at him as we got to the edge of the sand.

"You'll see."

We stepped onto the creaky wood, and I stopped walking for a minute, taking in how amazing it was. Little silver lanterns lined both sides of the pier, lighting the whole thing up just beautifully.

"Come on." He gently pulled on my hand again.

As we got closer to the end of the pier, I finally noticed the white box with a perfectly tied red bow sitting at the end.

"What's that?" I cooed.

He bent over and picked it up, handing it to me. "Happy birthday, Kacie."

I tugged on one end of the bow and it unraveled smoothly. Wrapping my hand around it so it didn't drop in the water, I lifted the lid of the box and moved the tissue paper to the side.

Confused, I frowned up at Brody. "My View-Master?"

The corner of his mouth lifted slightly. "Look at it."

I handed him the box to hold as I raised the View-Master to my eyes, aiming toward the lanterns for backlight. Blinking for a second so my eyes could adjust, the first picture I saw was of Lucy, Piper, and me in our matching Wild jerseys from his first home game.

"Oh my God!" I peeked over the top at him. "How did you do this?"

"Keep going." He laughed.

I pulled the orange tab down. The next picture was of Brody and me walking the red carpet on our way into the Wild Kids charity event last year.

"Holy shit! This is so awesome," I said, pulling the tab down again.

Picture number three was taken last fall, right in the exact spot we were standing in. It was one of my favorite pictures ever. The sky was painted pink and purple and the sun was setting perfectly right behind my mom and Fred as they exchanged wedding vows.

I anxiously blinked a couple of times to clear the tears from my eyes so I could go to the next picture.

This one was taken at Brody's parents' house. It was of Brody, me, his mom and dad, Shae, and her new fiancé, Ricky. The picture was a little crooked because we had Lucy take it, but you could clearly see Shae showing off her new engagement ring. Brody's fear had come true—his sister was going to be Shae May.

"This is just the coolest thing ever, Brody. I want to do this with all my pictures." I sniffed, pulling the tab again.

Picture five was of Viper, Brody, and the girls from the first time they taught them how to ice skate. Not many kids could say that the first time they ice skated was on a professional hockey rink with two professional hockey players as teachers. The smiles on their faces were priceless, just like this gift.

The next one was from my graduation ceremony several months back. I was grinning at the camera and holding up my certificate while Brody kissed the side of my head. One of my proudest achievements.

I pulled the tab for the next picture and my breath caught. I remembered taking it on Christmas morning. The girls woke us up super early to open their presents. After we were done, I was making monkey bread in the kitchen while Lucy, Piper, and Brody sat on the couch watching *Charlie Brown's Christmas*. I'd noticed it had grown pretty quiet in that room and tiptoed over to see what they were doing. Brody and the girls were lying down, sound asleep. Lucy and Piper were each tucked up under his arms with their little heads on his chest.

Picture eight was another favorite of mine, taken the weekend we spent at his house after his first game. The girls were grinning ear to ear, playing blissfully in the fort Brody had made them in his living room the night before. Diesel liked the fort too.

The next picture was of me, Brody, the girls, and Zach. It was taken last Halloween when we all went trick-or-treating together. It was the first time we all hung out together for the girls' sake. There had been many of those occasions since then, but that one would always be special.

I pulled the tab again.

"What picture are you at?" Brody asked.

I moved the View-Master down just enough to look at him as I answered. "The one of you and Andy from the night you were awarded the William M. Jennings trophy. You looked so hot in your suit."

Picture number eleven was from just a couple of weeks ago when we got another big rainstorm and Brody ran out and bought hot-pink rain boots for the girls so they could jump in puddles with him. This picture was the most breathtaking shot of Lucy's and Piper's ecstatic faces just as they hit the ground and the water sprayed up around them.

The next one was another recent picture. It was a big group shot of me, Brody, the girls, Derek, Alexa, Tommy, Lauren, and their new son, Max. Tommy had his arm proudly around Brody's shoulders, and the way Alexa was standing, you could really see her pregnant belly starting to pop. I had a five-by-seven of this one in my bedroom. I would never get sick of looking at it.

Picture thirteen was of a Ferris wheel. I sighed. Our first kiss.

I pulled the tab again and immediately recognized the barn from Brody's parents' property. I squinted my eyes to look closer and gasped when I realized that Brody was standing next to it, pointing up at red letters painted on the side that read:

WILL YOU MARRY ME?

#30

My knees suddenly felt like Jell-O and my hands started shaking. "What is this last pict—" I lowered the View-Master and froze.

Brody was down on one knee, staring up at me as he held a black ring box open. He hadn't even said a word yet, but tears started streaming down my cheeks faster than they ever had.

"Kacie, I've thought about what I wanted to say for a long time now, and I know I'm probably gonna mess it up, but here goes." He took a deep breath. "I love you. I love you so damn much it scares me. But what scares me more is the thought of ever losing you. I have no idea what the future holds, or where my career will take me, but I *do* know that none of it is worth looking forward to if you're not by my side. Please, let me love you forever. You *and* the girls. Will you marry me?"

I clutched the View-Master to my chest and let go of a sob I'd been fighting like hell to keep in while he talked. "Yes. Yes!" I cried, flying into his arms as he stood up. He caught me, thankfully, because I sailed into him with such force that I was surprised we didn't both tumble into the lake.

He wrapped his arms around me and squeezed tight, lifting me off the ground. "Say it again," he mumbled into my shoulder.

I cupped his face in my hands, staring into the eyes of my best friend, my soul mate, my fiancé. "Yes, I will marry you." I pressed my lips against his and closed my eyes, desperate to remember every detail of the moment so I could relive it over and over. He pulled me hard against him and slowly dipped his tongue in between my open lips. Our mouths moved together in slow, sensual waves, feeding off of each other's excitement and pure joy. My eyes danced around his face as I pulled back. "I'd marry you tonight if I could."

He wiggled his eyebrows. "We could be in Vegas in just a few hours."

"Okay, no. I take that back." I giggled. "I need my family there."

"True. Both of our moms would kill us if we eloped." He set me down and locked his hands around my waist. "Especially yours; she's been as excited about this as me."

I jerked my head back a little. "She already knows?"

A devilish smirk curled the corners of his mouth upward. "Who do you think set up the lanterns for me while we put the girls to bed?"

I looked around at the pier and shook my head. "I didn't even think about that. You sneaky little brats."

"I wanted you to be surprised."

"Well, it worked. I'm blown away . . . and so damn excited to be Kacie Murphy."

"Holy shit." His eyes widened. "I love the way that sounds."

"Me too." I pulled him down against my lips. He slipped his hands around my waist and tugged me against him, returning my kiss.

He pulled back suddenly. "Wait."

"What's wrong?" I was left needy, wanting to feel his lips on mine again.

"We forgot the most important part." He opened the ring box, which was still in his hand. "Let's make it official."

I'm not a high-maintenance jewelry girl, nor do I know a lot about diamonds or rings, but when I looked at the ring he'd picked out for me, it took my breath away.

"Oh, Brody." I covered my mouth with my hands. "It's amazing."

"It's simple but beautiful, like you." He took the ring out of the box and slipped it onto my shaky left hand. "I hope you never, ever want to take this off."

"Has my mom seen this?"

He laughed and shook his head.

"Come on!" I grabbed his hand and started pulling him back up to the house. "Maybe the girls are still awake. I can't wait to tell them."

"Let them sleep," he argued. "If you tell them tonight, they'll be too excited to go back to sleep."

"They wouldn't be the only ones. I don't think I'm ever going to sleep again," I turned and whispered as I walked up the deck steps.

Mom and Fred were sitting at the island drinking coffee when we walked in. They both turned toward the back door. I was barely through it when my mom covered her mouth with her hands and started crying as she ran toward me. We met in the family room and hugged each other tight, rocking back and forth as Fred came over and gave Brody a quick hug.

Mom pulled back from me and held her arms open for Brody. "Come here, my favorite son-in-law."

Fred came over and put his arm around my shoulders. "I'm so happy for you," he said as he squeezed me.

"Thanks, Fred." I laid my head on his shoulder. "How perfect is this? First you and Mom get married, now it's my and Brody's turn."

"Lucy and Piper will be excited to be flower girls again." He laughed. "They sure love dressing up."

"Definitely." I nodded, lifting my head and looking at my mom. "How long have you guys known about this? I can't believe you didn't slip. You're terrible at keeping secrets."

Mom waved me off. "What, Fred? Like two weeks?"

"Yeah." He nodded nonchalantly. "Since that day at lunch."

"What day at lunch?" I asked as I looked back and forth between them.

"A couple of weeks ago, Brody called one morning. He knew it was a day you were working and asked if we were free. He wanted to take us to lunch." Fred sat on the couch and took his glasses off, rubbing his tired eyes. "Anyway, he told us about his plan and asked for our blessing."

My jaw dropped as I turned to Brody. "You did?"

He shrugged. "I had to do it the right way."

"Brody . . ." I sighed, wrapping my arms around his waist. "I don't think it's possible for you to get it wrong. Ever."

ACKNOWLEDGMENTS

So many wonderful people contributed to the making of this book, and I want to take a second to thank them.

Thank you to Dina Lepczynski for your amazing eyes and proofreading this one last time for me.

To my sweet, fantastic editor, Megan Ward: I don't even know where to begin. Getting this book ready was stressful for both of us, but you never gave up on me, and for that, I will always be grateful. Thank you for cleaning up my messy story, thank you for pushing me to be a better writer, thank you for being my friend.

To my betas, Michelle Finkle, Chelle Northcutt, Kaci Buckley, Shelly Collins, Christy Elliott, Happy Driggs, Deb Bresloff, Pam Carrion, and Jenn Haren: the input from you ladies was crucial to this story, and some of your suggestions made everything ten times better. Thank you for taking the time to read, sometimes more than once, and share with me. I am eternally grateful.

To all the bloggers who have participated in reveals, tours, pimping, and supporting me: None of us authors would be where we are if it weren't for you. Thank you, thank you, thank you for all that you do.

A big ol' thank-you to Michelle Kisner Pace for answering hours and hours of questions, sometimes the same one more than once. Okay, a lot of times the same one.

To my CP, Melissa Brown: You have fielded more neurotic phone calls from me and read more rambling, insane messages than any one human should ever have to. Thank you for not changing your number and blocking me, and for believing in me when I didn't.

Happy Driggs: "Shut up and just write." If I had a dollar for every time you said that to me, we could go to every book event in all of 2014. And maybe 2015. I love you, asshole. Thank you for pushing me . . . even when I pushed back.

Tara Sivec: I'm glad our "babies" are being born so close together. We need to get them together for a playdate soon. Perhaps at the Subway in Sturgis?

To my husband and kids, and my mom: Your support is the absolute foundation of my career. Thank you for making it a strong one. I love you all more than anything in this world. (I know I said that in the last book, but it's true.)

ABOUT THE AUTHOR

Photo © 2014 Stacey Houston Photography

Bestselling author Beth Ehemann lives in the northern suburbs of Chicago with her husband and four children. A lover of martinis and all things Chicago Cubs, she can be found reading or honing her photography skills when she's not sitting in front of her computer writing—or on Pinterest. *Room for More* is the second installment of her popular Cranberry Inn series, which includes the novel *Room for You* and the novella *Room for Just a Little Bit More*. Contact her at: authorbethehemann@yahoo.com

Or follow her on:
Facebook: www.facebook.com/bethehemann
Twitter: @bethehemann
Instagram: @bethehemann
www.bethehemann.com